Exhilarated 2

LISA AUSTIN

Before you read

In the first installment of Exhilarated, there is mention of Lydia, Aphrodite's cousin and Gage, Goal's brother. The two have a short prequel titled *Euphoric* and I continued their story in this book. You DO NOT have to read the prequel in order to follow along for the small parts they play in this story but if you would like to, the link is below.

Take note that *Euphoric* is an exclusive and is not available on amazon even though it can be read on your kindle. If you choose to purchase, you'll get an email of instructions on how to read it. Again, it is NOT imperative that you read their story. EVERY-THING is broken down in this book. Y'all know I don't leave anything out lol. Thank you, and enjoy!

https://bit.ly/Euphoricpreq

CHAPTER 1

Quasie Lantis

TWO WEEKS BEFORE THE HOUSEWARMING

I'd been to New York quite a few times, but I'd ever been this damn nervous. Stepping off the plane into JFK International, I placed my oversized YSL shades on my face and pulled the hood of my hoodie on my head. Even though there was an unspoken law to wear comfortable clothing at the airport, that law never applied to me. I'd always dressed to the nines, even walking through the thick of the anxious crowds. Today, however, fashionable Quasie was left back in Jagoda Bay. Dressed in a white Hoodie with the matching joggers and a pair of Pink and white Nikes, I chose comfort. Instead of the XL black Chanel I normally wore at the airport, a pink Mia Ray Shopping bag rested in the crevices of my arm. My bag was usually packed with my laptop when I traveled and a few real estate books that I liked to reference because my trips were mainly always business. Since this wasn't a business trip, the usually heavy bag was void of books. In spite of Kilo's stupid ass breaking my laptop, my bag was light altogether, only housing my makeup bag, wallet, charger, wet wipes, hand sanitizer and lotion.

Making my way through the hustle and bustle of the airport, I followed the signs to baggage claim and sighed with relief when my suitcase was rolling by as soon as I made it down. Grabbing my luggage, I swallowed hard and reached in my bag for my phone, but before I could retrieve it, I felt a grip at my elbow.

"You're in my way."

His scent evaded my nostrils and had me closing my eyes to let it marinate. Four days ago, he'd all but fucked the wig off me. I hadn't been handled like that in... well, never and hadn't been able to get the scene out of my mind no matter how hard I tried. I'd even ignored his sister when she sent me pics of all of the furniture that arrived. I wanted to get the Kodas family out of my fucking head, but when Kilo popped up at my house calling me miserable, lonely, and the baby of a side bitch, I was on go mode.

"Maybe being in your way is where I wanna be."

I shuttered as I remembered him saying the exact same thing to me days ago, right before our bathroom rendezvous.

"Damn, you even look good from the back in these big ass sweats."

I chuckled as Eleven wrapped his arms around me. For the last two days, I felt a terrible tenseness in my body, but being in Eleven's embrace had me releasing it all and melting into his large frame. I didn't know this man. Not even a little bit, but in this moment, standing at baggage claim with hundreds of people bypassing us, I felt the safest I had in a very long time. The feeling was semi foreign, but I'd be lying if I said I wasn't craving this type of security. I opened my eyes, landing them on his tattooed knuckles that were trying to make their way inside the front of my sweatpants. I wanted to bite my lip and spread my legs to let him fondle the tautness out of me, but I remembered where the hell we were.

"Eleven Kodas, it's good to see you too." Turning on my heels, I placed a hand on his chest and stood on my tippy toes to kiss him on the cheek. He gripped my chin and planted a sloppy kiss on my lips, sucking and tongue, making me moan in his mouth and moist down below. I had to take Epson salt baths every night this week in order to get the soreness from my kitty. Eleven was too much to handle. *What the fuck are you doing here, Quasie?*

"Let's get the fuck up out of here before a nigga get you put on the no-fly list for bullshitting."

Eleven smirked, brown eyes mimicking the color of a bear's fur. They were like a light, dull, chocolatey brown, but they held so much sparkle. His medium walnut-hued skin, bare, chiseled chin, birthmark

2

in the corner of his eye that mirrored a teardrop, and low cut hair all made up the perfection of Eleven. He was looking so damn good in a light brown Essentials oversized tee, shorts that were the material of that swoosh swoosh jogging fabric we used to wear back then and a pair of Nike Air Dunks that had different color patches of brown in them. His fit was simple yet swaggy, and of course, his jewelry was present.

"What do you mean, before you get me put on the no-fly list? You're going to get both of us put on there," my breath hitched a little as he grabbed my hand, and pulled my luggage with the other.

"Nah, I fly private, mama. If yo' hard headed ass wouldn't have hit me up three minutes before you hopped on the plane, you could have flew with me."

Eleven gazed at me with a snarl on his mug, and that had me laughing so hard, I almost ran into someone.

"Watch where you going, silly ass girl. Come on, I'm right here."

When Eleven led me to a black Lamborghini, I silently appreciated the car. I'd never been in one per se, but many of my clients owned the luxury sports car. Deep down, I was low key excited because it was definitely one of my dream cars.

Eleven walked behind the car and handed my bag to a gentleman dressed in an onyx-colored suit, who added my bag in the back of a truck that was parked directly behind the Lamborghini before he climbed behind the wheel. Eleven then swaggered back over to me and lifted the doors before placing his hand at the small of the curve in my back to let me in. Questions were swirling in my head. I was hoping his ass hadn't given my shit to a stranger, but instead of asking, I stayed quiet for once in my life. My mind was too jumbled anyhow for that shit.

The new car smell mixed in with the butter black leather had me taking a deep inhale, and once Eleven was in the car, his scent overpowered both. I was shocked the car didn't smell like weed. I'd only rode shotgun with one man, and Kilo's ass didn't care how much he paid for a car, he smoked it out like a chimney.

Alicia Key's *City of Gods* played at a nice volume throughout the speakers as he swerved through the airport traffic. I was curious to see how he was about to get through this busy ass New York City rush. The

3

two times I visited, I stayed in areas that had the least amount of tourists, using a cab or Uber to get around.

As we comfortably made our way through the streets, I thought back to what brought me here. Yes, Eleven invited me. However, I had to escape Jagoda Bay. I needed to get the fuck away from the city because it wasn't big enough for Kilo and I. He'd pissed me the fuck off to no return, and at this point, I felt like he was just doing shit. When he knocked my laptop out of my hand, it took everything in me not to have Haddie in a big black hat standing over her grandson's casket as it was lowered to the ground. So, after two days of barely being able to function, I tossed shit in the bag, let Kassie and my other assistant know that I would be at a real estate conference in New York and headed out. I didn't realize I had no details of the trip, so I inboxed Eleven moments before takeoff. He'd followed me on social media as soon as I left his sister's home and had been all in my DM's, although I knew he had my number.

"Even though you was spontaneous as fuck with the shit, I'm glad you came."

Snapping from my thoughts, I glanced at Eleven's side profile and admired his nearly perfect sculpted face. He was too damn fine for his own good, and fine men like him came with problems. Problems that I had no intention on ever solving. Hell, I was still shocked that I was sitting in the passenger of his car while being thousands of miles away from Jagoda Bay.

"Do you have any baby mamas, Eleven?"

The further we drove into the city, the more my mind worked. I didn't know anything about this man besides how good his dick felt stroking my married ass walls, but now that we were once again in each other's space, I needed to know what the fuck I was getting myself into. I'd let the man slut me out in my client's home after not having peen from a real man in five years, so I deserved to know if he was even worth taking me down again.

Eleven slowly licked his lips and looked into the rearview mirror before switching lanes. *Damn, even the way he drove the car was sexy.*

"I would never label the mother of my child as a baby mama, Quasie."

I may as well have been a balloon, and he was the needle because I inflated right there in the front seat. I'd sat on this man's dick and didn't know anything about him. I don't know what the fuck I was doing with this man, but baby mama drama or children that didn't come from me were non-negotiable. Call me impractical, but those were my rules, and despite what the hell Kilo thinks, it's one of the many reasons I did stay single. Most these negros had a slew of BeBe's kids with a BeBe attached. No, thank you.

"I think this was a mistake. Can you-"

"I would never refer to my child's mother as my baby mama because if she has carried my child, she would fasho' be my rib. You ain't make no fucking mistake. You fucking with a real nigga this weekend. Ion got no fucking kids, mama."

I opened my mouth to talk, but nothing would come out, so I closed it. All of a sudden as the infamous tall buildings of the most popular city in the world came into view, excitement took over. Last time I was in the city was for work. I enjoyed two restaurants, but that was about it. I had always said I was going to come back and visit, but who the hell would I bring? My mama and Kassie? Well, I have the girls now, but shit, they have their own lives. Despite me being in a shitty mood, I was going to enjoy whatever came with this trip.

We pulled up to 5th Avenue, and I couldn't hide the smile from my face if I wanted to. Eleven valeted, and as soon as the doors went up, I was frozen in my seat. Eleven held his hand out for me to grab, but I shook my head no. I continued to sit in the seat, fingers tensed in my lap. If I was to flip the visor down, I'm sure my bare face would be cloudy with uneasiness. Oh Gosh! My face was bare! Behind these frames were bags deeper than Elon Musk's pockets. *Why the hell did I not beat my face? What the fuck am I wearing? Do my clothes in my suitcase even match?* I pride myself on style and grace. It wasn't just for social media or for my business; it was literally apart of my lifestyle. So, to be sitting here about to walk into New York's prime shopping location, I felt like a whole damn bum.

"You look good, mama. *Come on, I got you.*"

Eleven held his hand out, and those five words felt like ice gliding down a burning throat. Soothing. Placing my hand in his, I clutched my

5

bag and let him pull me from the low-sitting vehicle. The moment I was in his embrace, he wrapped his arm around my lower back and rested his chin on my shoulder. Eleven's chest was so solid. The coldness from his chain tickled my skin, and his cologne pinched my nose. This man was too damn much for me but, there was something inside of me telling me he was what I needed, even if for the moment. It puzzled my brain because for the last few years, all I needed was my business, my mom, my team, and my clients. Now, here I was halfway across the country with a man that I didn't even know. My pussy knew him, but Quasie Lantis didn't.

Eleven pulled back from me with a lick of his lips.

"What are we doing, Eleven?"

I wrapped my arms around my body and turned my head to watch the family that walked past us.

Rubbing his hand down his bare chin, he stepped back and gave me a slow, seductive onceover.

"I told you I wanted to show you a good time. Dick and bread, remember? Now, bring yo' lil' skeptical ass on. We ain't strangers. We done fucked in my sister's crib before she has."

My eyes expanded, and at the same time, Eleven pulled me by his side with his arms tossed around my shoulders.

"I still feel so bad about that, Eleven. Please don't bring that up ever again. Your sister is probably going to leave me a terrible review and not send me any clients. Then your mom was there! Gosh, I'm such a hoe!"

My skin grew warm with embarrassment. I would think about Eleven and I in the bathroom and then get turned on, but immediately after, I would become flushed. I was dead as wrong for busting it open for him in his sister's brand new home. Now I was going to have to update my employee handbook and add, *NO FUCKING ON THE CLIENT'S PROPERTY*. I don't know how I could ever face Earis ever again. Let alone Ms. Eya. Lord!

"Stop tripping on that shit. I'm a grown ass man, Quasie. My mama and sister know that shit. They not tripping. The still love yo' thick ass... Aye, what's good! Y'all ready for me?"

We stopped in front of a Hermes Boutique store, and my heart palpated. I had quite a few designer pieces in my closet. In all honesty, I had more than a few. However, I could never bring myself to buy a Birkin bag. I didn't even have the sandals or the belt because I felt like if I didn't have a bag, I shouldn't have an accessory. Now, I did gift my clients the blankets as a gift, and I had a few of the throws throughout my home as well, but that's where it ended. Just standing in the entryway of the store had me not only antsy but eager. If this man bought me a Birkin, I was popping this kitty all over this sinking ass city. I made damn good money, and before I made money, Kymani took care of me. I had everything my heart desired when I was with him, so when I no longer had him, I was determined to make shit happen on my own. So, having a man blow a bag on me was another foreign feeling because Quasie IS the table.

"Yes, Mr. Kodas. You're right on time. Ms. Bolston, welcome to Hermes."

I hadn't been called by my maiden name in over seven years, so the French sales associate had me taken back a bit. Still, I smiled and walked inside the luxurious store.

Looking around at all the leather goods had me feeling like I was a kid in a candy store. I'd heard that most Hermes bags were always hard to find or on backorder, but here they all were, out on display like they weren't a hot commodity. A slim Indian lady with long, black hair approached us with a tray of Giulia. Thanks to my boo Aphrodite, the burgundy concoction had become my favorite wine. I'd always thought it was bitter until she put me on. It had the right amount of sweetness, tartness, and potentness. I'd been pushing my little Stella Black to the side as of late.

"Ms. Bolston, would you like a glass of wine while you shop? If you want something a bit more elusive, I can get that as well."

"Wine is fine. It's become my favorite brand anyways. Thank you."

Lysa poured me a glass and then tried passing some to Eleven, who was standing behind me, humping my bottom every now and then.

"I'm straight. Leave the bottle for her though."

Eleven bent down and kissed the side of my neck before pulling back and turning me to face him.

"I'll be over there handling a lil' business. Go crazy, mama."

Before I could object, Eleven was sitting in the small waiting area, leaving me with Lysa. I was normally a shopaholic that could do major damage to my credit cards and be pissed when I paid the balances off the following month but standing here in the store of my dreams, I was stuck.

Another salesman came up to Lysa and I, and she handed him the tray but never pulled her smiling eyes from me.

"You can place the tray with Mr. Kodas. My new friend here will need a refill soon."

I hadn't realized I was downing the wine like it was water, and giggled when I noticed my glass was nearly empty. I was acting like a bitch that wasn't used to shit. I needed to contain myself, especially since I hadn't eaten anything.

"Would you like to start with our Spring collection first? Then, we can make our way to Summer and Fall. I assure you, aside from Spring, you'll be the first and only person wearing these goods."

This all sounded good, but I was still stuck. Looking back at Eleven, I had to squeeze my legs together seeing him gapped-legged, lounging in one of the brown chairs with one phone at his ear, another in his hand that he was scrolling on, and a third sitting in his lap. He wasn't even doing anything and I was turned on to the max.

"I...don't.... know what my budget is." I vomited the words that left not only a bad taste in my mouth but caused my skin to dampen a bit. I didn't want to pick out a certain bag, and it be more than what Eleven was willing to pay for. I would then put it back and carry my ass right out the store. I hadn't bought a Hermes and had no intention either. I was cool with my Chanel until my house was paid off. With no shame, I will carry my ass out of this store and buy me a cute little six thousand dollar Chanel before I lived beyond my means and splurged on a Hermes. If I had forty thousand to blow on a bag, I could add a hundred and forty seven more to that and get the deed to my house. One day, I would though. Right now, I had to be frugal about my business because although I made good, my overhead was a bitch.

"Ms. Bolston-"

"Quasie is fine."

"Ms. Quasie. I can assure you that Mr. Kodas has put no budget in place."

With a raised brow, I took another sip of the remnants of my glass.
"He hasn't?"

"No, as a matter of fact, he stated, '*if she wants everything in this muhfucka, wrap that shit up and give it to her.*' Excuse my language."

I laughed out loud at Lysa because she tried to wash away her Indian accent and speak in Eleven's tone.

"He rented out the store for your shopping enjoyment. Now, Spring collection first?"

I turned to look back at Eleven once more. He winked at me, and I almost fainted.

"Can I look at the Crocodile Kelly first, and then we can head to the Spring collection?"

Lysa spoke into the mic that was clipped on her navy blazer.

"Excellent choice. It's being bagged up for you as we speak."

"I said I wanted to look at it."

"Mr. Kodas said if you asked for anything not on display, just to wrap it, and you'll look at it later."

"Oh really?"

I didn't think I could be any more turned on in the moment. I needed a shower to wipe all the slime forming between my legs.

"Really. Now, let's do some damage, Ms. Quasie."

* * *

Not only did I do damage in Hermes, I ran rapid in Saks on clothing, heels, and accessories. I was sure I'd packed bullshit in my suitcase, so I had to make sure I was set for the weekend. The way Eleven hung back and let me do my thing, almost had me forgetting he was there. When he went to Saks, he did come in the dressing room and rub his hands all over my body. I had to pry his fingers off me every time I was naked. He let me have my way, and the way I didn't see him pay for a thing let me know he'd put his card on file the moment he closed down the stores. That or his ass shopped here way too much. The more the day progressed, I was starting to realize Eleven was not only a big dick mystery, but he had even bigger pockets.

After tearing the mall down, the black truck filled with all of my shopping bags trailed us to the heart of the city and stopped on Billion-aires Row. Now, I'm not licensed in the state, but being the real estate mogul I was, I'd toured a few apartments and condos on Billionaires Row. 111 West 57th Street is considered the tallest and skinniest building in the world. 1400 and 28 ft tall and only 60 ft wide. This place offered world class amenities, including a stunning indoor pool and a private dining room I hadn't had the pleasure of seeing in person. When the doorman came out and retrieved my bags, I knew it would take him a few trips to get everything up. Now that my wine was wearing off, I cringed thinking about all the damage I'd done in the stores. I'd really outdone my fucking self, and now I was having regrets. This man invited me on a trip and let me have my way in the malls, but I'd gotten outside of my body with the shopping. I felt like a damn gold digger, but when Eleven told me I could go crazy without a limit, I did just that. Every bag, shoe, scarf, belt and earring I batted my lashes at, Lysa had that shit bagged. I felt like a fucking Cinderella, but if he'd owned or was even renting an apartment or condo in Billionaire's Row, he had it to spare.

Bypassing the luxuriousness of the Gilded Age marbled lobby where a pianist serenaded the residents, we rode the elevator up to the seven-tieth floor. Once the doors opened, I tried hard to hold in my gasp. A beautiful view of Central Park and all of its green trees was in the back-ground, and it was breathtaking. This man wasn't just renting a condo or an apartment, this was a fucking penthouse. The house was fully decorated in an industrial style décor with a hint of Luxe. Brown and black leather adorned the space, and it worked well for this high rise.

Three bedrooms, three full baths, a free-standing wine cellar, office, large open living room, floor-to-ceiling windows, and a wide island with top of the line stainless steel appliances all made up of the magnificent space. The realtor in me kicked in, and I estimated that with the New York market, this had to be at least sixty million dollars. Prime fucking real estate. That's over three million dollars for the realtor. Damn. That was goals for real, but I couldn't see him actually owning this place. He had to be renting it. I mean, Eleven didn't have it like that. I knew people that had it like that, and his ass wasn't it. Still, I was going to flaunt and enjoy the weekend with him.

Eleven slid out of his shoes, prompting me to do the same. The door opened, and the doorman, followed by four other gentlemen that was dressed the same as him, brought my bags in. Eleven reached in his pocket and pulled off a hundred dollar bill from his bulging knot to each of them.

When they left just as quick as they came, Eleven walked over to me and pulled me into his chest. He began walking, prompting me to walk backwards, and when he led us to the balcony, the crisp cool air hit my face. Horns and breaks squeaking could be heard in the distance, and people down below looked like ants. When my back hit the railing, I gripped it firmly because I was scared out of my mind. Yes, I was a bit afraid of heights, but not to the point it made me hyperventilate. This building was so damn tall and slim that despite the genius of the architect, I felt like it was going to blow the hell over.

"You so fucking sexy. Come up out them joggers."

Eleven didn't give me a chance to respond. He spun my ass around, bent me over the balcony and pulled my pants down. With a slap of my ass cheek, I was stepping out of my thong that. I was embarrassed to see what it looked like.

"I been wanting to eat this pussy for so long."

My chest rose and fell as it pressed against the railing, and once he aggressively spread my ass, I squealed, feeling his tongue pierce my asshole.

"OHH FUUUUCK!"

Eleven was so nasty. He stuck his tongue as far in my ass as it would go and let it sit in there while swirling it around. The feeling was different but in a good ass way. I'd never had my ass eaten, and before now, I didn't think I wanted to.

I breathed lightly between parted lips as I began to count the trees. I didn't know what else to do to stifle my moans because although we were up way high, I didn't want the city of dreams to hear my cries.

After having his way with my romp, Eleven began sucking on Ms. Kitty. The slurping sounds he made as my silky folds were vacuumed into his mouth had my knees buckling. He began rubbing his thumb deliciously up and down the crack of my ass, and that drove me nuts.

"Fuuuuuuck! Shiiiit! Oh my God, Eleven!"

Fuck the trees. I saw the moon, the stars and the Statue of Liberty in a space suit as I creamed all over his bare face. I was panting as he whipped me around again to face him. My juices covering his handsome face was the most beautiful sight I'd seen all fucking year. His hands lifted my shirt above my head. I assisted him because I didn't want my bob going over the balcony.

"All I been thinking about is tearing this pussy up on this balcony. Fuck, you pretty as hell, mama."

His hands roamed intimately over my breasts as he enjoyed the view, and when he eased the lacy cup of my bra aside, my head flew back as he sucked on my pebbled nipple. Eleven's tongue made a path across to my other surgically-enhanced breast as he slid his hand down my taut stomach to the swell of my hips.

"That pussy taste so fucking good. I can eat that shit for breakfast, lunch, and dinner for the rest of my fucking life."

Eleven sucked hard on my breast, causing me to squeal out at the pleasurable pain. He then kicked my legs apart and trailed his tongue up to my neck and then my ear.

"but you ain't ready for that shit."

With his marked-up, knuckled hand, he gripped my neck, bent me over the balcony a bit more, wrapping my legs around his waist while elevating my body, damn near lifting me from the ground. Then he pulled his long, thick, pretty, veiny, walnut dick out and rammed it inside of my oasis.

"Oh! Shit! Fuck! Eleven!"

I didn't know what the fuck planet this man was from, but it was obvious that he'd been skilled with lovemaking. I felt like I was about to fall but was secure at the same damn time. Eleven's whole dick was pumping in and out of my stomach, all while he squeezed on my neck. I didn't know why I had so much trust in this man, but with the way he was making my body feel. I swear being at the top of the building was where I belonged because I felt like I was on cloud nine.

"Damn this pussy tight, mama."

Eleven's love faces were so damn sexy as he exposed all of his stark white teeth with his nose scrunched. I was sure I looked like the walking dead, but he didn't seem to mind. With one hand on my neck and the other at my hip, I was trying my best to take all of him without tapping out like an inexperienced schoolgirl.

"Pussy so fucking good! Fuuuuck! You got a nigga gone! Wanna go back shopping after this shit... hunh?? Wanna spend some more of my fucking money after I spray this pussy up?"

My stomach muscles clenched as he talked his shit, letting me know my orgasm was about to make her special appearance.

"You 'bout to cum on this dick? Cum, mama. I'ma give it to you as much as you want."

Eleven bent down and sucked my lips in his mouth, and that was enough to have me shaking like a salt shaker.

"Where you want this nut, mama?"

My eyes were rolling to the back of my head. I felt like I was out of my body with the way my body was floating.

"In...my...mouth!"

Eleven rammed in me even harder.

"Nawl, I want it in this pussy. Welcome to Billionaire's Row, Mama. Fuuuuuck!"

And that's exactly where he put it. After going two more rounds, I had to beg him to let me shower alone so that I could get dressed for our dinner reservations.

CHAPTER 2

Quasie Lantis Bolston?

STILL IN NYC

The sex between Eleven and I was so heavy on my mind that it outweighed anything else. I'd never done anything like what I was doing with Eleven. Unlimited shopping sprees with the stores being shut down. Mind-blowing sex that was not only next level but in the most unconventional place. If this was the Princess treatment the girls spoke about, I'd been missing out.

I was now feeling like myself after cleaning my body, popping a plan B that the doormen had brought, beating my face, and dressing in a short brown silk wrap Celine dress that matched Eleven's eyes. On my feet were a pair of gold matching strappy heels, and I went heavy with the gold accessories. I wanted to add some contrast to my look, so I grabbed the hot pink Hermes with the gold hardware that I was thirsty as hell to wear. I don't even know how many bags I left the store with, but it was well over ten.

Before we left the building, I had to refrain from hopping my sore pussy tail self all over Eleven because he was looking good as fuck in his denim and chocolate. Ms. Eya know she did her damn thing when she gave birth to her children. They were all beautiful, but she'd outdone herself with her firstborn. She ought to be a shame. Right as we were about to leave, I remembered I had his chain from our unauthorized fuck session at the closing, and when I handed it to him, he took it and placed it on my neck.

"It doesn't go with my outfit," I whined.

Eleven rubbed his hand down my forearm, causing me to shiver.

"You make everything look good, mama. Come on."

With my hand in his, we rode down to the lobby and in no time, he was zipping through Manhattan. We pulled up at Giulia Steakhouse, and I had to do a double take because it shared the same name as my new favorite wine. I made a mental note to ask Aphrodite if she knew the wine was named after a steakhouse since she was the one who put me on. After being led into the building, I was pleased at not only the dark, romantic setting but, the smells spewing from the kitchen. The restaurant was packed, but we were led to a private room that had gorgeous views of the Empire State Building.

"Eleven, thank you for all of this. It's only the first day, and you've done so much. This place is... Wow."

The waitress came in and brought us spring water and bread, along with crab cakes that had my mouth overflowing with saliva.

"The pleasure is all mine, mama. I should be thanking you for even giving a nigga an ounce of your time, let alone that magnificent pussy."

I bowed my head to hide my rosy cheeks. This man here. Was. Too. Much. I was already wide the fuck open, and the shit had nothing to do with him blowing a bag. It was his aura.

"You a trip. I know we are past that, but you're a mystery to me, Eleven. Even down to your name. Tell me more about you."

Sticking a fork in the crab cakes, he chewed and then looked up at me with a subtle smile.

"Your asshole was my *appetizer,* and now you want to know about a nigga?" He chuckled.

"Yeap. Start with the family dynamic." I put emphasis on the P and dug my fork in as well. The seafood was fresh, and the crab cakes were just like I liked them, not overcooked and well-seasoned to perfection."

"Yeah. Aite, but uh, I'm the oldest of four. The twins that you met, Earah and Earren. Then, my worrisome ass sister, Earis. You need to text her ass back too, before she pops the fuck up."

I looked behind me while covering my mouth.

15

"She knows we're here?"

Eleven laughed so hard it almost shook the room.

"Nah, shaky ass girl. I'm just fucking with you. She is here in New York, though. Grabbing the last bit of her shit."

I nodded. Earris did have an NYC area code, so it must've been where she did her schooling.

"I'm close as fuck with my family. They clingy, but I'll die behind them. I lost my pops about nine years ago to lung cancer. Stubborn ass man couldn't let the squares go, but he was the best man I knew. Not only am I close to my immediate family, but my entire family as well. I got a shit load of aunts and cousins and shit. All four of my grandparents are living. I been living in Jagoda Bay for a few years, but I split my time between here, Las Vegas, Cali, Miami, and Mexico."

It was just my mama and I. I had some family across the country, but we were never really close like that. Hearing him talk about his family caused a bit of jealousy to course through me because I always wanted that. I thought I was going to make a big family with Kilo, but that shit is so out the window and has been for a long ass time.

"NYC, Las Vegas, Cali, Miami, and Mexico. Interesting. Why those states and country?"

"Work."

Eleven kept it short, so I moved the conversation along.

"Okay. Your name. I know you all have the E names going on, but what's the story behind your name? Is it a street name? What's your real name?"

I took a sip of my water while Eleven dropped his fork and sat back in his seat while his brown orbs pierced through me.

"Street name? Nah. That's my government. My pop's name is Seven. He was born July 7th, 1967, so my moms wanted to keep that shit going. Once November 11th came around, she took that as a sign. Eleven Seven Kodas was born."

That was cute, but I didn't tell him that.

"You're not born in 2011, are you?" I joked.

"That would make me going on twelve. Do I fuck like I'm in middle school, mama?"

Fuck no!

Clearing my throat, I went to the next question.

"Okay. What brought you to New York this weekend? Is it work? Or to help your sister. I'm going to feel bad for intruding if it's the latter."

I low key hoped it was to help his sister because I didn't want to be caught up while he was handling his *work* in my presence.

The waitress came back out and placed a bottle of my wine on ice, along with the same champagne Eleven made it rain with at the house-warming.

"Nah, you good. She didn't even have to bring her ass back. I paid muthafuckas to do that. I guess she wanted to cry one last time."

"So, she's a nurse practitioner. What do your other siblings do?"

"Yeah, she followed my mom's footsteps. Earrah, she's in college. Soon to graduate with her degree in engineering, and her brother fucks with the ball. He nice with that shit too."

I swallowed hard because I knew the ball was more than likely some street lingo meaning an 8th ball of crack. A sip of wine drank away the anxiety I was feeling.

"You don't drink? I mean, I saw you pop the bottle at the signing, and you have a bottle of wine right there untouched and I've been drinking since I landed."

Eleven's gaze shifted toward the chilled spirit for a few moments before he was back focused on me.

"I'm not a fan of hangovers and shit. Anything that requires me to take medicine to cure, I stay away from. Ion fuck with pills and shit. Barely can swallow them bitches."

"Oh my god, you're childish. You can't swallow a tiny ass pill?"

Eleven shrugged.

"You know, there are more ways to cure a hangover than to take a pill. Plus, you don't have to drink much."

Eleven picked up the bottle, popped it, and placed it to his lips before the fizz could subdue. I don't know why but seeing champagne drip off his chin was so fucking sexy to me. I wanted to reach over and lick it off, but I'm a lady. Everything Eleven was so fucking sexy to me. God!

"Happy? Now, yo' turn."

Our food came out, and despite the fact that I didn't look over a menu, seeing steak, salmon, lobster, and all the fixings brought out hot had no complaints from me. Eleven must've requested everything on the menu before our arrival. Prompt, prepared, and a planner. Something new for a man heavy in the streets, but I wasn't complaining.

"Well, I don't have a big family like you. I wish I did, but I don't. It's just my mom and I. No siblings. My dad is dead as well, but I can't lie like he was amazing like your father. His ass gave my mama nothing but pain and suffering, so I would hope hell is as hot as it's portrayed to be for his drunk ass. I do real estate, as you know, and I love what I do. My brokerage and my team are my life."

I wanted to speak on my life with Kilo, but I refrained. The steak was so savory and buttery, I moaned onto my fork.

"And that nigga that put that weak ass ring on your finger?"

I looked down at my bare hand that was lighter than the rest of my deep brown skin in that spot.

"Kymani is my... it's complicated. I mean, we haven't been together in forever and have no plans on reconciling. He's been in jail for the last five years. Just got out a few months ago, and I hate it like hell too." I said the last sentence more to myself as I scooped scallops in my mouth.

"Damn, he can't be that bad. Don't wish the man back in prison. Then concrete walls and bars ain't no fuckin' joke."

I swallowed hard again because that let me know he knew from experience.

"Yeah, well you don't know Kymani Lantis."

"Why you ain't divorce him?"

That question caught me off guard and had me taking another sip of wine.

"Hunh?"

"You heard me, mama. Don't do that."

"Uh, I don't know. I will be though. Now that he's free. Kymani was my first love. We married young. Really young. He gave me the version of his world and treated me like a queen, but he was a cheater. He was also heavy in the streets. Once he brought two babies home from two different women, I was done. He moved on to another woman, not one of his baby mamas, might I add. Shortly after, he was locked up. We had zero communication in jail and have no communication now that he's out. I hate that man and wouldn't offer him a life jacket if he was drowning. So, yeah, there is that."

I hated the fact that the mention of Kymani's name, along with taking a trip down memory lane, brought so many emotions out of me. I'd been through so much with him, and just when I felt like my life had some normalcy, here his ass comes out of jail fucking my whole life up.

"Zero communication, but he got you way off your square?"

Sticking my fork in the wedge salad that could be on the cover of a food magazine, I paused just as the crunch of the lettuce could be heard.

"Excuse me?"

Eleven chewed his steak, never removing his earthy eyes from me, causing me to feel like an object being magnified.

"He got you off yo' fucking square. Quasie, I been seeing your posts for some time. Even saw you out a few times, including the grocery store. You always dressed like you fresh off a fucking Paris runway. You about yo' fucking business, but you're always smiling. I ain't no stalker or no shit like that, but Shirah ain't but that big. You at the airport without your face on and in sneakers got to be my favorite version of you, and if I had it my way, anytime you aren't working, that's how you'd be. That ain't really the *You* I've witnessed, though..

Plus, you let me know you were on the way when the fucking plane took off. Like you'd just got up and ran off impulse. I bet if I opened ya' suitcase, you got shit in there you wouldn't normally wear or shit that don't even go together. That nigga got you off yo' square because he wants that old thing back." Eleven took another gulp of his champagne.

He'd called me out. All I could do was drop my fork and play with the large gold ring on my middle finger. I'd been discombobulated since the day Kymani left my house the first time. I played the security cameras back a few days later and saw the moment he and his children entered my home. My heart pulled to the little girl he was holding because not only was her hair all over her head, she was barefoot. When they entered the house, I switched the camera view and saw that she was his twin. A perfect little girl and little boy that looked just like their father. I was shattered, but I didn't cry. I refused to cry. I hadn't seen the children since they were babies and refrained from visiting Haddie because she had pictures of them all over the house. Kassie had sent me screenshots of the baby mothers clowning me on social media in the past, but I never once desired to see the children. Kilo had lost his damn mind bringing his bastard children to my fucking house like they were moving in. I could have gone the rest of my life without seeing their faces and been perfectly okay. Now that I had, I was beyond hurt. This man had really gone out and gave two other bitches what he was supposed to give me.

"I don't want to talk about my husband. I just want to enjoy my time with you and forget all about my failed relationship."

I was having an amazing day. I went on the shopping spree of my dreams and got superb dick. I was away from my demanding business and had a change of scenery. All things Kymani was in Jagoda Bay, where I wanted it to stay.

"So, you drink occasionally but not really because you are scared of taking pills. Smoke?"

The waitress came out and refilled my water glass.

I determined right then and there, just like the wine, Giulia, this was now my favorite restaurant. The food, the ambiance, and the view, are for sure a ten out of ten. I could see myself now booking a flight just to come eat. I was going to have to bring Aphrodite and Tuscany with me just because Ditey had done her big one by putting me on.

"I don't smoke. If you smelled it on me at the signing, it's because my brother does."

Right, the one that's nice with the *ball*.

"What do you do for a living?"

"What do you think I do for a living?"

I pondered on the question when, in reality, I didn't have to. Eleven had hustler written all over him, but not an average hustler though. He was indeed somebody's Kingpin. Millions of dollars in real estate, Spending close to half a million dollars in the shops today that I was still shook about. I don't think it would become real until I'm at home placing the bags in my closet. He spent money like he printed that shit, and men that did that indeed made fast money on a large scale. Most rich men had accountants that watched their funds. They had to be intentional when spending in order to stay rich, but not Eleven. In true dope boy fashion, that man was throwing away money.

"Eleven, I appreciate this weekend. Hell, I appreciate Monday. You've spent more on me than I spent on my own self. Hell, you spent more than anyone has, and I appreciate that. Words can't fathom my gratitude. I've been fucking toys for years. So, being with you has been not only refreshing but invigorating. I don't want to get into something with someone in your... profession. I've been there done that. I'm beyond the bitches. I'm beyond dodging the police. I'm beyond the watching out for the robbers. I'm beyond that life completely. I have too much to lose behind dealing with a man in the streets. I just want to have a good time this weekend."

Eleven rubbed his hand down his low haircut before gripping at his groin. Sexy as ever.

"I told you I wanted you to use me for Dick and bread, and I meant that shit. I just want you to turn my fucking pockets inside out, mama, and wet this dick up until your pussy is my permanent stench. You ain't ready for a nigga like me, and I mean that with no disrespect.

"We can enjoy the next few days, and when I feel like you can't walk no more from being stuffed with so much dick, only then will I put yo' pretty ass on a jet and send you back to the city where that nigga's somewhere punching the air. When you get that situation under wraps, you can come holla at me, baby. I'll be here. Right now, though, I'ma fuck you like I'm yo' fucking husband." Eleven ended his statement with a drink of his water, and I was so turned on I was ready to get charged with public sex from pouncing on him.

"Eleven, you won't be here. I'm sure you have women lining down the block."

"It don't matter what the fuck I got. I know what the fuck I want. So if it takes yo' sexy ass three months or three years to get that hurt up out ya system from that nigga, I'll be here. Ion come with no baggage or none of that shit. So, what you can do is clear yo' situation and let a real nigga put a glacier on yo' ring finger. "

God damn.

"But yo' profession-"

"And? What the fuck about it? If you want to know some shit, don't assume. Ask me about me. I'm the only muthafucka that can give you straight facts."

I didn't have a reply. I finished my dinner, and after changing my shoes, we walked around Central Park because I was feeling too stuffed. When we made it back to the penthouse, I was still floored the same. He made good on his promise and fucked me like we'd just said I DO. That damn Eleven Seven Kodas.

CHAPTER 3

Tuscany Payne

TWELVE YEARS AGO

"**B**wuah! Bwuah! Ummmm... shit!"

The cheese pizza I'd eaten didn't stand a chance as it erupted from the pits of my belly into the toilet, almost too late. When I thought I was good, I stood but bent right back over and tossed up the rest of whatever it was that was sitting in my stomach. Besides the pizza, I hadn't eaten anything. I couldn't if I tried. For the last three days, the smell of food made me nauseous.

"Here, chile."

Still squatted in front of the toilet, I cocked my head left where a towel was waiting for me. Getting up from the floor, I flushed the toilet, grabbed the towel and wiped my mouth.

"This is the third day you've thrown up, and them there pads are still under the sink unopened. You know what this means, don't 'cha?"

Tossing the rag on the sink, I washed my hands while trying my hardest to blink back tears. I'd been avoiding the truth for a few weeks now, but when I could no longer stand the smell of food, I cried like a baby. My mama can't afford another mouth in her house. That was the first thought that ran through my head.

The nice man with the shiny car and generous pockets, who I thought was a dream, had been a fucking nightmare. That hot June day when he purchased groceries for my brother and I had been the day I unknowingly

23

sold my soul to the devil. Four weeks. That's how long it took him to put his hands on me. He beat me damn near 'til I was unrecognizable. At the same time, he climbed on top of my seventeen year old body and had his way with me. I'm far from dumb, so I knew the arrangement we agreed to would involve sex. Hell, I'd had sex with a boy in the hood for free, so why not lay down with a grown ass man in the comfort of his mansion if it meant my brothers wouldn't go without? I didn't think one of the stipulations would be me getting my ass beat for sport, though.

"What am I going to do, Ms. Giselle?" I cried.

"Now, now... shhhh. Come here, chile. It's gonna be alright."

I fell into Ms. Giselle's embrace and cried in her bosom. My mama is going to be so disappointed.

"I can't have his baby! He's a monster!...I'm only seventeen, Ms. Giselle! I want to...go...to...college!"

Ms. Giselle rubbed my back as I ruined her blouse with my snot and tears. My life was over. I officially hated myself. I'd done so good. Made honor roll every year since first grade, hadn't so much as missed a day of school, and now here I was, with child.

"Tuscany! Can we spenanite?" Tulscan appeared in the doorway of the bathroom, causing me to jump up. He looked at Giselle and me with a raised brow as he scooped an oversized spoonful of cereal in his mouth. This boy had just eaten fried fish, spaghetti, and salad but was standing here with a mixing bowl full of Captain Crunch. I tried to hold out on eating 'til after my nap, but since I'd thrown up the pizza, I was going to skip out altogether.

"Boy, go back down to the kitchen with that cereal. Greedy tale. Mr. Jose will be ready to take y'all home in the next hour."

Disappointment flashed my little brother's face, but he turned on his brand-new Nikes and headed back downstairs. I walked out of the en suite bathroom into my bedroom to close and lock the door.

"My life is over."

I plopped down on the queen-sized bed and let my back hit the pillowtop mattress. Two nights after he purchased our groceries, Gilberto took me out on a date. I felt like Cinderella because he took me to the mall, bought me threads and shoes for the date, and dropped me off at a salon where I got the works. That was the first time I'd ever had a T-bone steak and lobster. Ms. Jean across the street from my mama's house made the best imitation crab every fourth of July, but I'd never had real lobster. The only seafood we ate was fried catfish, and that was only when my mama could find it on sale.

That night, I talked as Gilberto listened. I don't know if it was the wine he ordered for us that made me have loose lips or the fact that I felt the prettiest and I felt FREE. My whole life, I'd been helping raise my brothers, so to finally be out and looking like a million bucks had me feeling like I was grown. I'd even told Gilberto how I shared a room with my mama back home. Luckily for me, I didn't talk about the future, just the present.

I thought Gilberto was going to have his way with me that night, but to my surprise, he dropped me off with an envelope full of money. It was five thousand dollars, crisp and fresh from the bank. I gave my mama half and kept the other half. That would be enough for her to pay the rent up for a few months. She wanted to ask questions. I could see it in her eyes, but we were struggling so bad that she didn't have it in her to ask me anything.

The next date was three nights after dinner, and that's when he took me back to the mall and let me ball out. I got so much shit for me and my brothers. I shopped not only for summer but with school in mind. I knew it would be starting back in August and wanted to make sure each of them had at least four pairs of shoes and a pair of slides. They could wear the slides and maybe one pair of shoes over the summer and save the other three pairs of sneakers for the upcoming school year. I don't even know how much we spent that day, but I do know my brothers had more clothes than they ever had, and it was all Nike, Polo, Jordan, and Adidas. I had to even stop and get hangers and containers so that I could put everything away. After that shopping trip, I didn't care what I had to do to keep this man. He looked black, but he spoke Spanish and was old enough to be my daddy, but I didn't even give a damn. I was just happy to be along for the ride.

One week after the shopping trip, he brought me to his house, and that was when he told me to dejar de hablar a menos que se le de permiso. I didn't know what it meant at the time, but I'd taken Spanish one and two and heard the word habla, which meant speak. So, I figured he wanted me to shut up since I was going on and on about how my brothers loved their clothing and shoes. That should have been a sign to me, but when the driver pulled up to this big ass mansion, all that went out the window. I roamed all over the house like a kid while Gilberto was in his office speaking Spanish on the phone. I learned very quickly he was a busy man and never talked about himself. Hell, he never even talked to me, he just listened until he told my ass to shut up. Before he took me back home that day, his housemaid, Ms. Giselle, cooked a Colombian dish that looked funny but smelled good. She even made enough for me to take back home to my brothers.

Week four, I was courtside at the summer tournament. It was just neighborhoods playing streetball against each other, but it was a big deal in the hood. I was cute as hell in my peach Nike dress, white Forces, and peach and white scrunch socks. Ms. Jean's niece had done my hair in micro braids, and I had even used three packs of wet and wavy human hair, so my hair was on point. I had always wanted this style, but at three hundred dollars with the hair included, that was damn near our rent, so I knew my mama would never. After my mama saw my hair, she wanted it, so I paid for her to get hers done too, but Roni Joe wanted hers straight. I was surprised she wanted braids because normally, Wanda, three houses down, gave her a roller set for twenty.

I was at the game looking like a hood celebrity, smiling, splurging, and soaking up all the damn attention. Gilberto called me on the cell he'd bought me right after the game to let me know he was pulling up. I had the big head, seeing all the girls roll their eyes at me since a shiny Mercedes was pulling up to pick me up. They had no idea that the man behind the tents was old as fucking dirt. The moment I slid in the back seat, Gilberto turned my ass every way but loose. Claiming I'd disrespected him. I didn't fight back because I was just that damn terrified. I'd been in a few fights with the girls in the neighborhood. My own mama didn't touch me, and here this man was, beating my ass like I was his child. That was when I knew I signed my fucking soul to the devil.

I glanced around the bedroom at the furniture that was perfectly placed and the purple drapes on the curtains and strongly wished this was my life but at my mother's house. Gilberto provided the perfect life for a hoodrat like me, but that shit came with a hefty ass price.

All I wanted to do was feed my brothers, take the burden off my mother so much and have fly shit. It wasn't worth having my ass controlled or beaten like a fucking runaway slave. My brothers were so happy, but I was drowning in misery. Now, I had to toss a baby in the fucking mix? A fucking baby? What the fuck was I going to do with a baby when I already had six of them? I couldn't even afford Tulscan, Tunan, Turo, Tulen, or Tuden! I had dreams. Big ass dreams. A baby was going to hinder that!

"Now you listen, and you listen good. I'm only twenty years older than you, so I consider myself young, but with a hint of wisdom. Gilberto pays me good money, better than any job I've ever had so I mind my damn business. I've been working for him for a year or so, and I've heard and seen some shit I refuse to repeat. What I'm about to say may crush you even more, but it needs to be said..."

Ms. Giselle was only thirty seven years old but looked every bit of twenty seven. She was a slim woman, but cooked like Big Mama. That wasn't surprising though, because most of us Memphis women were taught to cook before we could talk. Even if we weren't taught, we learned due to our survival and instincts. I haven't ran across many Memphis females that can not cook. Even if they weren't that good at it, they had at least one signature dish down to a science.

I wiped my nose with the back of my hands while watching Ms. Giselle place her slender hands on her slim frame. Ms. Giselle, although barely a hundred and thirty pounds, was fine as hell. She was definitely giving these young hoes a run for their money. When Gilberto first brought me around, I thought she was his wife or that they had something going on. She didn't dress like a maid. Her ass was always in the latest fashions, even while scrubbing toilets and stirring pots.

"You had no fucking business fucking on that grown ass man!"

Ms. Giselle's dark eyes glittered as she told me what I didn't want to hear, but for sure what I needed to hear.

"I don't give a fuck what he promised you! You should have kept it fucking moving! I don't know much outside this man. Hell, I don't even know his last name because no mail gets delivered here, and he pays me under the table. What I do know is he is dangerous as fuck. I saw the black eyes and busted lips. He knew not to pull that shit on you while I was here

because I would have beat his muthafuckin' ass. But like I said, you had no business spreading yo' legs for that fucking pedophile! Men like him prey on girls like us!"

"Us?"

"Yes, Tuscany, US! I was you once before, except my sibling and I are the same gender, but she was deep in her books. I wanted her to focus, so I was the one cooking and cleaning and caring for us while my mama did everything except raise us. You have a mama that works her ass off for y'all, but I had a mama that sold her ass for a hit. She didn't give a fuck about nothing, but getting high, and it got worse the older we got. I was the meek, shy ghetto girl that stayed to herself, but my sister was the nerd that was going to get us out of the fucking hood. Our life took a drastic fucking turn when a man came along and fed me the same fucking fairytale that Gilberto fed you. Except that shit wasn't a fairytale. It was a fucking nightmare! Nigga beat my ass 'til I was fucking blue! He then saw my sister and had his fucking way with her too. He knew we were always at home unsupervised, so he had the green light. The more I tried to fight him, the worse my ass whoopings got. I didn't have no fucking teeth in my mouth due to the nigga kicking 'em out when I was only sixteen years old! Sixteen!

I walked around for almost all of my adult life like that until Gilberto saw me out at a grocery in Cali, where my sister and I had moved to when she finally went off to college and offered me this job. I knew I was signing another deal with another devil, but I was sick of working petty jobs while my sister helped me out. She'd done the right thing and gone to college, so it wasn't her fucking job to take care of me. Luckily, it's strictly business with us, but I was prepared for the worse, if it meant making money.

"See, we are the same. You knew that man wasn't right the first time you met him, just like I knew his ass wasn't right. Our spirits told us; we just didn't want to fucking listen. Survival made us go against our gut, but the difference between me and you is that this will be your last fucking time making that decision. You're too fucking smart for this shit, Tuscany. If I got anything to do with it, you will get through this shit. You will be better than me and yo' mama."

Tears were now soaking my shirt. My belly was empty, but my soul was just as void. I'd successfully let this man come along and ruin not only my life, but my confidence as well. I was so disappointed in myself that all I could do was cry.

"We gone figure this shit out. I'm not even gone ask you if you want to keep the baby because hell no, you're not. We getting rid of this lil' motha-fucka the fast way. I know you're seventeen and won't be able to go, and being that yo' mama got six kids, I doubt if she's pro-abortion. I'll have to get me a fake ID made saying my name is your mother's name but I need you to get your social and your birth certificate. I'll make the appointment once we have all the documents and go from there."

Relieve washed over me. I didn't want this baby. I couldn't keep this baby. There was no damn way I was about to let this man's demon seed grow inside of me. It's been only a few months, and this man has took me down through it. Imagining sharing a child with him caused me to shudder, but I was glad that I had Ms. Giselle to figure this shit out for me.

"But when we do this, you got to stay the fuck away from Gilberto. The best way to do that is to move. I have some money saved, and I will come with you to yo' mama to convince her to move y'all. I'll even pay the rent up a few months, but you just have to promise me you gone keep yo' legs closed and never sell yo' fucking body for a hot meal and material shit ever again. That shit ain't worth it."

I swallowed hard and nodded, "I promise."

Two weeks passed by, and those were the hardest fourteen days of my damn life. I was throwing up left and right, and my mama had only caught me once. Luckily, Gilberto had been out of town, so he hadn't noticed, nor had I heard from him. And for that, I was grateful.

On Wednesdays at school, I had a half day, and I only had about fifteen more minutes 'til the bell rang. Most of the times, Ms. Giselle picked us up from school anyways or we walked, so my appointment being in the next hour was going to work out perfectly. Me and Ms. Giselle had gone over our plan at least a hundred damn times. She called the clinic a week ago after I had my documents, and she had her fake ID. My mother kept all of our important Information in the top drawer in our bedroom, so I had no problems there. Ms. Giselle kept getting the run around when it came to the fake ID, so that was what took a week. When she finally received it, she called around to three abortion clinics, and the third one had an availability. I'd even gone to the free clinic yesterday to make sure I wasn't too far along. I was only six weeks, which meant I could take the pill or get the procedure. I decided to get the damn procedure. I heard from girls around the way that the pill was torture.

My phone buzzed in my Coach bag at the same time the school bell rang. When I looked at the screen of my Motorola Razor, I cursed under my breath, seeing that it was Gilberto.

"What the fuck do he want?" I mumbled as I gathered my belongings.

I didn't want to upset him by ignoring his call, so I answered as I shifted through the hallways, squeezing past my fellow classmates. Everyone was lingering around, and I usually would too, to show off my fit, but today, I was trying to get the fuck out the building. This damn baby had been tearing my ass up, and I was ready to get rid of it.

"Hello, Gilberto," I answered with a roll of my eyes.

"I'm outside. Where are you?"

His voice was calm and laced in his thick Colombian accent as panic showed on my face. I could feel my forehead sweat, and my scalp itched underneath my fresh micro braids.

"Uh, it's okay. You can leave. Ms. Giselle is picking me up today. We have to run in Walmart and get some feminine products," I lied. Just sitting here and explaining myself to this man had me ready to bend over and barf on my icy white Air Force Ones. I wanted nothing more than to hang up the damn phone in his face, but I knew that shit would cause more harm than good.

"That wasn't a request." Click.

I looked at the screen to confirm he disconnected the call and went to send Giselle a text. I paused in my stride since I was close to the main doors, and I knew he was parked right at the front.

Me: Oh my God! Why didn't you tell me he was here? He's at the school! My appointment is in less than an hour.

Ms. Giselle: We have time. Just act normal. I'm sure he is bringing you to the house. I'm about to leave out of the parking lot and head back to the house. Don't worry, he not going to try shit while I'm there.

I flipped the phone down, tossed it back in my purse and walked out of the double doors. I spotted Gilberto's car immediately and like always the girls were giving it the googly eyes. They just didn't know. I would hand my position over to them in a fucking heartbeat. Wasn't shit good about the arrangement I had with this fucking sick ass man.

I climbed in the back seat and closed the door. Gilberto was sitting across from me, in his normal suit and tie, and slick back ponytail that highlighted his handsome features, puffing on a cigar. He didn't tell me much, but he did tell me that he had the cigars imported from Columbia. All I knew was that today, it stunk when usually the fumes didn't bother me.

Gilberto took one look at me, and instead of a scowl covering his face, he smiled. The cigars were starting to stain his teeth, but they weren't that bad. With all the money he had, I'm sure he was going to get his smile fixed just like he had done for Ms. Giselle.

"How was your day?"

I raised my brow because I couldn't remember the last time he asked about my damn day.

"Uh, it was alright, I guess. Are we going to your place? Ms. Giselle is waiting for me."

Gilberto broadened his smile, and that shit sent chills down my spine. I knew then he wasn't just being nice. Some bullshit was about to come behind him showing all thirty two or twenty eight.

"I know you don't know much about me, young Bonita, but I will enlighten you on one thing. I'm a very impatient man. A very jealous, impatient man. A very dangerous, jealous, impatient man. When I ask you these questions, it would be in your best interest to answer me accurately. Comprende?"

I pressed my English book into my chest since I had my arms crossed around it. After licking my dry lips, I slowly nodded.

"How far along are you?"

My heart dropped out of its place, and my stomach turned. I needed to throw up right here, but I held it in.

"I'm not pregnant."

Gilberto stared at me for what seemed like 'til the end of my pregnancy before pulling on the cigar and exhaling the smoke.

"Okay, let me rephrase myself. Your mother and brothers' lives depend on the question. I will kill them in front of your entire ghetto ass neighborhood and piss on their corpses without a care in the world. Now again, how far along are you?"

I wanted to cry. Big fat tears. I knew my plan to get an abortion was over and done. He knew. He fucking knew. There was no way he was going to let me get rid of his child.

"Gilberto, I can't have this baby. I'm just a baby myself! I have been taking care of my brothers all my life. My mom is struggling. Plus, you-"

"Plus I what? I what? I take care of your black ass, and your fucking brothers and your Madre! I fucking own you! You're my property! Mi Propiedad! You will not get rid of my fucking baby! I will lock your ass away and kill you after you push it out before I let that shit happen!"

Gilberto slid up in his seat, and I jumped.

"Please, Gilberto. Please. I'm only seventeen. I'm a child myself."

Me saying I was a child must have angered Gilberto because he reached back and backhanded me so hard, I flew into the window.

"You're a child, but you suck and fuck cock like a grown ass woman. If you're grown enough to fuck, you're grown enough to birth my child. I didn't do right by my first two seeds. They look at my own father as their father, but this boy here will be the one to love me. I will never let you take this moment away from me. I'll sell your ass to the highest bidder the day he slides out of your ripped pussy in you ever try to harm my son."

I was only a few weeks pregnant, and Gilberto had already put a gender on him. I cried until we arrived at his house. Then I ran into my room past Ms. Giselle and cried myself to sleep. I heard Gilberto yelling at her, but tuned them out. I knew going forward my life was never going to be the same.

For nine months and thirty seven days, I went through the worst times of my fucking life. My brothers had even stopped coming to Gilberto's house because they noticed the shift in energy, and he surely had stopped buying them things. Didn't even get them a stuffed stocking for Christmas. I hid my pregnancy from my mom clean through my eighteenth birthday, and at that point, I was able to go to my own doctor's appointments. Half the time, Ms. Giselle had to drag me to appointments, and the other half, Gilberto had to slap me to them. He still beat my ass like a Hebrew slave, but he dodged his precious son.

Right after Christmas and before the new year, my mama caught on to the pregnancy. By then, I knew the gender, and although I wasn't showing much, I wore heavy ass coats zipped to the neck every day.

When she placed the ultrasound that I had carelessly laying around on the bed, I could only drop my head. It also so happened to be a day she was off, and I was sporting a busted lip. Instead of going off, she walked out of the room, went into the kitchen, and started dinner. Ronnie Joe didn't speak on the baby the rest of the pregnancy nor did she ask me if I was receiving prenatal care. She didn't even call the police about all the bruises and black eyes I was rocking. For that, I began to look at my mother as an enemy and placed her right in the same pot as Gilberto. I packed up all my clothes and shoes, which took three trips and carried my ass to the Mansion of Doom. Some would say I was a fool to go to Gilberto's house, but at least I knew he was mainly out of town, and Ms. Giselle was there to love on me, cater to me, and make me smile. Except there was no smiles during the pregnancy. I didn't smile when I heard his heartbeat. I didn't smile when I saw the ultrasound. I didn't smile when he kicked me all day. I didn't smile when I found out the gender. The baby was nothing, but a fucking curse binding me to the man whom I hated more than life.

Prom came and went, and so did all the other fun senior shit, and I was sure to skip past it all. I was big as a fucking whale and went from the dusty girl to the fly, spoiled girl to that pregnant girl all in the span of 12 months. I wobbled across the stage to receive my diploma, and if it wasn't for Ms. Giselle, I would have come to graduation with a ponytail and sweats. She made sure I had a sew-in with Remy hair, took me to get my nails and feet done, had a girl at the Mac counter do my makeup and had me the prettiest blue dress and sandals since my feet were too swollen for heels. I'd gained about fifty pounds during pregnancy, and my nose had spread across my face, but seeing myself after the makeup had me feeling like a model. For the first time in a long time, I felt like myself. I even saw my mama in the crowd with my brothers, but I was still on my fuck her hiatus. Gilberto didn't come to the graduation, and for that, I was exhilarated. He hadn't been around much the last month, but when he did come around, he was on his Ike Turner shit. Thankfully, I had gotten too fat in his eyes, so he hadn't sexually assaulted me in months.

After taking a few pics with my brothers and ignoring the looks from my mama, I allowed Ms. Giselle to talk me into allowing my mama to come eat with us. Ms. Giselle took us to Jay Alexander and I pigged out on steak, mac n cheese, and mashed potatoes. Her and my mom talked, but I kept my attention on my phone playing Tetris and joking with my brothers every now and then. I was shocked that my mom paid for the hefty tab when the waitress came, but I still didn't leave with her. Ms. Giselle took me to the park to walk the baby down some since I was now full term and before we could reach two miles, I was dead ass tired.

"Come on, let me help you get in the car."

Ms. Giselle helped me into the shiny red Jetta she had been driving the last few days that I thought was so damn cute. It wasn't brand new, but it was in great condition, had leather seats and smelled like cherries.

I felt a gush of water come from my private and immediately knew what that meant.

"Ms. Giselle! My water just broke!"

She drove like Miss damn Daisy to the hospital, and after that, everything went fast. I was wheeled off to labor and delivery, and the pain was like something I had never felt.

"Oh my gooooood!" Cramps shot through my ass light lightening, and it felt like rocks were being thrown at my stomach from the inside.

"It's too late for an epidural, and the baby is crowning."

The doctor, whom I had seen once or twice during my pregnancy was on call, so she was delivering the baby. I went to a state clinic and there weren't any assigned Ob-gyns, just whoever had an opening on that given day. Gilberto gave me three thousand dollars every time it was time for my appointment or sent it to Ms. Giselle. I made sure to stack it and opt to use the free clinic. I had close to sixty grand and wasn't sure when I would need it, but whenever I did, I would have it.

Sweat poured from my head as the hospital gown that was open in the back fell down my shoulders. I had sweated my curls out, causing the twenty inch weave to stick to my face and neck.

"You got this. I did this and it's not so bad."

I snapped my head to Ms. Giselle.

"Wait, you had a child?"

"Another story for another day. Now, push."

I squeezed the life out of Ms. Giselle's hand and pushed Gilberto's nine pound son into the world. He came out calm as still waters, with a head full of black straight her and pink skin. Ms. Giselle saw that the nurse was trying to give me the baby and intervened by holding him first.

I cried like a newborn baby, and the baby hadn't even cried. Here I was pussy split wide open, being that the nurses were delivering the after birth, and I couldn't even stand to look at the baby. I thought that my motherly instincts would kick in, but that wasn't the case. I wanted nothing to do with this child, but I knew I didn't have a choice. This was my life now. A teen mom from the ghetto. All my hopes and dreams shattered.

Once the nurses left the room, and I was all cleaned up, Ms. Giselle made sure I was comfortable and went to check on the baby. The nurse had injected my IV with something to help with the stinging I felt in my cat since I had pushed the baby out all natural and had been split and stitched with three sutures. My mind was running rapidly. Every time a nurse walked into the room, I jumped, thinking it was Gilberto. For him to desperately want the damn baby, he sure did miss the fucking birth nor had he called my phone. As the medicine began to kick in, I just prayed he didn't walk in while I was sleeping and strangled me in my fucking sleep. The medicine beat my thoughts, and I stopped fighting my racing brain and let sleep take over.

I don't know what time it was that I woke up, but the streetlights from the parking lot shone in the room, and I was now in a much smaller room than that I delivered in. My vagina was numb, but I didn't feel too much pain besides the soreness still in my butt. I tried to look for the remote and was about to give up when the door opened to my room. My eyes grew wide and my left hand began to shake. Please no...

"Hey, Tuscany, it's just me. Mom."

The fear on my face was replaced with annoyance. Although deep down inside, I was so happy to see my mother. It's not until you are placed in a scary situation that you feel the need to have your mother's presence near.

"Hey."

She was still in a black midi dress with white tulips on it. However, her black wedges had been swapped for her black work slides that had seen better days. Roni Joe worked like a dog and had six kids, but she still held so much youth in her face, and at one hundred and ninety four pounds, her body was still banging. Although all of her children had a different father, we all looked so much like our mother. Same tawny skin, high cheeks and sleek eyes. When my brothers were born, people thought each one of them was girls until after their first birthday when they got haircuts.

"How are you feeling?" she hesitantly asked as she stood far away from my bed and damn near still near the door.

I shrugged, "I'm okay."

I was everything but okay. Today was supposed to be the happiest day of my life, but instead, I was living a nightmare. I hadn't bothered to apply for not one college, and I had five that I was interested in. Even though I had my ass beat and fucked to death my entire senior year, I still managed to graduate with a 3.4 gpa. I was shocked as hell each time I got my grades because there were a few times Gilberto beat me so bad, I had to miss days of school. Most of the time, I was able to make up my work, but there were a few times that I couldn't.

My mama ran her hand through her rollers set, and I knew Wanda that lived three houses down had done it. The twenty dollars that she charged would have your hair looking like you came straight from the salon. I could smell the products from the bed, and as always, it smelled so good to me. I guess I still had my pregnancy nose.

"I can't stand blood. I've been here since a little after you arrived, but I was too squeamish to see it. Plus, I didn't want to see you go through that pain. I did it six times all natural, and it hurted like hell each time."

"But I needed you, mama. I've been needing you. I know you had to work, but I needed you." I wasn't even speaking about the birth because she was off today. I was speaking in general.

When the tears left my eyes, my mama ran to my side.

"I know, Tuscany. I know. I know you needed me way more than I needed you. I was wrong. So wrong. Just because I had children by ain't shit niggas, that wasn't your burden to take on. I ruined your life-"

My mother, the woman I'd never seen show emotion, burst out into sobs. Making me cry even harder.

"Mama, it's okay. We gotta stick together, that's what you said. That's ...what you... taught me," I sniffed out.

"Yeah, but you should have never been made to raise my children. I worked all those damn hours to still never make enough. We were still struggling and y'all were still going without. I am so damn sorry for doing that to you. You didn't deserve to be handed over to a predator like that. I know you laid down with Gilberto for the sake of your brothers."

I gasped because I didn't even know she knew his name.

"Hell yes, I know him, and I pulled down on his ass too. Sick ass nigga was with another young bitch when I saw him. I told him if he put his dick in my daughter and hands on you one more time, I was on his mutha-fuckin' ass. If he wants to fight a bitch, he can fight me."

My eyes bulked as my mama wiped her face.

"Mama!"

"What? Don't mama me! He hasn't touched you, has he? Exactly! Got mine fucked up. Bad enough he was fucking on my underaged daughter. I should have been stopped that shit, but the money you were giving me and seeing my kids not wanting for nothing had me selfishly turning a blind eye. Never a fucking gain, though. That Spanish slick-haired Ike Turner got the game fucked up!"

I laughed through my tears because my mama made a face that looked just like Turo. He was the jokester out the bunch. He made jokes out of any situation and would check your ass 'til you cried.

"You know it was Tulscan's ass who roasted me a while back."

I cocked my head because Tulscan was a true mama's boy. Even now at his big age.

"Come again, say what?"

"Yeah, mane. Tulscan roasted the shit out of me. Called me trifling and unfit for letting her daughter get beat on by a grandaddy ass nigga. I guess the lie about you working for Gilberto that you told them wore out. He told me I should be ashamed for letting you sell pussy to a Feliz Navidad ass nigga. I was so damn mad, but I laughed about that shit when I calmed down. I did a whole lot of praying and asking God for forgiveness the next day and quit my job. I got a knock at the door, and it

was a group of folk recruiting people to go back to school. They were paying us to do so, and it paid more than both jobs together. I signed up, kept my first job, and in six more months, I'll be in medical billing and coding." My mama smiled.

"Oh my God, mama! I'm so happy for you!"

My mama had been having it hard since before I can remember, and she was smart as hell, so I was happy she was going back to school to be able to provide a better quality of life for her children. At the same time, I was also sad for my own damn self because I wouldn't be seeing a damn school probably ever.

"Yeah, the school has all types of programs, even a first time home buyers one. I plan on getting us a nice five bedroom home."

"Mama, I'm really happy for you! That is so amazing! I call dibs on a bedroom when you purchase because I'm definitely coming back."

I didn't care what the consequences were, I just wanted to be with my family. Hell, I was even going to offer her the sixty thousand dollars I'd saved up so that she could go ahead and find a house now. That should be enough for a down payment to pay the mortgage for a few months and fully furnish it. I just knew I had to get the fuck away from Gilberto. I refused to be his punching bag. Now that I wasn't pregnant, I'm not too sure how long my mama's warning was going to last.

"No, you're not."

I drew my head back in confusion.

"Hunh?"

My mother dug in her black Coach bag that I had gotten her for her birthday back in September. It still looked new despite her wearing it every day.

She pulled out five envelops and sat them on my lap. I picked up the first one and read through it. I then picked up the second, third, and fourth and the following two. By the time I'd finished the last letter, I was bawling.

"You will not be a fucking statistic! You hear me? You will not! I may have been a shitty mother to you and your siblings, but I listened. I fucked up a few times and had to sit in the line for hours with your guidance counselor for instructions, but I successfully applied to all of your colleges of choice. And as you can see, you have a full ride scholarship to all of them for the whole four years. Your guidance counselor applied to every piece of money she could get her hands on. You received so much aid, you'll be able to get a dorm to yourself or an apartment on campus. I will feel safer if you stay on campus."

My hands were shaky as I held all of the letters. I was so overjoyed I didn't know what to say.

"Mama. I... how... How will I be able to go?"

"Let me ask you this. Do you want to be a mother, Tuscany?"

I felt so bad, but I shook my head no. I had a beautiful baby boy in the nursery and I hadn't asked about him once.

"I know you don't. I love my grandbaby, but you shouldn't have to suffer because of my mistakes and because this monster shot up in you. Fuck him. He can raise that fucking baby on his own since he wanted it so bad. He got enough money and resources to do so. Ms. Giselle will make sure I can still see the baby if you feel comfortable with that, but in the morning, you are being discharged. All of your things have been packed in that cute Jetta Ms. Giselle got for you. Tomorrow at first light, you leave to whichever state of college that you choose and all of this shit will be behind you. We gone put you in an extended stay until you can move on campus early summer."

I couldn't believe it. Here I was ruling out college, and my mom had come through in a major way. I thought my life was over. I wanted so fucking bad to ball up and die, but now, things were working out in my favor. God hadn't forgotten about me, even though it had seemed he had.

"Mama... I... thank you, but I can't. I'm sure he is on his way up here since I had the baby. He will kill y'all. He said it."

"That bitch thinks you're being induced the day after tomorrow, so we are getting you out of here. I wish I could come with you, but I know he will be pulling up at my house. I got a few of the block boys posting up outside my house just in case he jump stupid. He not gone fucking kill shit because I got proof he was fucking with a minor. I let his ass know that day if he jump stupid, he will be deported. He ain't got that much fucking money to beat the system. We gone be straight. You just go get your education. We will be just fine."

"This is crazy. I don't want you to keep in contact with him or anything. Just let Gilberto have him."

"Are you going to at least name him Tuscany?"

I hoped he wasn't sick enough to abuse his son, but I had to choose me.

"I don't know. I... maybe... Tulsaire. It don't really matter to me what his name is. Is it bad that I don't feel a connection to the baby?"

"Nope. Fuck who don't understand. Make some shit of yourself, Tuscany. Your brothers need some shit to look up too. Them last three joining the football team at the community center. I'ma make them stick with it too. Now, what college you choosing so I can set up the extended stay?"

Without a second thought, I told her, "University of Jagoda Bay, but I don't need an extended stay. I'm going to leave you some money, but I had enough to get me an apartment."

The next day, I was wheeled out of the hospital on a early discharge and sitting in my new Jetta. Ms. Giselle didn't feel comfortable with me driving, so she had her neighbor, Amber drive me. Amber even stayed with me for two weeks while I healed, found an apartment and helped me settle. I almost cried when she left, but she promised to return. I dropped her off at the airport, and she made sure to keep that promise and had done so up until she moved out of Memphis up to New York and married a hotshot lawyer. We still spoke on social media though.

Jagoda Bay was different than anything I had experienced. It had the city life of New York, star power like Hollywood, Cali, gambling like Vegas, but the tropicals of Florida. I hadn't been out of the apartment much besides Walmart and Target runs, but I was ready for new beginnings...

I really had put my past behind me and hadn't felt guilty not once. I was told Gilberto had moved out of Memphis, prompting Ms. Giselle to move here since she was relieved of her duties and share an apartment with me for a few months until she found her own. I knew then the coast was clear to visit, but still waited 'til after the first semester. Going back to Memphis, I didn't yearn for the child I carried for nine months. I did still pray for him, and when Ms. Giselle said that Gilberto treated the child exceptionally well until he moved, I took her word for it and locked that boy in the back of my mind. It sounded cruel, and I knew no one would ever understand my story, but it wasn't for them to understand. Had I stayed, I would have been six feet deep somewhere.

Not once in twelve years did I feel an ounce of guilt. Even when seeing my man and best friend grieve their child. I had more of a connection with a dead Athena than I did my own blood. I guess because I knew she was made out of love and my child was made from survival, but now, my feelings have reversed.

Gilberto giving me the option to let Athena go, was a no brainer. I loved Baguette more than I loved anyone in this world and seeing him pained after the loss of his daughter hurt me. His focus was so off that he couldn't even fuck me some days. Just when it seemed like he was hopping out of his funk, here comes Gilberto. There was no way I would have been able to just go on with my life after I'd seen Athena's beautiful little face. So, if I had to die so that she could live and get to know her parents, then, that's just what it was. I owed my man that. I owed my best friend that. I just couldn't understand for the life of me why or how he'd pulled that shit off. It was sickening.

After dropping Athena off on Aphrodite's porch, Gilberto had us driven straight to the hangar, and we were now forty thousand miles in the air. He dragged me to the back of the plane, beat my ass again and then allowed me to shower and change. Now I was sitting up front looking out the window contemplating on jumping. I'd come so far from this all to be dragged back to Hell. I knew there was no way Gilberto would let me leave this time. I was stuck, with death being the only way out.

"Here you are. I asked the stewardess for some ice for your eye."

I slowly turned my head, and my heart began thudding in my chest, looking at the replica of my brothers and me staring back. He saw that I wasn't accepting his homemade ice pack, which was cubed ice wrapped in a fancy napkin, and pressed it to my eye himself. All the guilt and the shame I didn't feel the day I left him in the hospital came back to me full force. He stood tall, just like my brothers, and the curls from his fade fell over his forehead. There were braces on his teeth, and I thought about how Tulscan's cereal-eating ass had to get them when he was seventeen because his shits were so crooked. His looked like they should come out soon because his teeth were perfectly straight.

Tears burst through as I nodded.

"Yes, I am. I'm so sorry!"

My baby boy stood there for over thirty minutes while I stared at him until the plane shook him, making me catch him before he fell and place him on the seat next to me. I drew in a sharp breath, taking him all in. Despair gnawed at my guts. The pain of seeing my baby boy all grown up hurt worse than any time Gilberto put his hand on me. When I first laid eyes on Athena, my head was full of fog. I couldn't believe staring back at me was Ditey's entire face. Gilberto didn't have to make introductions. If her looks didn't tell me, the pull in my gut did. But seeing my own baby with traces of my DNA all through his posterior had my mouth bone dry.

I hesitantly took the ice pack from him and held it myself as I continued to study him through my good eye. He was so fucking handsome. The most handsome little boy I'd ever seen.

"Wh...what's your name?"

Pulling his head out of his handheld game, he looked me in my mirroring eyes and put his attention back on the game.

There were so many things I had to make right. So many questions I knew were swarming through his young mind, and I'm the only person able to answer. But first thing first, I had to do what the fuck ever to get my child and I away from Gilberto. Because I knew in my heart, Baguette wasn't coming to find me.

"Tulsaire. My name is Tulsaire Navarro."

CHAPTER 4

Aphrodite "Ditey" "Pretty Pretty" "AP" Greer

The million dollar home I was standing in front of, my best friend pulling up looking as if she'd been beat to a pulp, and the two guns pointed at the two most important men in my life didn't move me. As a matter of fact, nothing did in this moment. With my heart galloping the same as a thousand horses and hands that were trembling, my mind was on one person – Athena. Athena Dianne Cherman. *My baby girl.* She's alive. She's living. She's breathing. She was in my arms just seconds ago, and just like when I gave birth to her, she was snatched from me before I could get a good look at her. *How? Where? Who? AND WHY?* I had so many questions running rapidly through my mind, but I was going to have to turn the trivia off and soak this all in. Just in case this was some type of cruel dream. Please let this not be a dream. I wasn't a saint by far, but I didn't deserve for this to be fiction. If this is what Baguette felt each night when he closed his eyes, then I can see why he was barely making it.

Taking one last look at the shit show in front of me, I scoffed and shook my head. Baguette had a gun pointing at Goal's wavy fade, and a mini Goal had a gun resting on Baguette's temple. This was crazy, and my heart nor mind could take any of the energy they were dishing out. I had no words for them. Instead, I turned on my heels and walked back inside my home.

The loud music from the DJ could no longer be heard. Just sniffles and everyone talking over each other, probably asking the same thing I was questioning myself. *Where the fuck did Athena come from, and how is she not dead?*

I pushed through the sea of cream and lavender, not caring who I was forcing out of my way until I could see my mommy cradling Athena in her bosom while rocking back and forward, tears staining her aging cheeks while speaking in tongues. My chest swelled, and my hand instantly went to my mouth as I bent over and stifled a loud cry. For years, my heart had been shattered into tiny pieces. There were days that I was so empty, life felt like a nightmare. A hand on my back rubbing in circular motions jolted me from the millions of questions swarming in my brain, and I knew by the smell of the Burberry Her perfume that it was my cousin, Sora.

For years, I'd grieved my baby in silence. I cut myself off from the world and turned into a whole different person behind losing my baby. If it weren't for my mama and Baguette, I probably would have lost my fucking mind, but here she is, being crushed to my mother's chest while her little legs hung off my mother's lap.

"Can...Can...I see her?"

My mama was still speaking in tongues, so my auntie pulled Athena from her arms and handed her to me. Once she was back in my grasp, the warmth of her body sent chills all over me. Her little round face, heart-shaped lips, and light brown skin was all me. I buried my face in her ponytails, where I could see the hair grease shining in her scalp.

"You're so beautiful. You know that, right?" I choked out while cradling her.

Pulling back, she stared at me with big brown eyes. In that moment, she looked exactly like her father, although she was my twin. That was so scary to me. Like how can a person that should still be in the ivory porcelain casket be cradled in my arms, looking exactly like her father and I?

"I have to potty."

Everyone laughed, although Athena didn't say shit funny, but hearing her small voice for the first time that was cute and innocent had me laughing through my tears.

"Okay, baby. Let's go potty."

My family parted like the Red Sea so that I could get Athena to the half bathroom that was tucked right behind the living room. The entire time I walked, I had my eyes locked into her brown ones, letting my feet guide us by memory only. *My fucking baby.* I was going to be so mad if this was a dream.

Once we got to the bathroom, I stood her near the toilet and closed the door behind us. I wanted her to have some privacy, but I didn't want to let her out of my sight. I was afraid if I left her in here by herself, the moment I closed and opened the door, she would disappear. It took everything in me not to inspect her from head to toe. I badly wanted to check her entire being, but at the same time, I didn't want to scare her. Nor did I want her to feel like it was okay for strangers to touch her anywhere. Bad enough, she's been with a stranger since the day I pushed her out. A stranger. A fucking stranger TOOK my daughter, and Tuscany brought her back. My head ached followed by the muscle in my chest trying to make a connection, but that would have to wait another day.

A strong pain surged through me as I once again realized someone had held my baby girl captive. I turned on my heels to hide my silent scream as she pulled her underwear down to use the potty. My head was all over the place, and I felt as if I would pass out. I still didn't want to do that in fear that I would wake up, and again, she would be a mere figment of my imagination.

Once I heard the toilet flush, I wiped my face, followed by a few sniffs. I had to get myself together in order to be able to process my current predicament.

"Um...um...um."

She was on her tippy toes, with soapy hands, struggling to reach the handle to turn on the water. I immediately jumped into gear, picking her up, turning the water on, and thoroughly washing her hands. My body was in motion, but I felt like I was merely outside of myself, on autopilot, watching the entire interaction.

Once her hands were dried, I added a little of the citrus lotion I had sitting next to the soap dispenser for guests. After making sure she was good, I turned the light back out, letting the candle glow the space and cracked the door.

Whispers stopped as I stepped back into the living room. My family was looking confused, shocked, and some were amused. This was something none of us expected. When I woke up this morning, Athena coming back to me wasn't even a thought. Now, here she was. In my arms.

"Okay, y'all go back to doing what you was doing. I know everyone has questions, but let's just give my niece the time to process this. Don't nobody go outside nor look out the damn window. Enjoy this expensive ass food and drink these strong ass drinks. I got punch in the kitchen too. DJ, start it back up. Gone now."

My family began to clear the space, trying to look busy as the DJ played Celebration.

"Baby, go to the back. Let's not overwhelm her." My mama had finally stopped praising and was wiping tears and mascara from the crevices of her eyes.

Holding on to my baby as tight as I could without hurting her, I let my mom lead the way down the hall, and she didn't stop until she got to Athena's bedroom. When Goal presented this room to me on our official first date, I knew it would be just a place where I came when I was thinking about my child. Never in a million years did I think she would ever be inside of here. *This is insane!*

Once I was in the room, which still smelled of the hibiscus plug-in I'd added in here a few nights ago, my mom closed the door behind us.

I stood in place as I watched my mom pace a little with her hand on the small of her back. She was whispering a few things to herself before stopping in her tracks and facing us. Shock covered her face as she took a step back and shook her head.

"That's all you Aphrodite. I have to get used to that. Wow. Lord have fucking mercy."

Athena giggled and placed her hand to her mouth and the snickers that came from her belly were the cutest. I began tearing up again because this was my first time hearing my daughter laugh. Her giggles turned into a full blown mirthless laugh and while she was cracking up I was boohooing.

I was finally able to control my tears while my mom stood with her thin lipped mouth curled into a sneer. I was beginning to feel light headed so I sat on the side of her bed with her still in my arms, calming from laughter.

"You laughing at me," My mama asked with a sly grin.

Athena nodded her head.

"Well, don't pay me no mind. I'm just shocked to see you. I know you must be confused."

Athena tore her eyes from my mom and looked around the room. When her eyes landed on a pile of new toys tucked in the corner next to the overflowing gold toy chest she turned her attention to me. Most of the toys were ones I'd collected off her grave from when Baguette would leave them. After letting them stay out a few weeks, I would go and get them if the grave keepers didn't. I couldn't find it in my heart to give them away so I had them in the garage at the old house for the longest. Just the other day, I came across them in the new garage and decided to clean them off and place them in the corner of her room. Her toy chest was equipped with Toys Goal had purchased when he present the decorated home.

"May I please play with the toys?"

I nodded, "of course, baby."

"You got to let her go, Aphrodite," my mama reminded me.

I placed her on her feet and watched as her dress bounced along with her long ponytails as she skipped to the toys. Once she had the Frozen doll in her hand, my mama sat next to me and grabbed my hand.

"I can't believe this is real, mama."

I turned my face to hers.

"I know, baby. Me either. Me either. My God. God is real, baby."

My mama began rubbing my hand then moved a strand of hair from the front of my face.

"Just like she has questions, I know you do too, but right now, your daughter is all that matters. We will worry about the rest later. Okay?"

I heard my mother's words, and although my head gesture said yes, somewhere in the back of my mind had me feeling like nothing was okay and it wouldn't be for a long time.

CHAPTER 5
Brock "Baguette" Cherman

My stomach was in knots as my chest felt like a whole drum line was going off in that bitch. With my gun pointed at the one man I thought I would never raise it too, sweat lined my fresh cut. Goal's eyebrows were slanted into a frown as a muscle quivered at my jaw. It was hot as fuck outside, but a circle of ice seemed to ring my mouth.

"Ion usually explain myself to a muthafucka that threatens my life, and being that you got steel to my dome, that's the ultimate threat."

His words didn't mean shit to me. Not even the gun that rested at my temple moved me. Some shit was going on, and Goal was the number one suspect.

"Gang, you know just as well as I know, this shit left field for me too. Ion know where the fuck y'all daughter came from or why Tuscany mentioned Gilberto, but instead of worrying about shit we can't change, take yo' ass in the house and love on yo' fuckin' daughter, nigga."

My daughter. My muhfuckin' daughter. For five fucking years, I've been tortured with thoughts of her. Dreams of her. That inkling in the pit of my belly that's been telling me that my baby was still here wasn't an inkling at all. The shit was intuition. My gut will never lead me astray, and had I listened to that shit, I probably would have found my fucking daughter a long ass time ago. That shit had me sick too.

"Hold up? That's why we got our shit upped? Over Gilberto? Maneeeee. We don't fuck with that nigga!"

The youngin' with the gun to my temple was who I recognized as Gage, aka Big Gator, the number one quarterback in the nation and Goal's baby brother. The niggas looked just alike. Mixed ass pretty boys with fucked up attitudes.

"Put the gun down, hijo. Let us let them talk like men."

Their mother spoke up, speaking directly to Big Gator, but looking at me with nothing, but sympathy.

"You good, big bro?" Gage asked.

Goal reached in and lowered his brother's gun and then turned and lowered mine. I let him without hesitation.

"We good. Y'all go in the house. We will be in there in a minute," Goal spoke dismissively with his eyes still on me. We both held rage and fire in our orbs, and I could tell he was on the same type of time I was on, but still, this shit didn't make sense to me.

"Aite, I gotta piss anyway. Come on, mama."

"Watch your mouth. We're going to talk about that gun too, hijo." Their mother, whom I could see who they got their eyes from, spoke in a heavy Colombian accent, but I could understand everything she was saying.

Once they were in the house, leaving only her sweet perfume to linger, Goal and I were in a face off. My eyes glowed with a savage inner fire, and his were dark and unfathomable.

"He used a bitch to get to me and had my daughter this whole time."

"But you'n know that, though. Listen, this shit-"

Goal sighed and swiped his hand down the front of his face.

"This left field like a muhfucka, but right now, that shit gotta wait."

Finality was in Goal's tone, and although I wanted to feel where he was coming from, my fucking heart was broken. Knowing my baby been out here alive the whole time and hearing my woman drop her off had me feeling lost, betrayed, and broken. *What the fuck going on?*

Tucking my gun in the small of my waist, I walked inside the house, looking past nosey muthafuckas that wanted answers they weren't getting from me. I hadn't ate shit, but a banana this morning, so the smell of food should have caused my stomach to growl, but my mind was spinning with bewilderment. My fuckin' daughter. Some sick pussy really held my seed from me for what? This shit just wasn't adding up!

"They went to the back," Sora called out after seeing me walk in circles looking for them.

I wasted no time heading to the back. About three doors down, I saw a cracked door, and before I could burst through it, I had to take a step back and breathe. I was so overcome with emotions that I didn't know if I wanted to cry, scream, or shoot some shit up. After getting myself together as best as I could, I bust in the door and found Ms. Deborah Robin consoling Aphrodite. I turned my head in the opposite direction, and there she was, in a corner, playing with toys that were meant for her grave. I knew because before purchasing them, I would sometimes spend hours on the aisles doing research to make sure I was buying something my daughter would cherish and love. I never would have fucking thought my baby would be playing with the fucking dolls in real life yet there she was.

I stood in place, feet cemented on the tan plush carpet as I let her entire being etch into my mind. One...two...three... four... five ponytails twisted and clamped with lavender barrettes. Baby hair lined her oval-shaped face, and while she was tiny, her jaws were puffy just like the day she was born. She held up Elsa at the top of the ice castle, began humming *Let it go* before jumping her sister on the balcony with her as if she too had powers. Yes, I might've watched the movie a time or two on some high shit.

Athena was sitting Indian style, and that shit made me frown because she was wearing a dress. I could only see her view from behind her, but the way I was feeling, I wanted to snatch her lil' ass up and toss some jeans on her.

I don't know when I walked into the room and kneeled beside her, but when she looked at me; eyes wide with innocence, I dropped my head and pinched the bridge of my nose.

This shit was surreal. My baby girl. My only baby girl. Right here in my grasp. Taking a deep breath, I looked over at Aphrodite because I didn't know what she'd told her. I'm sure wherever she'd been, they didn't let her know what her real name was or who her real parents were. Just thinking about that shit had me boiling hot, but I had to dial back and let shit rock for now. Right now, the most important thing was my daughter.

Aphrodite shook her head, so I turned my attention back to Athena.

"I'ma give y'all some privacy. I'll be in the living room if you need me. See you in a few, pretty girl."

Aphrodite's mom took her stand, and that shit had me remembering I had to call my own damn mama. What the fuck would I even say? They were supposed to come today, but I had a sick uncle in Connecticut that they were visiting last minute. So much shit was resting on my shoulders now, but I needed to at least make sure baby girl was good.

"What's your name, beautiful?"

Athena Dianne Cherman was her name. The same name that was plastered over the wall in gold. When Tuscany came home and told me Aphrodite had a room specifically for our daughter, I was pleasantly surprised. This shit was fitting for her too.

"My name is Alba, and my middle name is Ramira, but you can just call me A or Ramira. I don't have a last name." She frowned.

When her brows furrowed, I had to bite back a smile because she had the same exact frown as her mama.

"Alba Ramira, hunh? Why you looking like you didn't want to tell me ya' name?"

Alba placed the dolls down gently and lowered her eyes.

"It's not that. It's just that Ricardo next door said my name was ugly, and his mom gave him time out, but he still says my name is ugly. So, I'm going by A or Ramira now. That's the first letter in my name. A."

She had the last sentence right, but all that other shit was bullshit. Her name wasn't no fucking *Alba,* and her middle name damn sure isn't *Ramira.* My daughter was way too pretty for those granny ass names.

"I'ma fuck Ricardo up. You know his last name-"

"Umm umm. Well, Ath- I mean A, you look very pretty today,"

Aphrodite complimented as she took a seat on the ground next to Athena. She even changed her posture so that she was sitting like her with a dress on, and I appreciated that shit.

Athena looked at her with a smile.

"Thank you. You're so pretty," Athena returned the compliment.

Aphrodite blushed, "Thank you so much, A. You like Frozen?"

Aphrodite picked up a doll and began placing heels on her feet.

"Yes, I love Frozen! I love Encanto, and Dora, and Doc Mcstuffins, and the Little Mermaid, and, well, I like a lot! I like all of these toys too? Who's are they? Maybe I can play with them with her."

Aphrodite nervously moistened her lips with her tongue, and she cleared her throat while looking from Athena to me. This shit was so crazy I didn't even know what the fuck to say. All I wanted to do was hug my baby girl and cry in her little arms.

"This room is our daughter's room. Her name is Athena, and we... uh thought...well...she passed away."

She dropped her doll in surprise and covered her mouth.

"Oh no! Was she almost five like me?"

"Yes. Well, no, well, she would have been five today."

Athena stood up in shock, putting both Aphrodite and I on alert.

"No way! Tomorrow is my birthday!"

Again, Aphrodite and I gave each other knowing looks, because today fasho was her birthday, not no fucking tomorrow.

"Well, how about we celebrate your birthday today, and you can eat cake and watch movies and sleep in our daughter's bed? Would you like that?" Athena nodded her head with a broad smile on her face, revealing dimples that she got from her daddy.

"I would-"

"Aw hellll nawl!"

Shattering glass had me jumping to my feet and reaching for the back of my waist. Aphrodite grabbed Athena, and I let her know to stay in here with my eyes. This had already been a fucking strange ass day. On God, ion have the time for it making another turn.

CHAPTER 6

Lydia "Litty" Greer

My whole life, I've done everything right. With my mother dying when I was in elementary, I wanted nothing more than to prove to her that her baby girl is good. After failing the first grade, I redeemed myself and went hard every grade after that. I went so hard that now during my senior year, I was graduating Salutatorian.

Being that I'm always on top of my studies, and due to the fact that I'm being raised by the best single father on the planet, my family goes over and beyond for me. My big cousin Aphrodite gives me whatever, and in return, I help her with her online boutique, Goddess Wears. Whether she needs orders fulfilled, pieces modeled, or help organizing her site, she knows outside of Auntie Deborah and Tuscany, I'm the girl to call. Then there is my big cousin, Sora. I love and adore my baby cousins, Rheas, Rayna, and Red Jr., so anytime Sora needs a babysitter I'm there. My family not only keeps my pockets laced, they make sure I want for nothing. Well, all except a car, and I was hoping graduation changed that. I was hoping to get my Kia Stinger in matte grey, even though my best friend Savannah thought it was a poor bitch car her words, but my actions months ago may have halted my car wish being granted.

In less than seven weeks, I'll be walking across the stage receiving my diploma and giving my speech that includes telling my classmates they can be anything in the world as long as they work hard, but the last thing any of them thought that I would be is a babymama. Most Likely to Succeed, Best dressed, Salutatorian, Honors Society, Chest Club Champion, and National Spelling Bee winner Lydia Greer. A whole baby mama out here. Pregnant as ever.

.

"I guess you not gone tell me I'ma be a God mama 'til you pushing this big headed ass baby out."

Kneeling in front of the toilet, my head popped up at my bestie. She was looking so cute in her ivory and lavender. I loved my chocolate bestie. Her curves were out of this world and had boys, young and old, salivating. Batting her long lashes that she'd done herself just this morning, she crossed her arms over her breasts and tossed her bundles behind her back. Hearing her speak something I was fighting against had me burst into tears. It had been so hard to hide this from my family. Aphrodite had to pay an extra three hundred for my dress because my hips and breasts had spread, and I needed it altered. Luckily, my stomach had a small pudge that wasn't noticeable. Prom was in two weeks, and I prayed I hadn't gained any more weight by then.

"Shhhh, best friend! Stop crying! You gone be okay! I didn't expect this shit from you, but you got me. You can still go to college and follow your dreams and shit. Plus, you already good with kids."

When I missed my January period, I already knew what was up. I made a doctor's appointment at the local clinic, and it was confirmed that I'd be welcoming a baby to the world in September. I would barely be a month into my first college semester!

I hadn't seen Gage since that night. I woke up around five in the morning because I was cold, snatched my shirt, and ran out of that penthouse. I left his ass in the cabana and Savannah. I didn't stop 'til I was at the hotel in the shower. I didn't regret what I did; I was just ashamed the next morning. I still scrolled past his IG every day, but hadn't returned to Sparkling City. Savannah had begged me to go with her since she and Jodi were a thing, but I refused. My girl was a whole stepmama out here.

"My family gone be so mad!" I cried.

"Girl, please. You're graduating salutatorian! They are going to support you even if they are a little disappointed. God makes no mistakes. Your family cool as fuck. Hell, look how they living. You and lil baby gone be straight. Now who the daddy? When you due? You been to the doctor?"

I nodded and wiped my tears.

"September. Yes, I been going to the clinic and paying out of pocket so my daddy won't see it on the insurance. I messed up so bad, friend."

Savannah's eyes grew wide.

"Hold up. I'm not no mathematician like you, but that means if you due in September, you got pregnant- Bitch, when you was on the balcony with Gage! That's why you left! It's his?"

I held my head low.

"Biiiitchhh! Tee Tee baby, rich as fuck! Bitch, you 'bout to have Gage "Big Gator" Navarro's baby? What the fuck? I keep telling yo' ass you God's favorite!"

Four months ago, my bestie talked me into driving to the school championship game, which was three hours away. She'd even used her big cousin's ID to rent a car since, at the time at seventeen, Savannah's license was restricted. I floored the rental to Sparkling City, where the opposing team, the Briarwind Gators, kicked my school's ass. Bayside didn't stand a chance with the game ending 60-26. We were slaughtered. Instead of taking my ass back to the room, I let Savannah talk me into going to an afterparty because she was dating number 33, Jodi Pruitt, on the Gator's team. The party was being hosted by the quarterback of the winning team in his brother's condo.

I stepped outside to answer my dad since the music was so loud, and in all honesty, I should have ignored the call. Well, I dropped my phone over the balcony and almost killing myself trying to chase it, and my crush was there to catch me before I turned into mush. We smoked, one thing led to another, and he was breaking my Vcard like the smitten schoolgirl I was. The dumbest decision of my fucking life. Now, here I was. A pregnant Salutatorian that was knocked up off my very first time. Tragic.

I placed my hand over Savannah's mouth. There was a full party downstairs, but she was too damn loud.

"Girl, I heard even if the nigga decided he don't want to go pro, which I doubt, he rich either way. They said his brother got that moneyyyyyy."

I didn't care about nun' of that. My future was on the line all because of the euphoric feeling this man gave me the night of the championship.

"When you gone tell him? Want me to get his number from Jodi? Because this nigga needs to step the fuck up."

I sighed. This was all making my head hurt.

"The baby isn't even here yet. I'm going to tell him, but he has too much going on for me to mess up his-"

"Nope, bitch. You have just as much going for yourself as he does. It's not fair for you to walk around all ashamed and shit. He needs to step.the.fuck.up." Savannah clapped with each word.

"Ion know. I want to forget it all for now. I will tell him soon, okay. Just don't tell Jodi."

Savannah shook her head, looked out the window, and did a double-take.

"I don't gotta tell Jodi shit. Yo, baby daddy here, boo. He walking up now. It's time to put y0'a big girl panties on."

I stood and looked out the window, and low and behold, the fine-ass Navarro family was walking up the yard, looking Godly in their off-white...

Shiiiit. Why is he here? They know my cousin? Fuck my life.

I closed my eyes for a bit and opened them back up due to Savanah grabbing my arm. Seeing Gage 'Big Gator,' pull a gun out of Baguette, my cousin's ex, had me clutching my pearls. I ran back to the bathroom and emptied more contents out of my belly. That's all I'd been doing since I came to terms of being pregnant was throwing up.

"Girl, yo' baby daddy done put the gun down! Come on back out here."

Savannah had her nosey ass head out of the window, watching everything unfold. I don't know why the boy I'd been crushing on forever had a gun to my cousin's ex head, but I would be lying if I said I wasn't holding my breath and praying God spared him.

"Bestie, they walking in the house! They walking in the fucking house, boo! Damn, I wish Jodi was here. This shit 'bout to get good!"

Snaking my neck around to my best friend since elementary, I rolled my eyes at the amusement in hers.

"This is not a game, Savannah. Nobody knows I'm pregnant! Why is he here and with a gun! He's the number one prospect in the country. He just led his school to a national championship in December! He can't have a weapon! And he lived three hours away in Sparkling City! Again, why is he here?"

I plopped down on the window ledge in frustration, not really needing this shit today.

Savannah sat down on the ledge across from me and pushed my curly hair behind my ear.

"Bestie, you be out the loops so bad. Okay, so boom, you remember when we went to the game, and that fine ass nigga, aka yo' brother in-law, sat next to us for a minute until he climbed onto the field?"

"Yeah, the one that was with that girl with the big, but?"

Savannah rolled her eyes, "Yeah, that bitch, but fuck her. Anyway, I think yo' cousin fucking with Goal?"

"Goal," I asked, confused.

"Yes, bitch Goal. Keep the fuck up. Goal is Gage "Big Gator's" big brother! Remember I told you that nigga like the plug plug?"

Savannah be telling me so much stuff, and most of it goes in one ear and out the other unless it's something of significance that I need to store about her.

"Okay, Goal, Gage's brother is the *plug - plug*, but that doesn't answer why he's here."

I wasn't as green as I appeared, so I knew my cousin's men and ex-men were heavy in the streets one time or another, but this is Aphrodite's housewarming. Although her and Baguette are close friends, they aren't together, so there would be no need for him to invite his friends over. If that was even the case.

The look of confusion hadn't wavered from my face, causing Savannah to slap her forehead.

"Okay, I think the plug done wifed up Aphrodite!" my bestie clapped with excitement.

My big cousin was indeed single and had been for five years, and although Savannah's info was usually rock solid, she might have hit a dub this time. Aphrodite didn't give men the time of day. I've seen her turn down plenty of handsome men. She was content with being single and sometimes that made me sad for her.

"No, you can't be right."

"Yeap, I can. Look."

Savannah pulled out here phone and went to Gage's profile, shoving the phone in my face. There was a slide of pictures of him standing in front of a pool rocking all white, and the thin diamond necklace on his neck and studs in his head had my heart fluttering. He was so damn fine!

Rocking that all white, headed to meet my brother's wifey. I wonder if he got good taste like his lil' bro.

"Read the caption, boo. He wrote that and popped up here. Plus, I remember seeing a video on Aphrodite's page and on God, Goal was in it. I just thought I was on some high shit when I saw it, and when I went back to check it, it was deleted. Baguette fine and all, and I'm sure if their daughter was still here, he would have been a great daddy, but GOAL IS MUTHAFUCKIN' ZADDY, BITCH!"

I placed my hand over her mouth just as the music stopped. It was crazy because I wasn't really showing when I got dressed, but now that I've eaten and Big Gator popped up, I had the biggest little bump ever. Fuck my life.

"Baby, your cousin the luckiest bitch alive next to you because on everything in my soul, I would be fucking both them niggas. A fine ass paid baby daddy and a fine ass rich ass boyfriend? Chooo Choo! Polygamy me, boo. Polygamy the fuck out of me-"

I placed my hand on top of Savannah's glossed lips because now that no music was playing, her loud mouth ass could be heard. The kids had the theatre room speakers loud, so I couldn't hear what was going on downstairs, but still, she was too loud, and anybody could be coming up the steps.

"My bad. Fine rich niggas just get me hot and bothered. I'm ready to risk it all and be a dopeboy's wife. Hell, these good boys with bright futures and shit got baby mamas too. Ain't no damn difference. Oops, sorry, friend. I was talking about my situation, not yours."

Savannah was dating Jodi, who was not only on Gage's team, but he too was a national prospect. My friend was a whole stepmama out here because he had a newborn daughter.

"Look, God gave you the stage. That young man is here and so is your whole family. Your belly poking in that romper, boo. You may as well tell the truth." Savannah shrugged.

A flicker of apprehension coursed through me and gnawed at my confidence. I wanted this to be nothing more than a nightmare. For four months, I've been praying to God that this reality be a dream. One night changed the trajectory of my future forever of not only mine, but his.

"I... can't. I'll tell my family because they will find out soon enough, but I can't do that to Gage."

"Oh, here we go back to this shit." Savannah scoffed.

"He's number one in the freaking nation for crying out loud! His mother and brother are down there! They are going to think I'm trying to trap him and ruin his life. He doesn't need a kid! Hell, he probably doesn't even remember me!"

Four months ago, Big Gator and I talked after he saved me, had sex, and now here we are. I'd been crushing on the man forever and had yet to say one thing to him until that night. His mom and I even made a connection at the game and then again when he saved me. She facetimed him, and we spoke. I didn't think he nor his family would be here in this house.

"Hey! Hey!"

I cut my eyes at one of my little cousins, who had a sly grin on her face.

"Y'all need to come down here. Aphrodite baby, not dead! She alive and here! Come on."

Before Savannah and I could ask her more questions, she ran her grown ass back down the stairs.

"If Presha lil' young ass lying, on God, I'ma beat her fast ass. I can't stand that lil' girl. Come on."

I didn't want to go downstairs, but being that my phone and purse were on the couch, I had to go sooner than later. Plus, there had to be something going on for guns to be drawn. I couldn't even wrap my mind around the possibility of Athena being alive because if that were true, then that was a blessing, but one that for sure was questionable. I remember like yesterday when my cousin cried her heart out about losing her only baby. It must've hurt her soul to come home from the hospital without a child she'd been preparing for, and although I didn't want this child, that was one of my biggest fears. I had dreams of dying during childbirth and others of giving birth to a dead baby. Heck, I'd even gave birth to a whole alligator one night, and when I pushed it out, the damn beast ate me. Pregnancy gives you the craziest dreams, I swear.

"Here." Savannah glossed my lips, dapped at my mascara and flattened my hair.

"You have just as much at stake as him, friend. You're the prize. That nigga knew what he was doing when he ran in you raw and didn't pull out. I got your back forever and always. Having a baby is not the end of the world. If you want me to be your on campus nanny, I got you. I'll follow you wherever, bestie. Just know, you're going to be a hot shot statistics lady, and this baby is going to be so blessed to call you mommy. Your family is understanding and loving. They will support you. We don't need Gage, and if he wants nothing to do with the baby-"

"Then I can do it on my own. See, bestie, you always got my back."

Savannah drew her head back and frowned.

"Hell nawl, I wasn't fitna say that dumb ass shit! I was about to say if he doesn't want nothing to do with the baby, we gone beat his ass and take that nigga straight to juvenile court. They too rich to get away. He gone help out too. Nigga better learn to balance a bottle and a football. Now come on, boo. Let's face the music."

Savannah pulled me up, rubbed my belly and locked her hand in mine.

"Now, let's see if we can get you one of these fancy ass houses."

Shaking my head, I let her lead me to the stairs, and before we could reach the bottom, all eyes were on me.

"Aw hellll nawl!"

My auntie screamed, and when I saw what was in her hand, I must've melted right there in the middle of the floor.

With narrowed eyes, hers landed right on me, and she began

stomping toward me. Savannah cowered, but stood in place right by my side as I waited on what I knew was about to be a tongue lashing.

"What the fuck is this, Lydia? Hunh?"

Auntie held up a sonogram that held my secret.

"You muhfuckin' pregnant? After all that fucking preaching I did to yo' ass? You graduating head of yo' class, got all these damn colleges at your doorstep, and you want to slip on a lil' ass dingaling unprotected?"

"What's going on, mama?" Sora walked up with Rhea, her three year old daughter on her hip.

I groaned inwardly as tears poured from my eyes.

"This lil ass girl is pregnant! That's what!"

Sora took the sonogram from her mother's hands, and sadness washed over her.

"Ima beat yo' ass! I don't give a fuck! You got us fucked up!"

"Mama, just wait. This true, Lydia?"

I could tell Sora had been crying prior to Auntie busting me out, and now tears were threatening to fall again.

"Hell yeah, it's true and look at the date! She past the abortion period! This a whole big headed ass baby on this picture. She 'bout to get ready to have this lil' muthafucka!"

"I'm sorry, auntie! I didn't mean to! I promise it was a mistake!"

"You can miss me with them tears! You don't make a mistake and fuck raw! When in the fuck do yo' nerdy ass got time to sex? You always babysitting or at a fucking chess club meeting! You done let one of them nerdy ass niggas knock you up! Brother! Brother!"

Auntie turned her head to look around for my daddy, and I took that opportunity and ran.

"Get yo' hot ass back here! Y'all catch her!"

Bobby tried to catch me, but I was too quick. I ran to the first door I saw, closed and locked it.

With my eyes closed and back to the door, I continued to cry because I never wanted my life to go like this.

"Uh, I guess I shoulda locked the door."

My eyes shot open, and my luck was just too damn bad because there was Gage, with his penis out, emptying a stream of urine in the toilet. My eyes bulged, seeing that it was still as big as I remember, and when he smirked, I turned my head.

Once I heard him flush and zip, I slowly opened my eyes again.

"What it do, gorgeous?"

Only my dumb self would smile through sniffles, and when he saw that I was crying, his amusement dropped from his face.

"Fuck wrong with you?"

Instead of answering his question, I watched as he washed his hands and shook them dry, skipping past the hand towels folded neatly in the black basket on the vanity and the lotion.

"I'm-"

Boom Boom Boom Boom. "Bring yo' ass out here, pregnant ass girl! I'm on yo' ass."

The beating from the door vibrated against the back of my head as I bit down on my bottom lip.

"Leave her alone! Baby, come on out. Let's talk. Auntie not gone touch you."

"See, that's the problem, Luda! You too damn soft on her! How the hell you let her get pregnant! Probably when she went to that hotel back in November."

"That was December and she went to a damn game!"

"Well, same damn thang!"

My dad and his sister continued to argue while I was hyperventilating. This couldn't be happening! Out of all the days! Why today?

Gage's eyes went from my tear-struck face to my belly and to my face again.

"Them yo' people?"

I nodded my head.

An expression that I couldn't read crossed his face, and he reached around me to get the door.

"No! Don't open it!"

"Look, I got you, aite? Come on."

As I stared into his piercing grey eyes, my cheeks burned in remembrance of the night we shared. My auntie would most definitely make good on her promise and beat me blue, but I wanted to kick my own ass for getting myself into this predicament. Gage's eyes hadn't left mine, but with renewed humiliation, I looked away.

Easing off the door, Gage twisted the lock, and at the same time, I cowered behind him and covered my head. I didn't want to get slapped by my heavy handed ass auntie.

"Uh, I thought my daughter was in here?"

My dad's gruffy voice was laced with confusion. I could tell by the way his sentence dragged the three beers he'd consumed had him on cloud nine. With the news he'd just heard about his one and only baby girl, I'm sure he will be sober in no time.

"Hi, daddy. I'm right here."

I stood on my tippy toes and peeped over Gage's shoulder.

God, he smells so good.

Seeing the gloss in my father's eyes confirmed my suspicions about him being drunk.

"I'm Gage Navarro." Gage held his hand out to shake my father's, and when my daddy left him hanging, I groaned.

Gage didn't take it to heart because he reached back and grabbed my hand, pulling me past my father and into the living room, where I knew my auntie was waiting.

"So yo' lil ass is pregnant? How in the fuck you gone be a pregnant muthafucka, Lydia?"

I wanted to question my aunt's incoherent rant, but I stayed quiet. I felt the eyes of my entire family on me and also the judgement in them.

"Lydia, are you pregnant?" Sora asked, still holding Rhea, with tears down her face.

"I... I..."

"Fuck all that soft shit! Who the fucking daddy? Where the lil' nigga at so that I can beat his muthafuckin' ass?"

Although my child's father was in this very room, right behind me, I would never out him. He did participate in getting me pregnant, but I hadn't even told him he was the father. Hell, we haven't spoken since December! The same night we met, the same night we created this child.

Instead of answering my aunt, I turned to Sora and nodded. My dad had now walked into the room with his arms crossed, and I could see

Baguette walk up. He almost looked pale in the face, and that brought me back to Gage having a gun to his head. I could see Gage's brother lowly talking in Baguette's ear, so I guess that little situation was all cleared up.

I took a step forward since all eyes were on me and decided to go ahead and bite the bullet.

"Yes, I'm pregnant."

Everyone's dramatic ass gasped, and Auntie's drunk ass was shaking her head.

"I know y'all are disappointed in me. To be honest, I'm disappointed in myself. I'm four months pregnant, but I don't know the sex yet. Although I've been hiding it from you all, I have been on top of my appointments by going to the local clinic. I let one night of fun change the trajectory of my future forever. I don't know what this means for my future, but I will provide for my baby on my own. I hate I let you down, and I appreciate everything you all have done for me my entire life, but I won't allow you all to bring me down with physical or mental abuse. I love my child, and I'm going to do whatever it takes to give him or her the best life."

I held my breath after speaking my peace and tried to lay eyes on everyone in the room.

"Fuck all that! I'ma beat yo' fast ass! Where the fuck is the daddy? You fucked up bad, but you damn sure not doing this shit by yo' damn self!"

"Aye, it won't be nun of that goin' on."

Gage stepped up behind me so close, I could not only feel him towering over me, but the hardness of his body against mine was calming.

"And who the fuck is yo' fine ass, light bright?"

"That's the father. Gage "Big Gator" Navarro. Am I right, son?" My dad spoke up, causing me to snap my head at him in question.

"What?" Goal drew his head back, and their mother's hand shot to her mouth.

I looked back at Gage, since all eyes were on him, and he had his head turned while scratching behind his ear.

"Fuck," he breathed.

"Hold up? You kin to fine ass over there? Y'all look just alike?"

"Mama, stop. That's Goal's lil brother."

"So Aphrodite set this shit up?" Auntie screamed.

"What? No, auntie! We met at a par-"

"Aye y'all, ion mean no harm or no disrespect, but the details of how and when or why it happened not even relevant. We slipped up, but I'm a man before anything. Litty and the baby already set for life. They not gone want for shi- I mean, nothing."

My heart fluttered at his response, but that didn't ease my anxiety.

"That sound good and all, but we not worried about no money. My daughter has been working hard her entire life. She's graduating number two in her class. I can take care of my daughter and my grandchild. My concern comes to Lydia and what she wants for her future. My baby has big plans, and even though I know it takes two to tango, I know with the type of future the both of you have mapped out, a baby is nowhere in those plans, at least not right now. I'm hurting for my daughter because I know her life will never be the same after this."

Seeing my daddy get choked up had the tears running rapidly down my face. Savannah came her scary ass from out of hiding and began wiping my cheeks.

"It's okay, bestie. I told you I got you."

"I understand y'all concerns, and this is a shocker for me too, but I can assure you all, the young lady's plans will go on without a hitch. My brother, as well as my family, will do our part. Now, you can all get back to eating and drinking unless y'all ready to dip. I cool with either or."

Everyone was quiet as a mouse as Goal spoke from his side of the room, and when the DJ started the music back up, he got his answer. Their mom walked up to me, looking as beautiful as ever, and Savannah stepped out of the way.

"It's nice to meet you in person, hermosa. Have no worries. All will be well." She grabbed my hands, kissed them, and then bowed her head and said a quick prayer in her native tongue. When she was done, she smiled at me and then shot her eyes up to her son.

"It's okay, hijo. We will get through this as a family."

"I know, ma. I'ma be back; I need to smoke."

Gage walked fast as hell out the front door, and Goal shook his head. He and their mom were following behind him, and I knew I wouldn't be seeing them again today. My head began to spin, and I just needed a moment to myself. I walked past everyone straight to the back and went inside of the first cracked door I saw. When I stepped in, I froze in my tracks. Aphrodite was holding a baby girl, and when she turned her head, all I remember is seeing the exact same face on the both of them before everything went black.

CHAPTER 7
Goal Navarro

As of today, I've had 33 birthdays. 33 years around the hot ass sun. 33 years to experience some of the best days of my fucking life. Even when I was a jit, and my mama was out on her ass, she always made sure birthdays were never the worst days. From her homemade cakes to her handmade signs, she used to make a nigga feel like I was the king of the world anytime my born-day rolled around. So, over time, I turned my shit into a national holiday. Usually, around this time of year, you could find me on an island that niggas never even heard of, getting my dick ate by a baddie. If I wasn't on that type of time, I was partying with the stars and shit or out in Dubai blowing a bag so heavy, the shit came with presidential treatment. But this year, of all my fucking birthdays, I was the most geeked. I went to bed, drunk as fuck and got some nasty, sloppy ass sex from the baddest. We fucked so hard, my dick was sensitive, rubbing up against my fucking jeans.

I left the crib to go get chopped, happy as fuck, and when I got back, she gave a nigga sloppy toppy in the shower. After getting dressed, and letting the caterers in, I headed out to make the three hour drive to Sparkling City to pick up my mama and lil brother. Aphrodite was rushing my ass back because she claimed to have a gift for a nigga that I was gone love. Truth be told, she was the fucking gift. I didn't expect shit from Aphrodite besides her fucking a nigga whenever she felt inclined to and continuing to grace me with her beauty.

Though today was my day, the shit wasn't even about me and for once, I was cool with that. My Pretty was happy, and from what I could gather, she looked forward to celebrating her daughter's very short life instead of dreading this day. What the fuck I didn't expect is to walk up and see her daughter in her arms and to have this nigga, B, look at me like I'm the fucking culprit. I could handle a nigga thinking I did some flaw shit. Even if it's from a nigga I would never cross out. But if Baguette was questioning a nigga's motives, then that means my bitch was questioning a nigga's motives, and that was some shit that had to be addressed asap, but until I could even face her, I had to deal with this other shit.

"Aye, bruh! Fuck you run out the house fah'?"

I caught the front door just as it was about to close. I knew like hell Aphrodite was going to get a HOA violation for all the damn cars that was lined up down the block, and I couldn't wait to curse their ass out when they issued it too. She 'bout one of the few, if not the only mutha-fucka in the community, that had the deed to her shit. They better tread the fuck lightly. It was dope as fuck seeing all her people come and show the fuck out for her, and if the circumstances were different, I would have been in there turning the fuck up. Her lil baby popping up on us from the grave was even some shit a nigga like me didn't expect, and I'd seen all types of shit in these streets. I was still trying to wrap my mind around it, but this young nigga in front of me had thrown me for a loop.

Big Gator was still walking and didn't stop until he was sitting on the hood of my Rolls Royce. He pulled a blunt from out his pocket and lit it as I took a stance in front of him. Scanning him from head to toe, it was almost sickening how much the nigga looked just like me. The only thing is, his ass just more lean and in shape than I was at his age, being that his ass had been running the ball since before he could tie his fucking shoes.

"Nigga, you gotta cut all that fucking smoking out too. High school was one thing, but college ball is a whole nother ball game. Just like the pro's gone be different than that."

Gage wasn't hearing shit I was saying because he inhaled smoke and let out a fat ass cloud.

"I fucked up, brother." With the blunt pinched in between his fingers, he dropped his arms and lowered his head.

"I got a whole fucking future I'm chasing. What the fuck I'ma do with a baby? Ion got time for no shit like this," he exasperated.

"Since the day Madre's belly started to grow, I came to terms that I had a responsibility. The thing is, I wasn't 18 with a laced ass bank account. Abuelo helped us, yes, but I was a young ass nigga that was already being an emotional support to our immigrant mother, and now a baby was getting thrown in the mix."

Knowing where I was going, Gage shook his head, shoulders still slumped.

"This shit different, big bro."

I drew my head back and crossed my arms.

"How, young nigga? How the fuck is it different? Nigga, I raised you when I was still a fucking baby myself! Ion even got no fucking kids, but there I was changing pampers, making bottles, and up all fucking night. I used to have the game controller in one hand and you in the other. You used to cry so fucking much that it drove Madre into depression. She had zoned the fuck out for a while, so I had to make some shake. The only fucking thing that used to shut yo' ass up is when I would play Madden.

When I noticed that shit, I started playing that shit 'til my thumbs hurt. Then, I tried my luck at putting the football games and shit on, and that shit used to keep you quiet. I would fall asleep with you in the rocker in front of the tv watching all the damn football game reruns and shit."

I chuckled, thinking about how the nigga came out obsessed with football. He gave us the blues, and the only thing that worked to calm him was watching niggas toss sheepskin and get their asses tackled.

"I didn't have time for that. I didn't even have a mapped out future, but I knew I didn't have time for no fucking baby. Madre winged it when she raised me, so her having to do the shit all over again 14 years later was a slap in the face. We made time though. We altered our lives to make sure you was loved, nurtured, and provided for. Even Abuelo. We all did what the fuck we had to do to make sure you turned out exactly what you are. Gage "Big Gator" Navarro. Number one in the fucking country! My lil bro. A baby? Yeah, it's life changing, but this shit is small to a giant, and nigga, at over 6 feet, we giants!"

"What the fuck I'ma do though?"

My little brother's grey eyes held so much worry, and all I wanted to do was carry his weight. It was my fucking job to carry his weight, but when it came to where he laid his dick, that was on him. He had to man the fuck up. Having a baby wasn't the worse thing in the fucking world, not when yo' ass is more than capable of taking care of it without a fucking job.

"Nigga, what you mean? You gone take care of yo' shit like a man! You stuck raw dick in her so you got dealt a raw ass hand. Play stupid games, and you win stupid prizes. Just like you got a future, so does she. You got my woman's baby cousin knocked the fuck up. You see how they are about her? She's the fucking apple of their eye! Salutatorian! That girl had a future as bright as yours, if not brighter! You a nigga, you can come and go as you please, but her? She the one carrying that baby. Not you. She gotta push that baby out. Not you. You gone step the fuck up like a man, talk to her and alter your shit around her. What's your top three colleges?"

I knew, but I wanted him to tell me.

"Southern Cal, Georgia, TCU."

"Yeah, that ain't gone work."

Gage kept his head down.

"You want me at Jagoda Bay University, hunh?"

"Damn right. If she wants to go away to college, let her do that. You came in and fucked her shit up, but just like I had to stay up all fucking night and deal with yo' ass while mama get her mind right, you gone do the same thing for your child. Even if you got to go to fucking practice with the fucking baby carrier on the sidelines. Let her go on with her plans. Don't mean you taking the baby or no shit like that, but you will support her. Financially, mentally, and physically. You didn't just get no ratchet bitch pregnant. She's the princess to her people, and her being pregnant let them down. You have resources that she doesn't have. You can still be everything you want to be, but you not gone run away from this shit. A football in one hand and a bottle in the other. We clear on that shit?"

I wasn't my brother's father, but I'm the closest thing he has had to one outside of Abuelo. I didn't run away from him, so he damn sure not about to be across the country living his best fucking life while that girl lost her damn mind trying to raise a baby. Women wouldn't even be able to get pregnant without us men, so I never understood why they had to be the ones to deal with all the responsibility while we dish out money, and some niggas don't even do that. Gage fucked up, but he was about to get his first lesson in manhood. *Sacrifice.*

"And lift yo' fucking head up. Shit ain't as bad as it seems. You ran outside and probably got ya' baby mama worrying her pretty little head. Don't do that shit no more! You a Navarro! You ain't no fucking pussy!" I boomed.

Gage lifted his head and shoulders, and when I saw that his eyes weren't red, it made me proud. Nothing wrong with being emotional, but this wasn't shit for him to cry about. He fucked and made a baby. Oh well. It happens to the best and the worst of us.

"Jagoda Bay U, though? I fuck with the city, and the coach of the program is a legend, but his team sucks ass. On God," Gage groaned.

"Well, you the best, ain't it youngin'?"

"Damn right, I am! Check the stats."

"Aite then, if you the best, you can go anywhere and make them the best. Simple."

His school wasn't 'bout shit until he and the starting line-up joined the team. If he can make them champions, he can do that shit anywhere, same with his teammates. Especially with a highly funded program ran by an Olympic gold medalist. I been telling the nigga to come fuck with JBU, but he didn't want to listen. Now his young ass didn't have a choice.

"Aye, my baby mama gorgeous as hell, ain't it?"

I shook my head at the devilish grin this nigga was wearing.

"Nigga, you was just out here about to cry, and now you talking about how pretty she is? Let me find out you got her ass pregnant on purpose."

I stressed the importance of rubbers to my lil' brother at a young age. I knew the nigga was handsome, and even if he wasn't ready, the girls would be on his ass. There was so much more shit he could get up with besides a baby. Bitches out here were foul and will have that shit and dead ass spread it to you without a care in the world just like niggas would.

"Cry? Never that. I didn't do it on purpose, but I damn sure didn't try to pull out. She was a virgin, G. Had me in there eating coochie and sucking toes and all type of shit. When I got up the next morning, I was mad as hell she was gone."

This nigga was wild as held.

"She got yo' nose wide open, but y'all young. Don't get all territorial over her and shit. You don't own her. Do what the fuck you gotta do as a man and be there for her, but also give her some space. We not one of them type of niggas. Just because she having your baby, don't mean she's your fucking property. Keep the ball on her side of the field. If she not on that with you, you got to respect that shit."

Gage hit the blunt and tossed it out just as he saw our mother sit on the porch. Someone had brought a chair outside, and when it was over, I was taking that bitch right back in. This ain't the fucking hood.

"I hear you."

His ass wasn't hearing shit I was saying, but he was gone learn the hard way, just like he did with running it fresh pussy raw.

"So what was that shit earlier? When you gone let me kill that Gilberto?"

Gage didn't know what the fuck was going on. He saw a nigga up the pistol on me so he upped his. That's how he was raised though. To be on go at all times on the field and in the streets.

"Ion know. I'ma get to the bottom of it though. Only thing yo' ass gone kill is the fucking opposing team on the field, nigga."

I clenched my teeth thinking about the shit Gilberto once again got me in the middle of. I wasn't doubting that he wasn't behind this shit because he was capable of anything, but what I hated is that he had me dead smack in the fucking center. I planned on eating good, drinking good and fucking good tonight, but now, I was about to play Ring around the fucking Rosie looking for his ass because after popping this child up from the dead, I knew his coward ass had jumped shipped. It was all good though. He couldn't hide forever.

* * *

I walked back into the house with my brother on my heels after calling up one of my folks to drop my Madre off to a hotel. The plan was to have her and my brother stay in one of the guest room's tonight, but with so much going on, Aphrodite was definitely going to want the house to herself.

"I know y'all got a lot of questions, but I think right now we need to give Aphrodite her space. We are all happy about the miracle that happened today, and my baby is very appreciative of the gifts. However, let's call it a day."

Aphrodite's mom stood in the middle of the room, and when nobody moved an inch, the auntie spoke up.

"Aite, muthafuckas, you heard my baby sister. Take y'all nosey asses on! My niece don't wanna see y'all drunk ass faces anyway."

Everyone started moving, including Gage, who was walking down the hall toward Athena's room. I gave a few hand slaps and watched as everyone grabbed to-go plates and drinks. Baguette could be seen from the window. He was in the backyard smoking, looking at the pool. I knew this shit fucked him up because it fucked me up, but what he didn't need to do was focus so much on revenge that he turned his back on his baby. A baby he thought was dead.

Thirty minutes later, once the house was cleared, Aphordite's mom walked up to me with her purse on her shoulder. Her daughter looked so much like her that Athena looked like her grandma's twin.

"I'ma go drop Bobby off and go by my sister's for a while. I'll be back later on. I won't be able to sleep at home anyway, especially without my grandbaby next to me."

She then turned her head and glanced at Baguette in the backyard before sighing and focusing her attention back on me.

"I know you and my daughter are fresh, but she's going to need you now more than ever. Don't let up. She's going to need Brock too, but their ship sailed a long time ago. Don't give up on my baby. She's a keeper. Men that tend to let her slip away still can't let her go." She placed a hand on my shoulder and then switched her thick ass out the house. *I see where Aphrodite get that shit from. Lord, forgive me.*

Instead of going on and dragging Baguette in the house, I went to the back, where I saw my brother go, and once I heard giggles come from behind Athena's door, I opened it.

Aphrodite was on the floor playing with her daughter, and although that put a smile on her face, seeing my brother and his newfound baby mama sleep in Athena's bed, had me frowning.

I walked to the bed and tapped his chest. His eyes shot open in confusion and were bloodshot red.

"Aye, all these guest rooms up in here. Go pick one."

Gage looked over at Lydia then back at me, and smacked his lips.

"She fainted a little once she saw...*A*. Your brother caught her before she fell. Once he sat her on the bed, she cried herself to sleep, and he laid down with her, Goal."

Gage stood and stretched as Aphrodite tried to vouch for the nigga, but I wasn't hearing it.

"The nigga still could have went to another room. "

Gage reached in the bed, grabbed Lydia and carried her bridal style down the hallway.

Aphrodite was burning a hole in the side of my head, but I was looking at Athena, amazed. I'd fucked with women that had children on some knock off type shit, but when I got with Aphrodite, it was understood her child was dead. Now seeing her in the flesh looking like twins had me in awe. It was unexpected, but I was happy as fuck for my baby.

"Do you think it's a good idea for them to be alone? Sora came in here and told me about their new little... situation."

I ignored Aphrodite and fixed the bed back up. They had her comforter and pillows looking all wrinkly.

"Goal-"

"What's gone happen, AP? She already pregnant. They needed to get the fuck up out her bed. She haven't even slept in her own shit, and they laid up in outside clothes."

Once the bed was fixed back to my satisfaction, I turned back to Aphrodite.

Reaching for her hand, I pulled her up and placed my arm around the small of her back.

There was so much sadness in her eyes, but her body was soft as fuck. The bodywash she used was still fuming off her skin, along with her perfume. Although my baby had been entertaining guests, she still smelled so fucking good.

Grabbing her chin, I made sure her brown eyes were peering into my greys.

"Shit weird. Ion know what the fuck going on, but I'ma get to the bottom of this. I put that on my life, I didn't know nothing about this shit. Ion even have a relationship with Gilberto."

Tears weld in Aphrodite's eyes, and I thumbed them away. Her makeup must have been waterproof or some shit because it was still in place.

"But you said my cars were a gift from your father. I just don't understand."

"Baby, it ain't shit to understand. I stole the nigga's card and bought 'em. Ion fuck with the nigga."

I looked down at Athena, who was now staring up at us, and hit her with a smile before focusing my attention back on Aphrodite.

"You focus on bonding with her. I'ma fix this other shit. I know she's confused enough, so I'ma go to the condo tonight, but I'ma have eyes on y'all. You ain't got shit to worry about."

I wanted to kiss AP, but since her daughter was looking, I refrained until Aphrodite was ready to properly introduce us.

I swiped a thumb down her cheek and bent down to whisper in her ear, "Seeing you in mommy mode sex as fuck. I'ma make this shit right, Pretty Pretty. That's on our next child."

She gasped just as I stood and turned out the room. Ion know what the fuck was going on right now, but this shit needed to get back on track asap. I couldn't even get no pussy tonight thanks to Gilberto's ole slick back-haired ass.

I knocked on the door of the first guest room past Athena's room.

"Aye, we leaving in fifteen, nigga!"

I was dropping Gage ass off at the room with our mama soon as we left here. I knew she was going to curse his ass out in both languages. I was going to let her handle her child because I didn't have the time to deal with Gage's fertile ass today. This kidnapping shit had to be handled. Gilberto had done some shit, but this time he'd outdone his fucking self. Nigga done snatched a whole baby. A baby that belonged to something that belonged to me. Yeah, his ass was done for.

"I'm going in there, nigga. I was just trying to smoke and praying this shit not a dream," Baguette blew out just as I walked into the backyard. Looking around the space, I nodded my head in appreciation. I was glad I poured another three hundred thousand in the backyard that Aphrodite didn't even know about. Had she known how much this house was really worth, it was no way in hell she would have let me just give it to her. The contractors had it looking like the Hollywood Hills back here.

"It's not a dream, nigga. This shit real. You a whole daddy out here, old ass nigga," I cracked. That got a slight smile out of B.

"Say's the nigga who turned forty today."

"I see you got jokes. Nigga, I'm young and in my prime."

We both stared out into the water and listened to the jacuzzi bubble.

"I been out here trying to process this shit, and this nigga really took my daughter because I no longer wanted to do business with him. You remember how Kilo went down on that charge, and we couldn't figure out how that shit came to play?"

I stroked my face, remembering how strange that shit was. It didn't make sense at all.

"The day we had her, everything was just...off... I'ma get to the bottom of that shit though, but I think Gilberto took her and sent Kilo to jail. The nigga was so fucking mad because we were his biggest moneymakers. I remember that shit. I just didn't think he would do some foul ass shit like that."

My trigger finger was itching like a muthafucka behind my sperm donor.

"G, we gone get to that shit, but for now, your everything is in the house."

"Shit, they know where she stay, so I gotta-"

"It's handled. I got three cars out front right now and four more on the way. Three men gone post up in the backyard while two sit out front. They good. They secured."

I had my young nigga Jett in charge of making sure they were protected in my absence. He was a beast with the sniper and had been handling pistols since he was nine. They were good.

Baguette stood up, held my gaze and then slapped hands with me.

Without another word, he walked in the house, and before the door could close, Gage walked out, eating a vine of grapes.

"Aye, I figured out why I been eating a lot lately."

Shaking my head, I walked past that nigga so I could drop him off.

"Nigga, yo' greedy ass be eating up everything anyway. Come yo' weak pull out game ass on."

After I dropped this daddy to be ass dude off, it was hunting time. I'd just found the love of my God damn life, and here go a muthafucka tryna fuck my shit up. Gilberto was fucking up my home, so I fasho was about to make his death a painful one. Happy fucking birthday to me and Athena. Bitch ass nigga.

CHAPTER 8

Aphrodite "Ditey" "Pretty Pretty" "AP" Greer

I don't know how long I had been staring at Athena as if I was a creep, but it had to be a while. Many of my family members had children, including Sora, and her kids mostly had their father – Big Red's whole everything. From the light skin to the boxy heads, her children were all him. Seeing my daughter in the flesh looking like a replica of me was surreal. I wanted to squeeze her with all my might and plant kisses all over her little brown face. I wanted to bury my nose in her thick, curly hair and inhale it's fumes. I wanted to love on her and release all of these feelings that were in the pit of my belly like a volcano on the verge of erupting, but I had to take everything slow. How do I even explain to her who I am? I could tell she for sure wasn't like the typical five year old because not once had she cried or asked to leave. Hell, she haven't even asked who we were. I could only ask the most high for guidance, but hell, I was looking at him sideways right now because why was my daughter taken?

After Goal came in and spoke his peace, I still was feeling uneasy about him. He had me questioning everything, and I was so mad at myself for even letting my thoughts drift to him. I did appreciate the fact that he didn't say anything to my child. I haven't even introduced myself to her, so I damn sure didn't want her to know who he was, especially not right off the bat.

"You good?" Baguette had entered the room, and I could tell he was good and high. I looked back at Athena once again and nodded.

"I'm good. You?"

Baguette rubbed his head and sighed, "Hell nawl, I ain't good."

Glancing at Athena, who was playing with her toys like she just hadn't fucked up all our lives by popping up, was bewildering.

"I really can't believe this shit. I'm happy as fuck, no lie, but at the same time, I'm hurt, I'm enraged, and I want that nigga's head."

I could understand everything Baguette was saying because I felt the exact same way. Happy, but most definitely mad at the world.

We both stood there staring at our child, watching her play without a care or worry in the world.

"We gotta tell her," I whispered.

"She thinks tomorrow is her birthday, it's today!" I squealed.

"Fuuuck!" Baguette groaned.

"Yo, A?"

She snapped her head up at us.

"Yes?"

Baguette nodded at the bed, prompting me to sit on it with him following. We left a space open for her to sit.

"Come sit up here. Let us holla at ya' for a minute."

Athena dropped the doll and walked toward us, with her dress bouncing with each step she took. I had to turn my head and bat away tears. God, everything she did, had me emotional. Is this what being a mother was?

Once she sat down with the help of Baguette, she turned to face him.

"You remember when I told you I had a daughter?"

"Yes. Is she my sister?"

Baguette and I shot each other a look before focusing back on Athena.

"What do you mean?"

"Well, the nice lady that brought me here told me she was bringing me to my real parents. She said my mom would look pretty like me and that my daddy would have dimples like me."

Athena turned and faced me.

"You're pretty and we look the same. So does the lady that said the bad word. And you-"

She faced Baguette, "You have dimples like me. You're my daddy, and you're my mommy. Are you two married?"

I cleared my throat and laughed nervously.

"No, daddy and I haven't been together for a very long time, but we are the best of friends."

My vision was clouded with tears, and I just let them fall. It was no point in wiping them away.

"Like me and Tulsaire?"

"Who?"

"He lived with me. We call each other brother and sister, but Gilberto says we are not. He can call Gilberto daddy, but I call him Mr. G," she explained and I could see Baguette sigh with relief.

"Well, he was right to not let you call him daddy because he ain't. You have your own daddy and the best mother. You were taken from us. If it were up to us, you would have been staying with us forever. I'm sorry that you had to live with Mr. G," Baguette choked out.

"Did he... did anybody hurt you?"

Athena shook her head no.

"Your real name is Athena. Right there on the wall. This is your room. Your birthday is April 16th, today. You were six pounds and seven ounces at birth. Your mommy's name is Aphrodite, that beauty beside you, and your daddy's name is Baguette, me. The flyest man in Jagoda Bay."

Athena's eyes lit up.

"You can fly?"

Baguette smiled, showing his one dimple, "Sum' like that, baby girl."

"If I stay here with you, will I see Tulsaire again?"

"I can't lie to you. I don't know who he is, so I don't know, but what I will tell you is, your mama would love it if you stayed here with her, and I would appreciate it if you spent the night at my house sometimes too."

"So you have a different house?"

"I do."

"Do I have a room?"

"Not yet, but I can get you whatever kind you like."

Athena placed her finger to her chin.

"Frozen and the Little Mermaid!"

I was glad my room for her was already coordinated because the room at Brock's house was going to look a mess.

"Then it's settled. The princess gets what the princess wants."

"If today is my birthday, where is my cake?"

Just as Athena asked, the doorbell went off. Baguette stood straight up.

He disappeared out of the room, and I took that time to once again study Athena. I just couldn't help myself. She was everything to me.

"Aphrodite! Y'all come in here."

I scooped Athena up and walked into the living room. I was pleased to see my family had cleaned up behind themselves.

"Happy birthday, baby girl."

Athena wiggled out of my arms and ran full speed toward the gifts and cake Brock was holding. I watched in awe as she ripped them all open, screaming at every last one. I was pissed that I missed four birthdays with my child, but seeing her happy had me cheesing and silently praying for Tuscany. She helped us out tremendously by telling her who we were and by bringing her home. I knew Brock was going to be hard on my girl, but I knew there was more to the story. As far as me and Goal, I just didn't know where that was going.

CHAPTER 9

Quasie Lantis

Mondays were always my busiest days. It didn't even matter if I had a showing or not, the first day of the business week was filled with my email full of inquiries, approvals, and all things Dream Team Realty. I'd gotten some much needed rest on Saturday and had an eventful Sunday, and now there were more than fifty messages that needed my attention. Instead of grabbing my tea from Starbucks and responding to the messages, I was on the way to Kassie's house.

Yesterday, she sent me a text that said to not come to Aphrodite's housewarming. I had already sent my photographers, and I wanted to go against what Kassie had texted, but my gut told me to just take my mama to dinner instead, so that's what I did. I tried calling Kassie, and she refused my calls. Just as I was about to pull my ass up on her, she sent me a text saying to come by her house before work. So, here I was. Kassie was off on Mondays, but being the workaholic she was, she usually handled all my business on Sundays. I knew she was shook about whatever went down yesterday because her ass hadn't gone in my email once.

I pulled up to her three-storied townhome and killed the engine on my Maserati truck. I was even shocked she was at home. Usually after the weekend, she would be curled up on Haddie's couch. She and her cousin were for sure grandma's babies.

Grabbing my purse, I got out of the truck and walked up the pavement to her front door. My mint green pumps clacked with each step I took. Today, I decided on a wheat-colored pantsuit and mint accessories. I didn't have any closings today, but I had three showings and two meetings.

When Kassie opened the door, the linen fumes from the plug-ins she loved hit me, but the way her ass looked like she was antsy hit me even harder.

"Come in now!"

Kassie all but snatched me into the house.

I looked around in admiration of what she'd done with the place. She'd completely redecorated from the last time that I was over, which was about three months ag- and a redecorating Kassie meant she was getting rid of some dead weight. Her and her dude must've broken up yet again. Anytime she put his ass out, she got all new furniture and decor.

Providing Kassie with a job after her cousin was locked up was a no-brainer. She was my girl through and through. Even back then. Although Kilo was her first cousin and best friend, she never once folded on me. She was the one putting me on game when it came to Kaisha and Ree, Kilo's baby mamas. I didn't have to worry about hearing shit from the streets because I always heard it from Kassie. My girl had also been in the streets heavy and not on no queen pin shit. She'd grown a nasty addiction to pills that had her almost on her deathbed. Still, I had faith in my girl. I still wanted her on my team. I never once judged her, even when she was down to ninety seven pounds. So, as my business grew, so did she. I have been trying to get her ass to go to real estate school, but with her up and down relationship, her focus isn't on any schooling. Still, she's the highest-paid assistant I know.

"Girl, what is going on?"

I took a seat on the peach-hued sectional and crossed my right leg over my left. Kassie shook her head, held her finger up and skipped to the kitchen. Kassie was a trip. When she came back in, handing me a wine glass, I took a whiff and smiled at it being Giulia. It was too early for me to be drinking, but I didn't turn it down. I'd been super obsessed with it as of late, and I wasn't sure if it was because it was just that good or it reminded me of him. It brought me back to my trip in New York at the restaurant Giulia's Steak House with Eleven, but I had to snap my head out of taking a trip down memory lane. My girl was stressing and needed my undivided attention.

"Okay, so boom! Everything was beautiful and whatnot. The house is astounding. Her family was so welcoming, and Bobby was busting my head on the dance floor."

I took a sip from my glass and looked at her over the rim.

"Why do I hear a but? Please tell me you have a good explanation as to why I had to take my mama out to lunch and shopping instead of the housewarming."

My mama asked me a billion questions as to why our evening was altered, and all I had for her was I had no clue, but I trusted Kassie enough to take heed. Kassie took a swallow of her wine and then began pacing. Once she ran her free hand through her bob-length sandy brown braids, I knew some shit was coming.

"Girl, so okay, why in the fuck that girl baby come back from the dead?"

I sat up in my seat and peered at Kassie with confused eyes.

"Aphrodite! The owner of the damn house! Her baby was on her beloved shit!"

"Aphrodite? Her daughter died at birth, I think." I remember that conversation vividly about Athena. Aphrodite and Baguette both are hurting behind the loss of their child, so if that was who Kassie was talking about, I needed answers for sure.

"Yes! Aphrodite! Her daughter showed up on her doorstep, and shit went up from there. Niggas was about to blow each other fucking heads off and some more shit!"

Raising my perfectly arched and penciled-in brow, I protested. "Impossible. She's dead, Kassie!"

"No, she's alive!"

Kassie placed her drink on her fireplace and began telling me the whole story. By the time she was done, I even knew about Aphrodite's cousin Lydia being pregnant by Goal's little brother. A brother I had no idea he had. I knew of Lydia because Aphrodite spoke very highly of her and had even shown us the prom dress she was having made for her. After Kassie filled my glass again and hers a third, I was spent and overwhelmed with all of yesterday's drama. We both were sitting next to each other now, looking off into space. An uneasy feeling was sitting in the pit of my belly and caused my mouth to dry. We were both stunned into silence, and I could tell that despite Kassie texting me last night that she was going to bed around ten and to be at her home this morning, she hadn't gotten any sleep due to the bags around her eyes. Although the situation was crazy and questionable as hell, I knew there was something else Kassie had to tell me. There was something she'd left out that had kept her up all night.

"What else, Kassie? Just tell me so that I can leave here and try and get through my showings. What are you not telling me?"

Kassie sat up on the couch and rubbed her hands down the front of her grey leggings. She paired the leggings with the matching crop top that showed her figure well. Although a plus size woman, Kassie looked amazing in any and everything she wore. Even in her longing clothing, she was killing it. She'd filled out nicely and damn near doubled her weight from when she was on pills, and honestly, I loved the curves on her. Everyone couldn't handle pounds. That's why I stayed my ass in the gym because I swelled up like a damn elephant anytime I gained a few inches.

"That little girl. I know her."

My head snapped so fast in her direction that I heard it pop.

Strange and disquieting thoughts began to race through my mind.

"What do you mean you... know... her? Kassie! How the fuck do you know a daughter that was supposed to be dead? Did Nardo had anything to do with this? Please tell me he didn't have you wrapped up in some bullshit?! Do you not know who Baguette and Goal are? This shit can be traced back to you-"

"Quasie, no! Nardo has nothing to do with this, but Kymani does."

Those twelve words knocked the fucking wind out of me. My heart refused to believe what Kassie had just uttered. The words flowed from her mouth like vomit, and suddenly my stomach soured. What the fuck did she mean Kymani had something to do with their daughter?

"Well, not Kymani per se, but Grannie. Quasie, I've been seeing that little girl since she was a baby. You know Grannie babysits for that rich family. Every now and again, she brings the children around when the parents are out of town. She isn't supposed to, so she makes sure they aren't in any of my social media. They know her as Athena, but I know her as A or Ramira. You should have seen how Baguette and Goal reacted yesterday. They are out for blood, and the first person they are going to come after is my grannie when they start putting the pieces together.

I know in my heart that she has no idea what is going on. All Grannie knows is that she has been babysitting these children for years. She has told me countless times that something isn't right with the dad, and the only reason she stays around is because she fears for the safety and well-being of the children. You know Kymani left enough money to make Grannie straight. Quasie, when they start putting shit together, they will automatically think-"

"They will think that Kilo had something to do with it."

"Exactly. My cousin is just as lost as my granny. I remember Baguette and Kymani were tight before he got locked up. Hell, Baguette and Goal both called me monthly, giving me money to put on Kymani's books. This is a whole child we are talking about. My grannie has been raising those kids for years. This shit is going to end bad for all of us, Quasie. I'm the cousin, and you're the wife. They are going to think we all were in on this shit, whatever it is. I know the fucking street, and you do too!"

My head was spinning. I felt a momentary panic as my mind jumped onto what was happening. It was impossible to steady my erratic pulse. What the fuck? What the fuck was really going on? I was just getting my back blown off overlooking the Billionaire's Row, and now I was caught up in a potential war?

"Kassie, what the fuck? Where the fuck is Kilo?"

"I've been trying to call him and Grannie-"

Ding Dong!

We both jumped hard as hell as the sound of the doorbell startled us. Fear and anger knotted inside of me as Kassie and I eyed each other.

"Who is that?" I mouthed.

Kassie picked her phone up and went to her Ring camera app.

"Fuck! Nardo's stupid ass disconnected my app. Hold on."

Kassie pulled a big ass gun from under the couch that had me gasping and stood to answer the door.

"Wait, Kassie!"

I tried to grab at her, but she was already up and down the hall that lead to the front door. I lowered my head, said a silent prayer, stood, and grabbed the mace that was attached to my small key chain. I'd left my gun locked in the safe at my house, and now I was wishing like hell I had listened to Kilo when he used to tell my ass to bring my gun with me everywhere. I sold fucking real estate, not bricks, but now, I wish I had the protection.

"Bring your ass in here!" I heard Kassie scold.

When my eyes closed, I said a silent prayer, and when I opened them, a fuming Kilo was standing over me with pissed-off expression.

"So, you went to New York with another nigga? Do he know he fucking on married pussy?" Kilo spat.

I wanted to take a step back, but the couch was in the way. I was boxed in. I had to take a deep breath and get my thoughts in order. Kilo looked so fucking good that it caught me off guard. He was standing here, dressed in his usual black sweats, crisp white tee, fresh out the box sneakers, head shinning, and smelling good as ever.

"Kilo, you got other shit to worry about. Real talk. Get out that girl fucking face! I been calling you and Grannie since last night! Even went by the house three times."

Kassie was talking, but Kilo and I were busy staring each other down.

Kilo snatched my left hand and held it up.

"And you not wearing yo' muthafuckin' ring? Yeah, you acting too brand new around this bitch. Don't that nigga know this my pussy? Hunh? My dick and tongue done been in every inch of you! Ion give a fuck how much time passed! You mine! 'Til death do us part, muthafucka!"

I nodded my head slowly. I hated so bad how he was able to bring out emotions in me. I went from fearing for his safety to hating what he did to us. No matter how good Kilo looked, being in his presence brought me nothing but pain. All the memories of me trying so fucking hard to get us on track and him in turn dogging me out. The shit hurt.

"Kilo, it would be in your best interest to listen to your cousin. Not that I owe you shit because we are separated. The ring is being cleaned. I was in New York at a real estate conference."

I don't know why I lied to him, but I needed him to calm the hell down and listen so we could figure this shit out. I love Aphrodite and 'nem. I have no plans to be tied into some shit that my ex may be webbed in. I'd finally found women outside of Kassie to develop a relationship with, and it looked like that was about to be snatched from me.

Kilo's expression softened, but he was still in my space.

"Ion know what the fuck you got going on, but stop fucking playing with me, Quasie. Now-"

Kilo turned his head to look at Kassie.

"Why the fuck you been blowing me up? I told you next time you called me about Nardo, I was wiping his ass off the earth."

"Nigga, get the fuck out of her face. This don't got shit to do with Nardo."

Kassie pulled Kilo out of my face, and the moment I had my space back, I breathed easily.

"That little girl that Grannie be watching? That is Aphrodite and Baguette's child! You know, the one that died at the time you went to jail? I was at the housewarming yesterday, and she showed up on the fucking porch."

Kilo drew his head back and squinted his eyes.

"What the fuck you mean that's their daughter? She dead, ain't it?"

Kassie ran the whole story down to Kilo, and by the time she was done, we were all lost in our thoughts.

"FUUUUUUUUUCK!"

Kilo roared and that had Kassie and I jumping again.

"Kilo, what the fuck are we supposed to do? Those are your friends, so you know how they think. They are going to assume we had something to do with this shit! I am barely thirty! I don't want to die!"

"Oh my God!" I screeched.

"Man, shut y'all asses up. Ain't shit gone happen to y'all! I'ma get up with Grannie and see what the fuck she done got tied into, and then I'ma pull up on them niggas."

"What if they pull up on us first?"

"What Quasie said!"

"I do business with these people. I have developed a relationship with these men's women. I don't want to be caught up in any of your street shit you got going on, Kilo!"

Kilo snapped his head at me and turned his lip up.

"Fuck you mean none of my street shit? This street shit made you who the fuck you were TODAY! You be fucking killing me like you above dope slanging! Stop acting like you didn't used to love this shit. I told you you straight! Both y'all. Them niggas know what the fuck it is with me! Ian never been no flaw ass nigga. Y'all good. Just keep living and doing what the fuck you been doing, and Kassie, put that big ass gun up. I'ma handle this shit."

Kilo walked toward the exit and paused before looking over at me.

"Be the reason a nigga is six feet under, Quasie Lantis."

I scoffed and looked off, but deep down inside, I was shaking in my thong. The look Kilo gave me before he made his exit was enough for me to shiver. Shit was crazy how this man really felt like he had president over my fucking life. He made his bed and now had to lay in it. Not only was he a serial cheater, he had not one, but two children outside of our marriage. I would drink fucking glass before I went back down the road with Kymani Lantis. He shitted on me when he went to jail, and now that he was out, he thought we were supposed to run off into the sunset? Absolutely not.

"We shaking in here like a college girl on amateur night, and this nigga leaves out all calm and shit. I swear to God it was so peaceful when his ass was locked up. Between him, his babymamas and Nardo, I'm gone end up having to check into the mental institution."

I bit my tongue when it came to the baby mamas. Call me petty, but I was still pissed that Kilo even brought them in my home. I know children are innocent, but I didn't want to see them or meet them. Hell, I didn't even want the daddy, so why the fuck would I be even looking at the fucking children? Fuck Kilo and his fucking seeds.

"I'm going to get out of here. I have no idea what your cousin has going on, but I want no parts. Can you send an email to the potential buyers and let them know I'm on the way to the North Star Property?"

Kassie nodded her head and picked up her phone to go to her email. Rubbing my hand down my slacks, I cleared my throat and gathered my purse.

"I'ma let you go view the property, but we are going to talk about how you haven't worn that ring in weeks and how there wasn't no damn conference in New York. I'ma let you rock for now, though. If you getting dick that isn't attached to my cousin, I'm all for it."

I blushed, tucking my strands behind my ear. I replayed Eleven and I's fuck sessions over in my head way too much. We hadn't linked up since New York, but we texted every other day. I was feenin' for him again, but I had to make sure it was on a day I didn't have work the next day. Eleven tended to take all of my energy with his aggressive ass fucking, and I was the type of person that needed all of my charge. He claimed he wasn't fooling with me until I got my situation under control, but it wasn't anything to get under control. I wasn't interested in anything beyond sex with Eleven's street ass. So my situation shouldn't have even mattered.

"Quasie, be careful. Not just with Aphrodite and 'nem, but with Kymani as well. I know you are hurt and no longer want to be with him, but make sure you close that door all the way before you open another. Two boss ass niggas going at it never ends well."

I cocked my head at Kassie and crossed my arms.

"I never said there was someone in the picture, but even if there was, how you know he a boss?"

Kassie pulled her face out of her phone and tossed her head back in laughter.

"Your bougie ass ain't fucking with a nigga unless his sack right. I done seen you turn down all types of millionaires in five years. If you fucking with a nigga, his pockets real heavy. Plus, you've worn three different Birkins in the last few weeks. The same bag you vowed to never spend a dime on. I'm happy for you, but like I said, be careful."

I gave Kassie a quick hug before hopping into my truck. Shit had been parked only an hour and was already scorching on the inside. After applying more lipstick to my lips, I pulled off and headed to my showing. My relationship was the least of my worries right now. I needed to see what the fuck was going on with my girl Aphrodite. Kilo plays crazy, but he not running shit over here.

CHAPTER 10

Aphrodite "Ditey" "Pretty Pretty" "AP" Greer

One week. That's how long I'd shut off the world and had been wrapped up in all things Athena. My phone had long ago died, and I had yet to put it on the charger. I'd done a huge restock the day of my housewarming on my site, so I knew I had packages that needed to be shipped, but at this point, I didn't give a fuck. My daughter was my one and only priority, and I was afraid that the moment I snapped back to reality, all of this would be a dream.

The next morning after the housewarming, one of the guys Goal had watching the house, who introduced himself as Jett, knocked on the door and handed me Target and Saks Fifth Ave shopping bags. On the inside was everything Athena needed. There were clothes, underwear, bodywash, hair care products, toys, and snacks. Goal had texted me that morning asking me to look inside her dress and shoes for her size. Besides that, I haven't heard from him. Right after that, my battery died anyway. Baguette also hadn't been back. He left as soon as Athena fell asleep that Sunday night and hadn't shown face. The selfish part of me didn't care though. I was just happy to be wrapped up in the world of my daughter. My mom, my aunt, and Sora had all come by. I left all of them at the door though. I just needed a moment with my baby. I didn't care where she'd been. I didn't care about the lost time. I just wanted to be smothered in her embrace.

"Aphrodite, I'm finished."

Athena's soft voice pulled me from my thoughts and caused me to wipe the fallen tears from my face. I'd been crying nonstop to the point my daughter was probably sick of me. The guys had been dropping off food three times a day even though my fridge was stocked to the brim, and I appreciated that because I was barely functioning. However, I hopped up the moment I heard that little innocent voice. I would cook ten times a day if Athena wanted it. I ate enough not to feel sick, but food wasn't a priority for me. I was just so fucking happy to have my baby. God had given me a second chance, and although I had questions, I was drowning in excitement. I was so overwhelmed that I didn't care what was going on outside of my doors.

"Okay, baby. Let's get you cleaned up."

Athena loved her some crab legs and lobster tails. She told that to the Jett when he was guarding the door on the second night, and every night for dinner her little self-had been delivered seafood boils. Since it was fairly early, she had just finished lunch, which was pasta from Red Lobster. I swooped her up in my arms like she was a baby and carried her to the bathroom inside of her room. That is where we had been spending most of our time. In her bedroom. I slept in the bed with my baby and held her so tight every night that she could barely breathe. She slept exactly like her father. Mouth slightly ajar, on her back, with an arm tossed over her face. It was the cutest thing. I never knew I could be obsessed with another person, but when it came to Athena. That's exactly what I was.

"I want the princess bubbles this time!"

I smiled at Athena as I ran her bathwater. She had pasta sauce all over her face and fingers, so although she took a bath last night, she needed another one. I could have washed her up, but she enjoyed playing with her toys in the bath.

Once her bathwater and bubbles were to her preferred temperature, Athena removed her clothing. I turned my back to give her some privacy, and when I heard the water move around, I turned and sat on the toilet next to the tub.

Seeing her dip the Mermaid in and out of the water brought a smile to my face and had my eyes glossing. I knew I needed to get a damn grip and that I looked a hot mess because outside of showering and handling my hygiene every morning, I didn't put any effort into my looks. Every day, I grabbed a lounge set and had my hair pulled at the top of my head in a bun. I didn't care about me, but looking at Athena's head and the barrettes and balls dropping from her hair, I knew I had to get her right. Her hair was the same as it was when she was dropped into our lives. Outside of the pajamas from Target, that's all she'd been wearing each day after her baths. I've been smothering her with kisses and watching movies, playing toys, and admiring the mere being of my daughter. For so long, it was believed that she didn't exist, so seeing her breathe was enough for me.

I didn't feel one ounce of guilt for shutting the world out. I'd been that person for everyone for so long that I needed to be here for my own damn self. Just like my mother, I was a flame and those around me were moths. This time, I needed to close myself off from the world and bask in my blessing. My baby girl was here. Fuck the outside world. Nobody missed her more than me and I needed something that was robbed from me for five years – *time*.

"Athena, would you like it if I did your hair? How about I let you pick out your own clothes today? I know you're tired of wearing pajamas."

Athena pulled her mermaid out of the water and stood her on the side of the tub. I picked up her pink sponge, squeezed baby Dove body wash on it, and began washing her gently. Once I had her face cleaned, she looked at me with those big brown eyes.

"Can I pick a dress out, Aphrodite?"

I smiled and nodded.

"Yes, baby. You can."

I hadn't gone through the bags, so I didn't know if there were dresses in them, but I was hoping there were. I wanted to give Athena any and everything her little heart desired. She was already rotten and hadn't even left my home.

Athena let me call her by her real name. I'm guessing because she hated the one she was given by whomever had taken her, but she was still calling me by my first name instead of mommy. I didn't mind, though. I knew all of this was a lot for her. I wasn't expecting her to understand that I was her mother right away because she was only five years old. As long as she was in my possession, that was all that mattered.

Once I had my baby cleaned, I let her pick out a light pink and purple Fendi Dress. I had to go through a few bags to find the matching lavender Fendi Sandals. I was grateful for Goal in that moment. He'd gone all the way out with my baby's wardrobe with nothing but designer. It was only about twelve outfits, and I knew she would need more clothes, but for now, that was great.

After getting Athena moisturized, I pulled out the hair supplies. I was able to use the lavender barrettes that were already on her hair and added a few pink ribbons. Her soft, long, spongy coils were so easy to comb. I decided to give her a different style from the simple one she was sporting, and by the time I was finished, I was in awe of her shaking her head in the mirror, admiring the six crisscross Bantu knots I placed at the top of her head followed by the ponytails in the back. My daughter was drop fucking dead gorgeous. Her sienna-hued skin, heart-shaped lips, small-pointed nose, and sleek eyes were everything. She was most definitely a little beauty, and the new hairstyle pulled her looks out even more. Wow, I can't believe we thought she was dead all this time. I tried not to let my mind venture there, but it was truly disheartening.

"Wow! I look so pretty! Can we watch Frozen today?"

I tossed my head back in laughter because Frozen had been on repeat. I knew the damn film word for word now, and that shit was driving me insane. However, if my baby wanted Frozen, she was getting Frozen.

The doorbell ringing had me standing and pulling Athena in my arms. It was too early for her dinner to be delivered, but I knew it had to more than likely be one of the men watching with something.

"Is that my daddy?"

Athena asked as I descended the stairs with her on my hip. That question caused my heart to swell and had stunned me to silence. She hadn't asked about Baguette in the seven days she'd been here, and now that she was, I was wondering the same damn thing. She hadn't called me mommy, but was damn sure asking about her block head ass daddy. I knew Brock though. He was somewhere combing the city, trying to make sense of things. Although he was happy as fuck to have his daughter, I knew he wouldn't be able to enjoy his child until he had some answers. When he was in his feelings, he liked to speak his peace and be to himself. He'd been dreaming of our baby for years, and as of late, she'd been haunting his thoughts. I knew it was overwhelming for him. At this point, I didn't care. My daughter is smart, wasn't harmed, and seemed to be mentally okay. She hadn't asked to go back to wherever she came from, so that was all that mattered.

"Uh, I'm not sure, baby. Let's see."

"Okay."

I placed a kiss on her plump cheek and looked through the blinds before I opened it. I saw two black trucks parked across the street, but seeing the guest on the porch, caused me to snatch the door open.

"Omg! Hiiiii, Athena. You're so darn pretty! I really have to get used to the fact that she is here and has Baguette's whole smile."

I playfully rolled my eyes at Lydia and stood back so that she could come in.

"Umm, no, she's my twin. Bring your ass on up in here."

Lydia adjusted her cross-over bag and searched for Athena, who happily hopped in her arms.

"What are you-"

"Bitch, you bet not close the door on me and my kids!"

Sora barged in, holding a Thank You bag with carryout containers in them, and another brown bag was clutched at her chest, and I knew that was liquor. Sora's kids hugged my waist and barged in the house.

"We let you have a week to yourself with our baby. It's time to let us in now!"

I shook my head, stuck my head out of the door to make sure no one else was coming and locked the door. I felt secure as ever with the twenty four hour security, but I still felt like someone was going to pull up and snatch my baby away from me.

"Not you still got these flowers and shit up from the housewarming."

Sora switched through the foyer and into the kitchen. I followed behind her, heart beating out of my chest. It took everything in me not to go pull my baby from Lydia's arms.

"The cleanup crew came on Tuesday, but I wouldn't let them in. If they come this week, I will. I don't want gnats and stuff to start forming. You know they are like roaches. They multiply, but never die." When I was living in Canquoy, I'd acquired gnats more than I'd like to admit. I wasn't having that at my new house.

Sora pulled the wings and fries from the bag, and just then, my stomach growled loud as hell.

"Don't I know it. When have you eaten, Aphrodite?"

Sora placed her hands on her wide hips, and seeing her sporting the ripped shorts and graphic tee that was from my last summer drop had me feeling good. She finished her look with white Forces. Her makeup was non-existent, but she still looked pretty with her lashes and arched brows. If my phone was charged, I would snap a picture. I was thinking about stocking the shorts again for the upcoming summer season.

"They bring food every day, but Sora, I can't eat. I can't even sleep, and when I do, it's with Athena in my arms. I find myself waking up out of my sleep, clutching her to my chest. I spend my days just watching her, thanking God, and crying. I'm just so happy she's here. Eating and shit is just not even something I'm focused on."

Sora cocked her head and stuck her foot out slightly.

"Aphrodite, how crazy does that sound? You not caring about eating? You have literally lost weight since last Sunday. That's not good, cousin."

Sora's expression softened when she saw my eyes water.

"Look, I don't know what the fuck is going on, but I'm just happy Athena is here. We all are. This shit is like a sick, cruel April Fool's joke, in all honesty, but she's here. You have to take care of yourself. I haven't seen you like this in five years. Damn near to the day. You have her. We have her. You got to make sure you're good though, cousin. Being a mom is hard, and now you have to dive head first with no instruction manual. She's the most beautiful little girl. I mean, outside of my daughters, but she needs you healthy.

"Has Baguette been here? Your damn phone goes to voicemail, so I didn't know what the fuck was going on. I had Big Red reach out to Goal since I couldn't contact you or Baguette, and he let our asses know to leave you the fuck alone. That was four days ago. I didn't give a fuck what that fine ass nigga was talking about, I knew today I was pulling up."

Thinking about Goal had me feeling all fuzzy inside, but I couldn't think about us while my daughter had just popped up. My relationship didn't matter. It was fresh and still up in the damn air anyway. Athena Dianne Cherman was all I was worried about.

"No, Baguette hasn't been here. I really don't care one way or another, but she asked about him."

Baguette could wreak havoc in the streets 'til his legs grew tired for all I was concerned. I knew when he was ready, he would pull up. I wasn't pressuring him. I knew what type of man and father he was. I knew he needed some time, and I was giving him that.

"Fuck you mean you don't care? You looking like you haven't bathed in a week, cousin. You need him here. You lost just as much as he did. Y'all both should be here getting to know your daughter. That street shit can wait. Niggas be killing the fuck out of me. He better be glad I love him like family."

I waved Sora off and bit into a wing. I wanted my daughter all to myself anyway. He could do him as much as he needed too.

"Aphrodite, I put your phone on the charger. I need to get your orders packed. I've been seeing comments on your IG page."

Lydia walked in with Athena still on her hip and Rhea, Sora's youngest daughter at her side. Lydia knew the ends and out of my business down to being able to order merchandise from my vendor. I was on fuck them orders time, but I was happy that she was over to be able to help me. I still needed to keep my income flowing so that I could be able to take care of my child. Damn. *My child*, I really had her here with me. That was so crazy.

"Well, look at you, little beauty!"

Sora grabbed Athena out of Lydia's arms and tickled her belly. Athena tried pushing Sora's hands away and tossed her head back in laughter. Her little laugh was my favorite.

"Mommy, can ha' play with me?"

Sora traced Athena's baby hairs with her pointer finger.

"What do you say? You want to go play with my daughter?"

Athena nodded her head.

"Okay, go play. When y'all get hungry, come back in here."

Both girls ran out, and I started toward where they'd went, dropping my chicken wing back on the plate.

"Aht, aht, aht. They will be just fine. Plus, Lydia will pop in on them in between orders. Right, Litty?"

Lydia gnawed on her bottom lip before eagerly shaking her head.

"Um, Savannah is on the way. She just finished up with her last lash client. She is going to help me with the orders, if that's okay?"

Sora crossed her arms.

"Umm humm. Don't think we're done talking, Lydia Greer! Go 'head on. Tell Savannah to bring her lash equipment. I need a refill." Sora picked at her lashes while dismissing our little cousin. Lydia wasted no time scurrying out of the room.

"I swear I'm so pissed at her. I'm trying so hard not to be hard on her, but she just don't know what this has done to her future. She was just a damn virgin yesterday, so I'm confused as fuck. Salutatorian. I thought that fast-ass Savannah was going to end up with a damn belly before Lydia. Shit so out of order around here."

I'd forgotten all about Lydia being pregnant. In all honesty, I had so much going on that I couldn't even focus on that. Was I disappointed that my little cousin was pregnant? Yes. However, babies are a blessing, and it's not like she was pregnant by a little knucklehead. She was having a baby by Goal's little brother, and although both of their futures were bright, they had the resources to still be able to follow their dreams.

"Back to you. Baguette hasn't been here, Auntie hasn't been here, so I know Goal hasn't been here. Aphrodite, I want to say take all the time you need, but remember you still have people that love you. It's not healthy facing this shit alone. I'm here for you. We are all here for you but act like you don't know who Goal is. That man gone break in here and snatch yo' ass up soon if you don't answer that phone."

I dipped another wing in ranch and took a bite. Thinking about Goal was enough to make me lose my appetite and not because I had any disdain for him. I knew in my heart he had nothing to do with my daughter. I loved him. Loved him. I was the first one to blurt it out when he gave me the best orgasm I'd ever known. It wasn't even about just the sex. I mean, yeah it's amazing. Fuck am I kidding? It's the best, but Goal was just – a lot. Right now, I had more pressing matters than a fine ass grey eyed, Aqua man demon. Fuck. Why'd Sora bring him up? Now I was going to have to find my Rose.

"Ion think I want to be with Goal like that," I lied through my damn teeth.

Sora's eyes bulged at my revelation. She pulled the mixed punch out of the bag, followed by two cups. When she walked over to the fridge and filled both cups with ice, she poured the cups to the brim and slid me one.

"Yeah, bitch, put some more food on my stomach and take a drink. You talking fucking crazy now."

"I know, but I don't know. With my daughter being here, I had time to think about a lot of shit. This street shit is the reason my daughter was taken from me for five years. Baguette is out of the streets now thank God, but Goal is not only in them, he's head of the Navarro Cartel. I can't risk my child's life nor can I risk mine. Hell, what about his life? Ion know, cousin. I'm content with owning my boutique, making my six figures, and living my life peacefully. All the shit that comes with a street nigga isn't worth it to me.

To each their own, but Baguette and I are the only ones that had our child taken. We went through some dark ass times behind that, and to find out it was all a lie. I don't even know why she was taken because they are still trying to get to the bottom of it, but that don't matter. She was snatched from us. I was robbed. Baguette was robbed, and that shit damn near killed us. Goal is bigger than Baguette, and Big Red combined when it comes to this street shit. What's next? One of us getting killed?"

I took a sip of the punch.

"Nobody but Brock knew what the fuck I went through in those five years. I hid my emotions well. I did, but every day, I was dying inside. I had to be strong for Baguette. I had to be strong for my mama. I had to be strong for Baguette's parents. I had to be strong for everybody, but the moment my head hit the pillow, the reality of losing my child crushed me like a wrecking ball. I know most people would be like, they only lost a baby at birth; it's not that traumatic, but it is. My baby was made from PURE LOVE. She was wanted. She was needed. I'd prepared for her. Baguette and I weren't together, but we wanted our baby. Now that I have her again, I can't fathom losing her again."

Salty tears entered my mouth, and I was surprised my body could still produce tears. I'm sure I was dehydrated, yet they still fell.

Sora reached in and aggressively wiped my tears.

"First off, I would never dismiss your feelings. Losing a child is hard, period. Whether you lose them at ten days pregnant, ten weeks pregnant, at birth or when the child is ten weeks. You lost a child, and I never was insensitive to your situation. That's why when you closed us out the first time, I gave you your space. I had my newborn baby. I couldn't even come around you because I didn't want to rub my daughter in your face."

I parted my lips to talk, and Sora held her hand up.

"I know you wouldn't have felt a way, but still, I cared about your feelings way too much. Still do. I couldn't do that to you. Now, while I get where you are coming from, I can't let you shut Goal out. That man has not only bought you a house, two cars, got the whole U.S Army set up around your house, but he is combing the fucking streets about y'all. Hell, how long y'all been a couple? A month or two? Who the fuck coming behind a bitch like Goal? Ion know too fucking many.

"Hell, ion even know one. That man is crazy about you, boo. Nigga gave you a million dollar home before he saw what the pussy was hitting for. Don't shut him out, cousin. Don't shut any of us out. We love you and Athena. We are praising God for bringing her back home. It's a miracle, but you got to let us be there for you. Nothing is going to happen to you or my baby, cousin. Y'all are the safest people in the city."

I chewed on another wing before taking another sip of the spiked punch. I heard everything Sora was saying, and even though I'd shut off from the world, I was happy she'd shown up. I was tired of crying. I just wanted to enjoy my life with my baby. I didn't want Athena to start getting upset since I was sad all the damn time.

"I hear you, Sora. Thank you for coming. I know over the years I've been a terrible cousin and pushed you away at times."

Sora smiled and took a sip from her drink.

"Of course, cousin. You know I love me some you. You was a mean bitch when you was with Baguette, so I thank God that ship done sailed, but the new you, I was starting to see was the old you. It's time for us to get back to the old us. Concerts, shopping days, trips, all the shit we was doing as young bitches shitting on these hoes in the city. Now we can actually do playdates and shit. Athena's ass is already dripped the fuck up. Her cousins got to step their game up when it comes to her, and you know Rayna is going to want to you to do her hair the same way. So, get ready."

Sora and I chilled and drank the whole night. I even let her wash my hair and deep condition it so that my curls could pop. I felt like a new woman, and seeing my daughter interact with her cousins had me on cloud nine. I was happy that my baby would have kids to grow up with because I wasn't having any more children. I now know that Athena coming out a stillborn was a hoax, but I was still scared to push out a dead baby. I'd experienced childbirth and pregnancy once, and that was enough for me.

Sora ended up leaving around one a.m. when Big Red called and made her ass come home and after promising Rayna that I would let her spend the night next weekend I was cleaning up our mess. I got Athena ready for bed, tied her hair down, and helped Lydia and Savannah with orders. I had over six hundred orders so I knew we would be at it a few days. Lydia was a lifesaver. She even recorded us packaging and made a status letting my customers know that Goddess Wears would be giving them a 15 percent off coupon on all the orders for the one week delay. It wasn't until I printed off a label and packaged an order that I realized how much I missed my business. Savannah and Lydia had agreed to spend the night since they had the next two days of school out due to Senior relief days, and although I had never heard no shit like that before, I welcomed all the help I could get. Around 4 a.m., I crawled into my daughter's bed, cradled her in my arms and called it a night.

CHAPTER 11

Aphrodite "Ditey" "Pretty Pretty" "AP" Greer

The next morning, I was up early, opening the door and getting our breakfast. I guess the watchers must've seen that Savannah and Lydia hadn't left and made sure they got more than enough breakfast for all of us. I had so many fast food boxes and containers in my trash it made me cringe. I had to get my damn life together. I didn't want my baby to be accustomed to fast food. It took everything in me not to ask what type of foods she'd been eating the last few years. I was trying my best not to let my mind go back to when we didn't have her.

When Athena, Savannah, and Lydia ate, I took a three pound container of ground turkey out to thaw. Dinner would consist of spaghetti and fish, and I prayed my baby liked it. She fucked that pasta up yesterday, so I was sure she would enjoy it. All kids loved spaghetti.

"I know you tired of me telling you, Aphrodite, but your daughter is so pretty. Ohh, friend, I hope you're having a girl."

Lydia cringed at Savannah, and Savannah immediately stood and gathered everyone's empty Waffle House containers.

Last night. when we were packaging orders, I still didn't pick up my phone, but I did listen to their little high school drama. Savannah also talked about her little baby mama drama. It was still comical to me that she was a eighteen-year-old step mama. Litty's baby didn't come up, but now that it had, I knew I had to address it.

"You want me to wash your hands, pretty girl?"

Athena nodded at Savannah, with her hair wrap still on.

"Come on, we can watch Frozen too."

Savannah mouthed out, *Sorry*, to Lydia and took Athena out of the kitchen. Lydia looked like she had the weight of the world on her shoulders, and I was pretty sure she wasn't feeling too well due to the pale color of her skin.

If you lined all the women up in our family, you would know we were related. Lydia, much like the rest of us, sported curves even though she was on the slimmer side. She'd begun to spread since that baby was sitting under her damn rib. The extremely fine hair shooting from her roots was hereditary from her mother's side. Although I was young when she passed away, I remembered how pretty she was, and Sora and I loved to brush her silky coils. Lydia had us, but she still didn't experience the guidance and wisdom from a mother and for that, I was sympathizing with her. But I was disappointed. She'd broken my heart for sure.

"Lydia, I'm not here to talk down on you. I know you've been getting that from everyone. Plus, I have so much shit going on right now, I don't even have it in me to say what I really feel. What I will say is I am disappointed. Disappointed in the choices you've made. Disappointed in you being careless. You worked so hard for your future. You want for nothing. We all work our asses off to make sure you have everything you deserve."

Lydia tucked her hair behind her ear. My cousin is such a beautiful young woman. I knew as she got up in age, it would be hard to keep the boys off her. We didn't worry too much because she was so deep in her books, and boys weren't her focus. If she wasn't helping me with Goddess Wears, she was studying or babysitting Sora's kids. I would have never thought she would have a damn baby.

"You know, I learned how to do hair because I used to have to babysit you while uncle worked. Sora and I both did. Uncle Luda was so upset when you failed first grade that he made a promise that he would make sure you were on top of your studies. You've been through a lot, baby cousin. You know why I spared no expense on your prom dress? Because you're a good kid. You don't give us any problems. You make straight A's. You're respectful. You do whatever we ask. *Goddess Wears* wouldn't be able to thrive without you. I am disappointed in you, but I love you. Despite your mistake, I am still proud of you. You just hurt us with this one, Lydia. A baby is hard work. Both you and Gage have scholarships and promising futures. A baby being thrown in the mix is going to be challenging, but I'm here to help in any way that I can."

Lydia lowered her head, and when she lifted it, tears stained her dull cheeks.

"You know I met him at the state championship. I mean, I'd had a crush on him forever, so I've always known him. I practically stalked his social media. When I saw him standing on top of the counter at the afterparty, I knew I had to have him. I was a virgin. I promise I listened to everything you all told me, but when I got in his presence, it's like all of that went out of the window. I didn't care about the safe sex speeches or the saving yourself for marriage commitments. I liked him, and I wanted him. My future wasn't even on my mind. Then, it hurt. Sex hurt so bad, but it was special because it was with him. I got to be the dumbest girl on earth to get pregnant on the first try. I know y'all are disappointed in me because I'm disappointed in myself. I don't know what I'm going to do."

Lydia placed her face in her hands and wept, causing me to hop up out of my seat.

"Lydia, it's okay. We all make mistakes, but a baby is not one. Babies are a blessing. Plus, you did nothing wrong. You couldn't get pregnant without him. I'm sure he knows he was supposed to strap his lil' wacker up. You're stronger than you think. We will figure it out as a family."

I rubbed Lydia's curly hair and let her cry on my shoulder. I know she's scared as hell. I got pregnant when I was fully grown, and my ass was terrified.

"So, y'all don't talk at all? You and Goal's brother?"

It was still crazy to me how they had hooked up. Then, when I saw his face, I couldn't even be mad at Lydia because he was an exact replica of his brother down to the grey eyes. Hell, had I met Goal before

Baguette, my ass would have been pregnant in high school too. Those Navarro's were the type of sexy that should come with a warning label.

"No, we were never together. It was like a one-night stand, I guess. Since the party, we still haven't talked. I know he's probably processing the information. I'm not pissed at him. I just hate myself for not taking a Plan B. I wanted to get rid of it because I never wanted to be a teen mom or a girl to trap a boy, but I couldn't do it. Something was holding me back."

I grabbed Lydia's chin and wiped her tears.

Hearing her say he hadn't reached out had me pissed. It brought me back to Sora saying Baguette should be here for my daughter. Lydia was scared as fuck, and the thought of Gage not being there for my cousin infuriated me.

"For what it's worth, I'm happy you are keeping the baby. Gage will come around. For now, try not to stress and prepare yourself for prom and graduation. I know I'm about to prepare my pockets because I have to get your dress fitted yet again, and prom is in a week? At least now I know why your ass is spreading."

Lydia laughed and wiped her tears.

"I don't know if this is a good thing or a bad thing, but our prom date is now pending. Bayside High booked the same day as another school, and even though it was an error on the vendor's part, our school has to find another venue."

"So that means your ass is more than likely gone have me paying for two more fittings? I should send Gage's ass a request since it's his damn fault you gaining," I sassed.

"Oh no, please don't, cousin."

I leaned in and kissed her forehead before pulling her in a hug. I know she was frightened of the unknown, but like always, Sora and I would be there to hold her crown up. Lord, she was about to have a Baby Navarro.

"Now go in there and start on them orders. You got to work for this prom."

We both giggled, and Lydia hugged me again.

"Thank you again, Aphrodite. I remember everything you've ever done for me, and I appreciate you so much. I don't know what the future holds, but I promise I won't let you down. I'm also happy that you are getting your fairytale. You deserve it. Athena is the best, and Goal is fineeeeee." Lydia blushed.

"Aht aht. Focus on your Navarro brother and him keeping that little Peter in his pants."

Lydia stood, "Cousin, it isn't little. At all. I know he and I aren't together anyway, but just know you never have to worry about me getting pregnant by him again because I will never lay back down with him."

I clutched my invisible pearls as Lydia ran out of the kitchen before I could get on her ass. If he was anything like his brother, I understood where she was coming from wholeheartedly.

I cleaned up the kitchen a bit, and just when I was about to go retrieve my phone so I could call my mom, the doorbell sounded.

"I got it, y'all!"

I wasn't sure if they heard me being that I could hear Lil Durk blasting from my office. Between that and Athena watching Frozen loud as hell in the living room, I knew their asses couldn't hear me.

I placed a kiss on the top of my baby's head and then headed for the door. Without looking through the blinds, I snatched it open and felt like I had been punked.

I closed the door back, counted to five, and opened it again.

"Where the fuck is Goal?"

The last bitch I expected to be on my doorstep was standing there looking like she was headed to the club instead of being dressed as if it was eleven a.m. With long blond tresses flowing down her back, skin-tight Louis Vuitton leggings and the matching jacket that showed her belly. I smirked because this bitch really had the balls to show up at my house.

"Daphne, I know you not stupid enough to bring your ass to my house, bitch?"

The question was rhetorical because obviously, her ass was bold enough since she was standing in front of me, with her long lashes, ant shaped body, XL nails in the flesh. Her makeup was a bit much, especially for early in the morning, but knowing this cum guzzler, it was probably her face from last night.

"Girl-"

She waved her long ass nails in the air.

"This was my house. The nigga probably still got my name on the deed. I'll call and get your ass escorted from the premises! You got my fucking leftovers! Just know, I'll be getting me a brand new one that's bigger and better than this lil' shit. Hand-me-down house living ass hoe!"

Crossing my arms over my chest, I leaned against the door frame and smirked. This bird brain ass, ran through ass bitch still was rocking the grey contacts. She wanted to be Goal's twin so bad! I remember when she was fucking with Baguette, this hoe went and got that piercing in her jaw on the same side as his dimple just to mimic him. Tragic.

"Oh, bitch, its lil' shit because you not in it? Newsflash, hoe. Your name ain't on shit over here. Now, I'm going to give you some grace because it is obvious you still drunk from last night. You standing here with another nigga's dick on your breath asking you about *my nigga*. Bitch, he up my ass. Now reach in there and pull him out," I challenged.

Daphne is a bitch that I really forgot about. I hadn't thought about the bitch since the day Goal embarrassed the fuck out of her the day I viewed this property. It was crazy how when I met up with Quasie, even she had issues with Daphne fucking her nigga. This hoe's pussy was hanging on by a thread, and she was still fucking going.

"You think you the shit, hunh? Yeah, you in the house for now but bitch, Goal is mine. For eighteen years, bitch."

Daphne turned her phone around so that I could see the black and white ultrasound and then reached in her breasts, and pulled out the actual folded up paper. Seeing the small peanut on the black and white picture that had her name at the top, along with the hospital and today's date, had panic rioting within me, but I kept the stale expression on my face. This bitch wasn't about to get the satisfaction.

Jett hopped out his truck, pistol at his groin, but he was good. I didn't need him for this peon ass hoe.

"Okay, what the fuck you telling me for? You got his number, call him. Just know the next time you show up to my house, I'm mopping my lawn with your wig. Daphne, please stop taking my kindness for weakness. You know it ain't never been no hoe in my blood. I done already kicked the cum out of you before. That fucking baby won't save you from an ass whopping. I didn't lay down with you, Goal did."

This was one of the main reasons I didn't want this house. Daphne knew where the fuck I laid my head. I didn't trust that bitch. She was so fucking envious, it was no telling what her scorn ass would do.

Daphne turned her nose up, "Girl, please. If you touch me while his baby cooking, we both know he gone kick yo' ass. Goal ain't never been afraid to lay his hands on a bitch. Ion know what the fuck he see in your average ass. I'ma let you have this lil' house though. You not the first bitch Goal done put up. I let my nigga have his fun, but just know when he not here with you, he with me."

I wanted to say that Daphne's words about Goal's infidelity didn't get to me, but I would be lying. The bitch was known to snatch niggas no matter how tarnished her name was. Ion know what it was about her, but the niggas loved her. Yeah, she was fun and had a banging ass body, but her reputation was shot.

"You done? I have a business to run. But bitch, he ain't scared to put his hands on A BITCH, not THIS BITCH. Goal will never in his life raise a finger at me. Ion play them type of games you *go for whatever* ass hoes do. Never have! You better ask around, bitch. I done told you the last time we had an encounter that I'm not letting you lick my pussy. Now, if you'll excuse me, you got Goal number."

I could see it in her eyes that she wasn't done though. She was the same ass bitch that literally stalked me and then begged me to bring me to an orgasm with her mouth. The hoe was so intimidated by Baguette and I's relationship, and now she wanted problems behind Goal. I knew the shit was bound to happen though, and that's why I wasn't trying to give his fine, persistent ass no play. Daphne was the type of bitch that liked to poke the bear. I just prayed that she didn't poke this mama bear because, with all this tension I had built up, I was liable to kill this bitch.

"No bitch, I'm not done. I guess since I took your nigga, you think you gone take mine? Think again, hoe. Just like I had Baguette sucking on this pussy and coming home to kiss you, Goal gone do the same. You can't even bring a live baby in this world. What the fuck my nigga want with – ahhhhhh!"

Pulling my pajama pants up, I took off on this bitch. Serving her straight-face shots with every one of them connecting, her ass was trying to get away. The more she ran, I hit her ass harder.

"Bitch...I ... told... yo' ... ass to leave! Keep my fucking....daughter... out...of...this!" I was hitting Daphne so hard, my fist hurt. She tried running to her truck and slipped, and I was sure to kick this bitch straight in the stomach.

"Ahhhh, bitch! I'ma kill you hoe!"

"Hoe, shut the fuck up! I told you to leave!"

Remembering back when Tuscany, Baguette and I were sitting on my couch at the old house in Conquoy, and my bestie said if she caught Daphne, she was going to *stomp the holy ghost out this big nose bitch*, I did just that. Stomped her ass to the ground, and some way, she hopped back up, but I didn't let up.

"What the hell!"

I looked up, and Savannah had run her little ass out of the house and was alongside of me giving Daphne the business. Savannah pulled Daphne's whole damn wig off, revealing a stocking cap the same as her yellow skin tone.

I lifted my barefoot and kicked her in the stomach again. I kept knocking the wind out of her ass until I was snatched off her.

"Aite, that's enough, Aphrodite! You whopped the hoe. Y'all stop for these white folk call the laws."

Jett pulled me and Savannah off Daphne, and he better be glad he had because I was going to make this bitch cough up an organ.

"Let me the fuck go and help that hoe get in her car before I'm on her ass again. I never seen a hoe so happy to swallow dicks! Bitch talk too fucking much! And stop ordering from my website! I'm sick of blocking all your accounts! I never seen a bitch so obsessed with another bitch! Hoe riding my pussy so fucking hard! Meta morphing ass bitch. I'll shit in yo' mouth! Garbage ass hoe!"

My heart was hammering, my breathing ragged, as anger rippled down my spine.

"Yes, bitch, you need to leave before I slice you like a food stamp pizza, bitch!" Savannah screamed.

"Bitch, your hating ass aimed for my stomach because you big mad! Y'all hoes jumped me!" Daphne winced, fighting back tears.

"And did, hoe! You been mad because no matter how many dicks you suck, you still gotta slave at that hospital, bitch! You was mad that Baguette had me on a shelf, you gone kill yo' fucking self when you see how YO' NIGGA really got me PUT UP! I'm two for zero times two, bitch! Two times I done handled yo' ass to yo' zero."

"That's one," Savannah co-signed while holding up the number one with her index finger.

"Two balling ass niggas that fell the fuck in love with my vibed out ass to yo' zero!"

"That's two! Checkmate, bitch! Get the fuck off her property! You snooze you lose duck ass hoe," Savannah laughed.

"Mommy-"

Hearing Athena behind me had me freezing up. She hadn't called me mommy yet, and her first time doing so was seeing me act out of character.

"Go back in the house, princess. Your mama just talking to a friend," Jett instructed.

"We good, fine ass. You can go back and post up."

Only Savannah's lil' young taken ass flirts in the middle of a damn fight.

"Come on, Princess. Want some ice cream?" Jett tucked his gun so my baby wouldn't see, but Athena didn't want to hear shit dude was saying because she came to my side. In turn, I scooped her up and placed her on my hips. Daphne's eyes grew wide as saucers. All the color drained from her face as she looked from Athena to me. I guess seeing the resemblance had her putting two and two together.

Daphne got her ass up from the ground, holding her belly, and struggled to get in her Rover. When she pulled off and burnt rubber, I stormed back in the house. This hoe had pissed me the fuck off. Had me all out of character in front of my child and shit.

"Are you okay? Did you fight?"

Athena asked me as I locked the door behind Savannah

I nuzzled my face in her neck, smelling nothing but maple syrup. Her presence calmed me tremendously.

"I did, and I'm sorry you had to see that. That lady is not a very good person."

I didn't want to lie to my daughter. Athena nodded, kissed my forehead, wiggled out of my arms, and ran back to the tv.

"What the fuck, Aphrodite? Excuse my language, but what the hell? Is she crazy coming to your house?"

I shook my head, fuming. Savannah's fists were still balled as I began to pace.

"She got to be! I'm so tired of this bitch! She lost her God damn mind coming to where I lay my fucking head! I'ma whoop that hoe every single time I see her. Ion give a fuck! Bitches think since I got a business now, I'm weak. I just let these hoes have that bullshit! I stay my ass in the house and out the fucking way. This hoe got me so fucked up!"

Daphne was like a thorn in my fucking side. I was too old to be doing the shit I did with her all them years ago. I handed her my nigga, and he still didn't choose her. Bitch so fucking wack.

"Well, now she my enemy. Anytime I see her ass it's up!"

Savannah's little ass was turnt. One look at her and you would never know her ass had hands. I mean, she had the shape of a grown-ass woman, unlike my little Lydia, who was slim thick, and still growing into her shape. She was all right with me though, because I knew if she rode with me, she would ride with my cousin.

"What's going on?"

Lydia walked up with raised brows and yawning.

"When your ass was taking that unauthorized nap, I heard a commotion and saw that the Daphne bitch was outside getting her ass handled. So, I jumped in," Savannah explained.

Lydia's eyes bucked, and she started for the door.

"No, you're pregnant, and she gone anyway." I stopped Lydia in her tracks. She was a smart girl, but her ass was raised up in the projects. The Bricks, to be exact. She could fight, me and Sora made sure of that.

"Are you serious? How does she know where you stay anyway?"

I waved Lydia off.

"Long story. The bitch will be asking for the grave if she come back though."

"What did she want?"

"Goal. Where my phone?"

"In the office. What does she want with Goal?"

I walked past Lydia and went for my phone. I was off the grid, but it was time to make a call. I was so mad my fingers were shaking. Walking into my office, I couldn't even appreciate the orders that were lined against the wall. Snatching my phone from the desk, I did the face recognition to unlock my device and called up Goal. I had so many missed calls and notifications, but they weren't a priority.

The phone rang four times before Goal picked up, "Wassup, lil Mayweather?"

I drew my head back because I saw his ass had jokes.

"You need to get your hoe under control, Goal!"

"Damn baby, no good morning Papi, how you been? You just gone go straight in on yo' man?"

Hearing his voice after a week had my core creaming and my kitty thudding. I didn't know how much I missed him until I heard his deep, rustic chords. Still, I was on ten. I hadn't fought in years, and here come this bitch bringing a side out of me that I'd grown from.

"I'm not playing, Goal! As a matter of fact, lose my number! You can have this house and the cars! I bet not stay where yo' hoe can pull up on me! My daughter here, nigga! Fuck both of y'all, and if Baguette around you fuck him too! You niggas sick for fucking hoes behind each other constantly anyway! Bye!"

I handed Lydia my phone since they were now in the room.

"Don't answer for that nigga. Matter fact, block him."

I went into the living room, got my daughter, went to my bedroom and put it on The Little Mermaid. I wasn't up for hearing another damn Frozen sing-a-long. I laid with my child and let her giggles and singing drift me to sleep. I was sick of every fucking body!

After a failed attempt at a nap, I got out of bed once Athena was down and headed to the kitchen. The cleaning company had come about three hours ago and got everything back in tip-top shape. My home now smelled of lemon zest. Savannah and Lydia were giggling and fixing orders when I peeked in on them. With the way the packages were starting to bury them, I knew I had to figure out where I could continue to box future orders. I walked outside, retrieved a few things, and went into the kitchen to cook.

It took me no time to make my spaghetti. I wasn't in the mood to fry any fish, plus I'd forgotten to take out the catfish filets anyway. I topped the dinner with garlic knots and a fresh Caesar salad. I had a thudding headache, so I ate a little something, fed Athena, and crawled my ass back in the bed. I even let Athena stay out with Lydia and Savannah. I was still pissed the fuck off that this hoe had really come to my place of residence. I loved this house, but if this bitch was going to be pulling up anytime she felt like it, I had to roll. I real life was going to kill Daphne if she kept playing with me.

It took three episodes of Game of Thrones and two Tylenol for me to count sheep. I hated to go to bed upset because I knew when I got up, my head was going to be thudding. I just prayed that by the time I woke up, I would be rid of these thoughts about Daphne because I was on the verge of pulling down on the bitch.

* * *

The rumbling of my stomach had me waking up from my slumber. There was no light peering into my dark room from the windows, so that let me know it was late. Sitting up in the bed, I stretched my arms above my head, pushing my sore limbs to the limit. A warm Epsom salt bath was my next step. First, I needed some light. Reaching over to the nightstand, I switched on the stone-textured lamp and nearly jumped out of my skin.

"What the hell? Goal, why the fuck are you in the dark?"

None other than Goal Navarro was posted in the Sherpa cloud chair nestled in the lounging area of my bedroom. This nigga was slurping on a plate of spaghetti. His legs was gapped wide open and body slanted in the chair all while fucking the food up. His jaws caved as he slurped a long, noodle in his mouth, leaving a saucy residue on his lips, and when he licked it away, I had to clamp my legs together.

"What's that shit you was talking on the phone, AP?"

I opened my mouth to talk but closed it again when the words wouldn't formulate.

Goal's sexy ass smirked at me before forking the last of his spaghetti in his mouth. I never wanted to be a fucking noodle so bad, and I was mad at myself for even wanting to go there with him. I was pissed. Pissed that he had even given this Daphne bitch the inkling that it was safe to ever pull down on me yet again about another nigga. We'd done that rodeo too many times with Baguette. I refused to do it with a new nigga.

Goal placed his plate on the small table next to the chair and stood. He towered over me even though I was a few feet away sitting in my bed. The very bed that we'd been sharing up until a week ago. I let my eyes roam his lengthy frame. His toast-colored skin, neatly trimmed goatee, thin mustache that sat above those pussy pink lips, and the wavy hair on top of his head all made up a perfect fucking man. I hated how fine he was. I hated how he may have been friendly with his dick before me. I hated that he had the ability to lick his lips and bring me to my knees like a weak bitch. My life was perfectly fine without Goal coming in the mix. At the same time, him coming around led to a series of events that had me getting my daughter back.

I hated how much I was so unsure of the role he played in my daughter's disappearance. Some days I knew he didn't have anything to do with it, and then others, I was so fucking torn until I had to just bury all that shit in the back of my mind and focus on what was important. My child. Me bonding with my baby to precedent over any fucking conspiracies. Still, I hated how fucking smitten I was with this man, and I didn't know why.

"Goal, I'm not in the mood. I thought you were giving me some space until I figured us out?" I crossed my arms over my chest. My cover was up to my hips, covering the black boy shorts that phat ma was soiling, but my breasts were on display, with only his thin wife beater covering my upper half. I didn't want him to see how pebbled my nipples were just from the mere sight of him.

Goal slowly trudged in my direction, causing my heart rate to increase times ten. I discreetly admired his attire. Goal was clad in clay-colored shorts that came a little above the knee and a matching hoodie that was sleeveless with the words AMIRI etched across. Two thin diamond necklaces layered his chest, but they were gleaming brighter than the lamp to the right of me. His watch was on froze, and as he closed in on me, I was able to smell the signature cologne he'd been wearing as of late. His mouth was void of his diamond grill, and I was grateful for that because it was something about the diamonds in his mouth that just took me there. I don't know what type of magician was in the room when his mama and daddy made him, but being that they did that shit times two, they shouldn't ever in life be able to procreate ever again. They did that shit way too well, and I hated to even admit that especially being that his father had something to do with the disappearance of my daughter. Goal was the be all end all. It was no topping him, and he knew that shit.

No, he didn't walk around like a fucking pretty boy. As a matter of fact, he was as rough as they came. However, the little smirks he cut at me when he caught me watching, the faces he made during our love session when he saw me cumming just because I loved the way he looked and the way he kept himself dazzled in the latest, gave off he knew he was that nigga.

"Goal."

"Wassup witchu, Pretty Pretty?"

I scoffed as he stood over me. He was so close that I had to look up to be able to see his face. I took a deep breath, inhaled all of him, and had to close my eyes to slow my racing heart.

"Why are you here?"

I don't know why I was being this way toward him. It was childish. I was acting as if I was the same age as those girls packing my orders. I'm a grown ass woman but playing childish ass games because I was mad at myself for falling for a man that had a roster as long as his dick.

"Nah, you mad because a nigga *haven't* been here. You asked me to give you some space and out of respect for Lil Pretty, I did that shit. I ain't even pull up on you when you lost yo' damn mind by letting yo' weak ass phone go dead."

Goal pulled my phone from his pocket and tossed it on the bed. A picture of us at his underground restaurant graced my lock screen, and the time displayed was three a.m.

"So you decide to come here at three o'clock in the morning? You could have just stayed where you were if that was the case," I spat bitterly.

Hearing Daphne's ugly ass words in my head had me ready to hop up and smack fire from Goal. *When he isn't here with you, he's with me, bitch.* I wasn't going to act like this bitch's words weren't true once before. Because yes, back then, when Baguette wasn't with me, he was most definitely with her.

"We not doing that shit, Pretty Pretty."

I hated how calm he was. I was on Rah time, and his nonchalant attitude was pissing me off. Knowing better than to push him out of my way, I scooted to the other side of the bed and stood with the cover still at my waist.

"No, we are doing this shit! I was good. I was perfectly fine around this bitch single, running my fucking business and wearing my Rose out! Me and my pussy were good! Then here yo' ass come fucking with me. Five fucking years! I stayed out these hoes way for five years! But, you just couldn't stand the fact that a bitch like me was out of nigga's reach and had to fucking push until you got me!"

My thoughts were racing dangerously, and although I knew I needed to stop while I was ahead, I kept going. Goal was standing there licking his bottom lips, hands crossed at his groin.

"You had a bitch pull up on me! A bitch I used to beef heavily with over my last nigga! A bitch whose ass I done whopped way too many times over some shit that was supposed to belong to me! This shit is just history repeating itself! I let the bitch have the nigga, and she is still stalking me! Shopping with my business, leaving fake reviews and bashing me on social media! I let the shit go because I knew the hoe was hurt that I let her have the nigga, and he still didn't choose her! Then, I had to go and fuck with yet another nigga who had been sucking on her pussy. This bitch was so bold that she came to my fucking house! To my fucking house where my daughter lays her head! I can't do this shit with you! I did it with Brock!"

Holding the cover up with one hand, I used my free hand to swipe up the nappy-ass blonde wig and ultrasound that was on the left nightstand. Tossing both at Goal, with the wig hitting his chest and the piece of paper flying in the air and landing on the sheet, he looked unfazed.

"You need yo' pussy ate? You not yourself when you horny. Come lay down. I need some dessert anyway."

I had to look away from his grey orbs because I was being drug into his embrace. When Goal was around, shit was different. Intensified. There was an air of efficiency around him that fascinated me. I hated that. I hated that, yet again, I'd formed another soul tie to a man that was destined to not only break my heart but make me look like a damn fool in the process.

"Did you not just hear me say Daphne; I mean, your baby mama pulled down on me today? Go suck on her pussy!"

Seeing the smile on this bitch face as she presented that ugly ass ultrasound had me wanting to press rewind and kick her ass again. That hoe had some fucking nerve!

"You my only baby mama. And stop putting her pussy and my mouth in the same sentence. Ion never been on that type of time when it came to her. The only pussy that be in my mouth is yours. Ass too. Daphne knows that shit too, especially since yo' mean ass told her I was up your ass," Goal snickered. A mischievous smirk covered his sexy ass face, and I knew when his ass left, I was definitely going to have to take a long hot bath featuring my Rose.

"Well, the bitch may not be pregnant no more due to me stomping her the fuck out. Only one Navarro baby on the way, and that's from Gage and Lydia. That hoe wasn't about to have a baby by my nigga and flaunt it around Jagoda Bay!"

Goal stuffed his hand down the front of his pants and shook his head.

"She shol' ain't, baby. Let that hoe know this yo' sperm. You the only one gone be totting my seed." This nigga was amused as hell while I was ready to cut his dick off for even giving it to Daphne.

"I should really make you take me to that bitch, so I can beat her ass again and dump her in that big ass shark tank you got at the lounge! Then, I'll take her remnants to Sparkling City and let the other fish finish her ass off!"

Goal shook his head, expression never wavering.

"I'm tryna figure out if this dick made you crazy or you been that way?"

He had jokes, and each time he smiled, I became even more turned on. That pissed me off even further. I been crazy, yes, but he came along and had a bitch delusional. That's why I wanted to part way before his sweet Colombia mother be burying his ass. I would hate that for her.

"Goal, get the fuck out. Go find another one of yo' homies bitches to fuck. Our time has expired. If I find out you had something to do with my daughter-"

"What?" He boomed.

Goal's playful demeanor vanished. His grey eyes darkened like angry thunderclouds. I wanted to cower under his glare, but I refused to show my fucking hand.

"I sai-"

Goal rubbed his hand down his goatee, and that simple gesture was enough to stop me this time while I was ahead. That subtle movement alone had me aware that I had took shit too far, but I wouldn't be a real bitch if I didn't voice my feelings.

"I'm not gone lie, Goal; I'm confused. I'm hurt. I'm tired. I'm disgruntled. I have been trying to put all this shit in the back of my mind like it don't matter, but the fact of the matter is that it does matter. My daughter has been missing for five years. Perceived dead. Before that, I was in a relationship where I was dogged out. I got over that. I forgave Baguette. I made peace with the fact that my daughter was dead. Even put up with bitches throwing dirt on my name. I stayed the fuck out of the way and got my money, but here you come. Doing everything right. Applying the right amount of pressure. Shit was good. Too good. Then, here comes my daughter.

My best friend drops her off on my porch and says your father is the reason my daughter has been missing, kidnapped or whatever. Then, my daughter is in perfect condition. Not a hair out of place. Despite her being away from me, she has been raised right. She has manners. She is beautiful. Why would someone take her just to raise her up good and give her back? If that's the case, why give her back? I just feel like it's more to all of this, and I don't like that fact that I feel like it revolves around you. My mind is cloudy, Goal. I can't do this with you until all this shit comes to light."

Goal's toast colored ass was the most beautiful, powerful, thugged out man I'd ever come across, let alone laid with, but I'd be a fool to ignore the obvious. Some shit wasn't right, and there was no way more shit wasn't about to follow. I was starting to feel how Baguette was, and now I felt bad for dismissing his claims. He'd always said something wasn't right and that the day our daughter died was a perfectly planned day. Damn, I wish I would have listened. Shit needed to come to light. Until it did, I wanted to be done with us. We had to be put on pause.

"The day you was at the club, and I had yo' ass snatched up and brought to my office?"

I cringed thinking about that day because Goal's rough ass had snatched the breast tape off both my nipples. It was the worse damn pain ever, but what the fuck did that have to do with what I'd just voiced?

"That nigga that came in with those other fake macho ass niggas is Gilberto. My fucking sperm donor. That nigga raped my fucking mama, AP. He raped her and I was created. Then he raped her again fourteen years later, and my brother was created. I don't fuck with that nigga. At fucking all, Pretty Pretty. You saying I had something to do with your daughter is the same as you calling me a flaw ass nigga and questioning my intentions. Baby, ain't no way in the hell I would have come to you knowing I aided in your heartbreak. If I wanted to fuck, I would have fucked you the same day on the counter when you toured this house.

"After I got done playing in your pussy, I would have made you get on your knees and suck my dick before I bent your thick ass over the island and fucked the shit out of you. I fuck with B, yes. But, that nigga and I ain't never been the best of friends. We do business. He ain't have a problem with me pursuing you, so what the fuck you keep bringing it up for? I told you he knew what it was when he put you in my path. B, know my type. He knows what the fuck I like. Has it occurred to you that he probably wanted us together? Ion give a fuck if he didn't and had a problem with it, I would have still went at you."

Goal licked his lips, and that shit had my eye twitching. Lord, why the fuck this nigga couldn't be ugly? I did feel bad as fuck hearing about his mama. I didn't know that, and I wished I could hug her. She and I didn't get to meet at the housewarming for obvious reasons, and now I'd wished we had.

"Yeah, I fucked Daphne after him, but I *wifed* you after him. He fumbled the ball, and now I got that shit. The fucking game is paused because I'm standing in the middle of the field holding you and handling that shit with care. Ion give a fuck about the game forfeiting. You MY bitch. Foreva. Fuck who had you before me. To me, I'm yo' muthafuckin' first. That old shit don't count. Had I known this nigga had your daughter, I would have retrieved her the moment he snatched her from the hospital or whatever the fuck he did. If you don't believe that then, baby, ion know what the fuck to tell you because I ain't going no fucking where and yo' ass ain't either. You stuck with a nigga. I ain't never agree to give you no space from the relationship. I agreed to give you one night to bond with Athena. I just got caught the fuck up trying to piece this shit together. Remember? When I getchu to myself, it's murdaaahhh." He sang the last sentence, sounding better than Sonder. *His singing ass.*

"I'ma give you a pass for questioning my character, because like I said, you not yaself when you horny. Now, lay yo' muthafuckin' ass down so I can suck on yo' pussy. I need to get a couple nuts up outcha before Athena bring her ass in here at 8 a.m. sharp."

My entire face was red and my body was hot. Every being in my body felt as if it was about to implode. I was so fucking turned on by the way Goal had bossed up on me that it was a shame. Still, I didn't want to give in.

"Umm, I haven't took a shower."

Goal rolled his neck and licked his bottom lip.

"Ion give a fuck. You should have been showering when you was stomping bitches in the stomach."

I squinted my eyes at him.

"Do they report everything to you?" I was referring to his watchers.

"Ap, I see everything that go on around here. You think I'll just put y'all's safety in some niggas arms alone? How the fuck you think Daphne was able to even get near the house? I told them to let her when

I saw her coming. I figured you had some stress to blow and wanted to beat her ass. I was right too. Now lay down. You owe me some more birthday pussy."

I immediately felt bad because the day everything went down was indeed Goal's birthday. He shared his with Athena. Baguette and I were still in shock, but we made sure we celebrated her, and the next day, I still let her swim and eat more cake and ice cream since that was the day she recognized as her birthday.

Before I could stop myself, I was letting the cover fall to the ground and slowly crawling in the bed. Goal bit down on his bottom, heighted his lip in a way that looked like he was grilling me. God damn, he was so fucking fine.

Spreading my legs, I let them droop on each side of his since he was standing on the side of the bed.

I laid there looking dumb as Goal stood over me, eyeing me seductively.

"Next time I tell you to bring me my pussy, don't let it be a next time. Bend over."

Holding my breath, I assumed the position. I really wanted to go take a shower. All types of thoughts began rushing through my head like, did I take a shit today? I mean, anytime I did number two, I was sure to use wipes, but still. I didn't want him to be sucking on my ass and dookie balls be back there.

I felt a smack to the ass that stung my cheeks so hard that it felt like my skin had ripped. Goal's aggressive ass pulled my boy shorts down, spread my cheeks open and dived head first.

"Shiiiiiit!"

I saw the sun, the moon, and the stars, and his tongue glided down my folds. His large hands were massaging my buttocks as he began sucking my clit, sending my legs shaking. His mouth covered my pussy hungrily, and the warm breath from his nose shot directly down my ass crack.

"Pussy always tastes so fucking good."

His words sent chills all over my body as slurping sounds filled the primary bedroom. Goal dug his nails in my flesh, and the pain mixed with the pleasure of his mouth was enough to send my body vibrating with liquid fire.

"I'm cummmminnnngggg! Shit!"

I didn't care that I was loud enough to wake the whole house up. The pleasure that Goal was bringing me with his mouth had me spent. I'd completely forgotten about not only Daphne, but my suspicions of him taking Athena. None of that shit mattered no more, and this just wasn't some cum-filled haze.

"Umm humm. Let that shit go."

I was still cumming as he munched on my box. I felt like I was seizing and was confused as hell as to why I couldn't stop. A burst of liquid shot from me, and I know it was all over his face.

"Wet a nigga up. Fuuuuck! That shit so sexy. Papi make you cum hard as fuck, don't I?"

"Unnnh hunnnh! Yesss, Papi!"

"I know it. Now take this dick."

I don't know when Goal freed his dick, but being that I was wet as fuck he was able to ram his shit right in my hole, and that had me falling from my doggy-style position.

"Aht aht. Toot that ass up."

Goal caught me before I could fall and pulled be back on his dick by my hips. My ass was moving without my permission as he banged in and out of my kitty.

"Hol...Hol...Hold up, Papi!"

WHAM! WHAM! WHAM!

"Shut the fuck up. Yo' tough ass can take this dick. You let a week pass by, and you close up on Papi? Spread that shit open."

I tried to reach back and spread my ass cheeks open but kept failing tremendously. Goal wasn't letting up. His strokes matched my heartbeat. If it could thud any harder, I would be going into cardiac arrest.

Goal grabbed my arms, placed them where they needed to be and gripped my wrists as I spread my ass cheeks open. This shit was feeling soooo good that not only were my eyes stuck at where my lids normally were, but slob was spewing from my lips. This nigga was giving me the fucking business up in here. My loud screams did nothing to slow his motion. I was literally praying that he was about to cum.

"Fuuuuuuck, this pussy so good. I'm cumming, baby. I'm fitna nut all in this pussy. I like seeing you in mommy mode."

With that, Goal shot off like a rocket, and at the same time, I was wetting him like a broken faucet. Goal was cumming so much that I could feel the warm gooey nut ooze out of me.

I plopped down on the bed, felt Goal move across the room, and moments later, the shower was going. Once he scooped me in his arms, he entered the free-standing, rainforest-style shower and placed me on his lap that was on the bench.

His mist-colored eyes were almost imitating the same color as the smoke around us. I pulled the wife beater over my head and tossed it to the floor.

"I love you, Aphrodite. Ion never loved no woman besides my mother before. Yeah, I was buying Daphne a house because the pussy was straight, and she was my bitch. I'm a rich ass nigga, and she wanted us to have a house, so I did that. Long before the house was finished, I found out that bitch was fucking a bottom feeder. I picked out all this shit. All the finishings, but the décor, that shit all you. Don't ever let that bitch feel like you got her fucking leftovers.

Truth be told, she the one that got yo' fucking leftovers. I was made for you, Pretty Pretty. I was just out here playing with these other bitches until you came and got me. I been out here trying to piece this shit together but best believe, every fucking night, I watch you sleep and not on no cameras and shit neither. I be here physically. I watch you cry in yo' fucking sleep while holding your daughter. I haven't slept in a fucking week, but watching y'all be able to lay your pretty little heads down at night gives me a sense of gratification. A nigga took your heart and crushed it to pieces for five years. I can't have no peace until I figure the shit out, AP. I got you, baby. I got us. When this shit is handled, I promise we gone live it up. If you would let me, I'd marry yo' gorgeous ass right fucking now. Average ain't even in yo' vocabulary. I keep telling you I'm not a street nigga. I'm THE street nigga. Let me the fuck in, baby."

Tears shot down my face, causing Goal to thumb them away.

"I'm sorry. I'm just so hurt. How could anybody take her? You see her? She's so perfect. She's my everything. I missed five whole years, Goal."

Pain like I'd never known before welled in my throat. My stomach clenched, and it was impossible to steady my erratic pulse. The thought of losing my baby again was one that I couldn't fathom.

"So the next five years, we gone double that shit up. Yes, you lost time, baby, but you got time. You got all the time in the fucking world to give her the best love. Let me handle giving y'all the best life. You think the house and the cars were something?"

Goal chuckled, "This ain't shit, my baby. This shit small. I got you. I got y'all. I'm yo' nigga. I'ma play the background with Athena until you ready for me to do more, but when it come to you, I own yo' fucking heart. I know that shit sound scary and possessive, and it should. I ain't going nowhere, baby, and I meant what I said about you owning me. This yo' dick. This yo' mouth. These yo' pockets. This your Cartel. This yo' fucking soul. Ion know what the fuck you did to me, but if you wanted me to kill off every muthafucka on the planet, it's done."

The seriousness in his expression sent a coolness all over my body.

"I'm sorry. I love you too, Goal. I'm just scared."

"My bitch not ever sorry or scared. Not when she got the grim reaper for a nigga. Now, if you want to apologize, give me a kiss."

Reached in, I sucked on his bottom lip, tasting my juices before we tongue wrestled. The hot water poured down on us as smoke made it nearly impossible to see. Once we were damn near dizzy from kissing, Goal pulled back.

"You got a gangsta kissing you and shit. You know I love yo' ass. Now get on yo' knees and suck this dick. I got a few more times to make you cum before I leave."

The thought of him leaving caused that panic to make its appearance again.

"Will you come back tonight?"

Goal gripped my thigh and smirked.

"I ain't never left. I told you I come back every night, baby. I'm just gone before y'all get up. If you want me to come and give you some dick before you go to sleep though, I will."

Goal standing over me, watching us sleep was sexy as hell. I still wasn't ready to make formal introductions to Athena because I wanted her to myself a little longer. Plus, I didn't want her getting a bond with Goal before she did her own father.

Dropping to my knees, I got eye level with his python.

"Yes, give me dick before I go to bed."

Taking him in my mouth, I made sure to deepthroat him, which caused me to gag. Goal gripped the back of my head.

"I got you, Pretty Pretty. Suck yo' dick, Mrs. Navarro."

CHAPTER 12

Kymani "Kilo" Lantis

It had been damn near three weeks since I left Kassie's house. I pretended like shit was all good with Baguette and Goal when it came to B's lil' girl, but a nigga was low key fuming. I'd been unsuccessful in getting in touch with my grannie, and that shit had me worried as fuck. Kassie had been calling like a muthafucka trying to get answers, but I didn't have any for her. I had no idea where the fuck my OG was, and I was trying my hardest not to panic. When she first told me about her job when I was locked up, I was pissed but chopped it up to her needed something to do. She had grown an attachment to the children she was watching, but as long as the people were treating her well, I was cool with it. I knew how old folk got when they didn't have shit to do, so I let it rock and didn't even look into it. A nigga was so fucking consumed with life, baby mama drama and being angry that my freedom was snatched away from me and my wife leaving me that I didn't care enough to ask questions. Now, I couldn't even fucking reach my grannie.

I didn't know what the fuck she was tied up in nor did I know if she was even safe. Thoughts of her no longer having life had me sick as a fucking dog. I'd been riding the city for answers, even asked a few of her friends, but I got nothing. My back was against the fucking wall.

Kassie told me about Baguette's daughter being dropped off on the porch, and ever since then, I'd been trying to get up with the nigga. My last resort was to reach out to Goal, but I wanted to speak with the source directly. I'd been around his fucking daughter a handful of times. That shit fucked me up that my nigga thought his daughter was dead, but I'd been in her presence unknowingly. Even bought her ass a few toys. She was smart as fuck too. I hate that I never made the connection being that she looked just like the nigga.

Pulling up to Houston's, I had to shake my head as I walked through the doors. I remembered vividly how I ran into that nigga here. I was meeting my grannie for lunch, and she had both the children she watched. My grannie was so attached and protective of those kids. Whatever they weren't allowed to eat or do, she made sure to run that shit down anytime they were in Kassie and I's presence. Kassie and I often joked that she kept them up to par better than her and I. Shit was wild.

My mama died a few years before I was locked up, and Kassie's mama died at birth. My grannie never really brought them up, and being that my mama had been living with the other family she created out in Cali had me not ever giving a fuck about her. Hell, I didn't even ask questions about her funeral because I knew I wasn't attending that shit. Every so often, my grannie told me some shit about my mama. Fuck that dead ass lady. It was my grannie 'til the world blew. She was all I fucking needed. That's why I was praying hard as fuck that she was good somewhere and just oblivious as me when it came to this shit.

I requested a booth at the back of the restaurant, placed an order for two triple shots of Dulce and waited.

A shadow cast over me as I scrolled through my phone, bypassing all the texts both my baby mamas had been sending. I had too much going on than to be dealing with their bullshit. They were just one big happy family, and now their asses were beefing. Long as my kids didn't get caught in the mix, I was good.

"It took me to come in here for you to pop out? Had I known that would have saved both us gas, I would have been pulled up."

With eyes low and red from either Za or weary, Baguette slid inside the booth and threw the shot back the moment the waitress placed the drinks in front of us. He looked much different from the last time I saw him, and not in a good way. Baguette got his name because the nigga stayed iced the fuck out, but here he was sitting across from with not a lick of jewelry on. Being that it was light rain outside, droplets of rain sat on his navy blue Nike windbreaker jacket, and before he sat down, I could see he was rocking the matching Air Max. I hadn't done much of any shopping besides for my kids and a few things for day to day, and honestly, I didn't know when I would. The money my wife blessed me with had come thru for a nigga, and the cut I was getting from Big Red had my pockets deep as fuck. With this shit knocking me off my square though, I didn't give a fuck about none of that. My grannie being good was my number one priority.

"You know I been following you."

Taking a sip from my drink, I lifted my hand for the waitress. I hadn't ate shit and wasn't trying to be throwing shots back like water on an empty stomach.

"Hell yeah, nigga. We both came up in these streets together. You know as well as I do, an unaware man is a fucking dead one. I figured you was trying to feel me out, but I know you came to the right conclusion."

Baguette gnawed on his bottom lip.

"And what's that?"

"That I ain't have shit to do with yo' daughter, nigga. I thought she was dead just like you. You think if I knew she was alive, I would be holding that info from you? I-"

Goal slid in the booth next to Baguette and I had to sit back in my seat.

"But I bet you ain't know *I* was following you, nigga. So, depending on how this conversation go, you just might be a dead nigga."

Baguette looked over at Goal like he didn't even know his ass was in the mix, but we were all here now.

"I hate to tell y'all this shit, but ion know what the fuck goin' on."

"Give me a bottle of what these niggas drinking and a glass with ice. Also, bring out three orders of salmon dip, three steaks medium rare, all with mac n cheese and three house salads. I'ma place a to-go order too a lil' later."

This nigga ordered for us and dismissed the waitress.

"What the fuck can you tell us, nigga?"

I chuckled and tried hard not to take offense to this shit. I knew both of these niggas were looking for answers, but that made three of us because I was looking for them too.

"My grannie got that job when I was locked up. She was forever preaching that she wasn't the babysitter to my kids but went and got a nanny job. Anyway, she fell in love with the job, and it kept her occupied. Between my jail sentence and my ignorant ass baby mamas, she needed some peace. The folk flew her around the globe and all types of shit. It seemed legit, so I never asked no questions. To be real, my focus was not losing my fucking mind in that bitch."

Goal nodded in agreement.

"So yo' grannie was my daughter's nanny?"

I nodded.

"Yeap. She been their nanny for five years. It's like the moment I got locked up, she got the job. When she told me it was a newborn baby girl, and a seven year old boy, I told her ass to go the opposite way. She told me she wanted to stay, so I let it rock."

"So it was two kids?" B asked with a raised brow.

"Nigga, yeah. Two. When I got out, she brought them around for the first time, and I instantly knew why she wanted to keep her job. I asked her the name of the rich muthafuckas she worked for, and she told me some shit I had never even heard of. Again, ion ask no questions. Now, me and my cousin can't contact her. Ion want to think the worse, but this shit killing me."

I hated how noncaring I looked in front of these niggas. I knew better. I should have been all in my grannie's business. Maybe this shit would have been avoided. Haddie Lantis was my fucking world. She raised me and Kassie when our own fucking mamas didn't want shit to do with us. Deep down inside, I know my grannie knew them kids needed her, and that's why she stayed on.

"Well, she was working for Gilberto. This whole fucking time, that was her employer, but you know that already. Because yo' cousin was at the housewarming that day."

I sat up in my seat and said fuck the food and downed my drink.

"Yeah, and every time I think about shit, it makes me sick to my fucking stomach. I don't know how the fuck I let that shit get past me. Why the fuck would that nigga hire my grannie? I know he did a background check and connected the fucking dots."

This shit was getting stranger and stranger by the minute.

"Nigga, yeah, he did. He targeted her because she yo' peoples. I hate his ass," Goal grumbled.

That explained why Kassie said she saw Goal and Baguette about to kill each other. Baguette must've thought Goal had something to do with this shit.

The salmon came out, so we paused and started back up when the waitress was out of earshot.

My fucking head was spinning trying to process all this shit. I remember when I decided to part ways with Gilberto. As a young nigga, I was happy as fuck to connect with the plug. I didn't know what the fuck a Cartel was until I hustled my way up and found the plug. The cocaine was pure as Alaskan Snow, and the prices were lower than low. I ran up so much fucking money under Gilberto. I always thought the nigga was shady, and his energy was off, but as a young nigga that had become rich overnight with this shit, I disregarded all that shit. When I heard that his father had stripped his privileges of the cartel, I was still willing to do business with the nigga. Me and Baguette. But the nigga started moving foul. His son came along with cheaper prices and was cool as fuck, so we went through with the move. All this shit happened five years ago.

"I got no doubt in my mind that Gilberto planted that shit with you, Kymani. The nigga shipped you off to prison, thinking yo' ass would get more than five, and he took your daughter, B. Ion know why the fuck I wasn't able to put that shit together at the time, but that's what the fuck happened. The nigga a whole bitch. On top of that, he been trying to get me to bow out gracefully and hand the cartel over to him, knowing damn well grace not even in my fucking characteristics. I should have killed his ass a long time ago, but Mi Abuelo is the reason I haven't offed his ass."

The waitress came back with the bottle of Dusse' and ice, and Baguette immediately poured him a glass full.

"This nigga played with my heart. Had me around this bitch going fucking crazy. Had me talking to an empty fucking grave and shit, and the whole time my daughter was alive. Judging by how long you said your grannie been working for him, she been right here in Jagoda Bay. How did I miss that shit? In plain fucking sight. How did I not run into her?"

"Let's not act like Jagoda Bay isn't big as fuck. Shit is huge. They could have been anywhere in the city. Especially being that he had hired help and shit." Goal scooped salmon on a piece of bread.

"You did run into her, my G. Here. Remember when you saw me in Houston's, and I let you know I was meeting my grannie?"

B was in thought until he chuckled.

"The little girl that ran into my knee. Shol' in the fuck did. I be having so many dreams of Athena it's hard to flip flop that shit from reality. It's crazy because the same way she looks in my dreams is how she looks in real life. Now I feel like I have seen her more than once in real life. Shit got me feeling like I'm losing my fucking mind, G."

I felt bad as fuck for my homie B. I had two children that I loved to death despite the bullshit that be going on with their mamas. I hate them fucking girls some days, no lie, but my kids are the best part of me. Losing them isn't an option. That was one reason no matter how much I love Quasie, I will always choose my kids over her in a heartbeat. She still can't fuck another nigga though.

"She here now, and she need you, nigga. I got this shit. We got this shit." Goal gave B a look and then tossed me the same look.

I was all the way in because now, this shit involved my fucking grannie and my freedom. Gilberto was sick as fuck for this weak ass shit.

"It's wild that this nigga tried to take us out by snatching my freedom and taking your child. Why not just kill us? Or someone close to us?"

Goal shook his head.

"Because that nigga knew his father would have put a bullet in his shit. Y'all were an intricate part of our operation and loyal as fuck. Had some foul play gone down, we would have automatically knew it was Gilberto. So, he studied y'all and found a way to break y'all down. I couldn't figure the shit out at first, but after thinking on the shit, I figured it out.

Him hiring your grandma and staying in the city was a way to fuck with your mind. B, you probably have seen your daughter on more than one occasion. That nigga wanted to taunt you. He wanted to drive both y'all crazy. What I'm confused about, though is why would he just show his hand now? And what the fuck Tuscany got to do with this?"

Goal lowered his head and chuckled.

"Cartel Games."

"Hunh?" I quipped.

"The nigga playing Cartel Games. He mad because I won't hand the fucking operation over to him, so he's showing me how far his reach is and how far he's willing to go. Then, he saw me with Aphrodite one day in the office and I fucked around and showed my hand. Letting the nigga know I was rocking with her. He even made a fucking comment about how I should focus on starting a family with AP. That's why he made Athena appear and snatched Tuscany up. B, yo' bitch don't have shit to do with this. He playing fucking Cartel Games."

A deep scowl covered B's face.

"Man, fuck that hoe. It's been three weeks and she still hasn't shown face. For all I know, she was in on this whole plan. She watched a nigga mourn- Just, fuck the bitch. I got a bullet with her name on it if she ever shows face."

Goal and I sat in silence. I could tell B was hurt by his bitch possibly playing a role in all this. He needed to check the facts though before just killing her ass off. Good women were had to come by once you cross the line and lose the forever.

"From what I see, Gilberto is calculated as fuck. I used to think the nigga was a cold-hearted ass, bitch boy that used his muscle to get his way. I ain't never had no problems with him because I got my product and was never short. I have seen the nigga in action though, and Cartel killings were never pretty. The nigga pockets suffered behind us, so he was willing to go to the extremes. He went to the extremes. This shit is just mind-boggling." I'd lost my fucking appetite thinking about this shit. The nigga really did too fucking much, but I was with Goal. I don't think Tuscany had anything to do with the shit, and I don't even know shawty.

B's expression softened.

"So, you been around my daughter?"

I nodded slowly.

"I have. Smart lil' sum too." I smirked.

"You know sum' 'bout her? Like what she like and shit?"

I thought long and hard. Although I'd been around her a few times, I never sat with Grannie and the kids for too long.

"Frozen. The Little Mermaid. But fasho Frozen. She always wants to watch that fucking movie. She allergic to some shit-"

"Peanut butter and Almonds," B answered for me.

"Yeah, that's it. My grannie call her Ramira and sometimes A. I taught her how to tie her shoes, and she learned that shit in an hour too. Besides that, ion know too much, homie. She a good kid. Pretty too."

I prided myself on having a beautiful daughter and Athena was just as gorgeous. I shook my head thinking about the hell Baguette and I would have to cause behind them in the future.

"You know the best way for you to get to know her? Nigga, go be with her. She been cooped up in the house with her mama for three weeks now. You know Aphrodite a damn homebody. Go see 'bout her. That nigga Gilberto is off the grid. I know because I been hunting the nigga since April 16th. We were taught by the same man, so I knew his ass was gone be hard as fuck to find. I'ma catch his ass, though. We just got to keep our ears open and have patience."

Our steaks were placed in front of us, and Goal said a quick silent grace before cutting into his beef.

"The quickest way to catch a nigga slipping is to make him think shit sweet. Go back to living but do that shit cautiously. Yo' grannie alive. He ain't kill her, trust. If she was dead, he would have delivered a body part to you by now. Cartel Games. You got to be smart when it comes to niggas like Gilberto. He pulled the wool over y'all eyes for five years, but I been woke. I hated that nigga since I sprouted from his nut sack."

Goal popped a piece of steak in his mouth. I had to force a piece of steak in my mouth. Thinking about the possibility of my grannie being caught up and then sliced into pieces had me sick.

"Let this shit ride out. Chasing the nigga just gone wear us out. I got his fucking Visa, so wherever the nigga at, he in the States. He wanna play, let the fucking games begin. Me and my gators real fucking patient."

CHAPTER 13
Tuscany Payne

I don't know how long it's been since I've been locked in the dark. The moment the plane landed, I was tossed into the back of a truck and knocked out cold. When I woke up, I was on a hard floor. I laid there and cried for I don't know how long. I cried over my foolish decisions. I cried for Brock and Aphrodite. I cried for my mother, who must've endured torture in my absence and hid it behind smiles anytime I visited. I cried for my child. A child I didn't think about once in the last twelve years. My first time seeing him, and all the love I thought I never had for him, came rushing back. He was so handsome. A perfect blend of all of my brothers, but with the color of his olive skin and wavy hair, his mixed roots shone through. I hated so bad that his father was Gilberto.

By the time my bones were aching, I got up from the floor and barely saw a closed door. Pulling myself from the hard floors, I opened the door and determined that it was a bathroom with no windows. I took a piss, wiped myself and just sat there on the toilet. I tried flicking the light on but noticed there wasn't a light switch. My mouth was so dry, but I didn't even have the energy to try and drink from the sink. I wanted life to be over at this point. Whatever Gilberto had planned for me was worse than death. Had to be. I'd been on the run from him for over a decade and left him with a child. If he wanted me dead, he would have done so already. He was going to keep me alive, beat me, and pump me with his evil babies. Just the thought of him getting on top of me was enough for me to hop off the toilet and dry heave. There was no food on my stomach, so there wasn't much to throw up. Suddenly, I became light-headed. I needed to lay down. Even if it was back on the hard concrete floors, I needed to lay down.

Walking back out, I walked in the opposite direction of where I'd come from and stubbed my toe. I knew that cracked my acrylic toenail, but I didn't give a damn. Bending down to feel what I'd jammed my toe on, soft fabric ran underneath my palm. I pressed down, and when I felt a springy mattress, I eased my battered body onto it. No sooner than my head hit what I assumed was a pillow, I was back out like a light. Another day or so went by, and by then, my body was all slept out. My hunger pains were so intense that I had no choice but to find my way back to the bathroom and feel for the shower. I ran cold water and removed my clothing because the scent of tart and musk was starting to make me feel sick, and lord knows I had nothing in me to throw up.

I let hot water cascade all over my body and then switched it to cold so that I could drink it. Cupping my hand under the shower, I drank until my stomach felt full. When I was done, I got my wet ass back in the bed and laid in the stillness of the dark. No one was coming for me. Brock and Aphrodite hated me. I just knew they did. I looked flaw as fuck in their eyes. Even if by some miracle I was led back to them, there would be no way in hell I could face them. What would I say? Everything that came out of my mouth would make me look flaw as fuck. I had no idea this man had their daughter. Hell, I didn't know Gilberto knew Brock! I was on the run from his ass! But that shit didn't matter.

I'd been walking around on eggshells around Baguette because he was grieving for his child, and I knew the day would come that I would have to bear his babies. I didn't want a child because I'd raised kids most of my life, but the real reason I didn't want a baby is because of the guilt. I'd already carried a baby to term, pushed him out and handed him over. How could I do that shit again? How could I love my baby with Baguette out loud when I had a child that I didn't care if he was living or breathing? That shit had me questioning my own damn self. Was I just as evil as Gilberto? Now that I'd seen my handsome baby boy, he was all I was thinking about to keep holding on. I closed my eyes and thought back to that day since all I was left with was images in my mind since I couldn't see shit.

"Are you okay?"

I was just pushed in the back of the car behind what I knew had to be Athena. I was so fucking confused. Had Gilberto beat me to death to the fact that I was seeing this girl? The same little girl that was presumed dead. I'd never seen Athena a day in my life outside of the baby pictures from the day she was born and died, but this little girl had the same exact face. Not only that, she was Aphrodite's twin. I prayed Gilberto didn't do know shit like that.

"Take this bitch to their doorstep and make sure she gets right back in. If she tries anything or says anything other than Gilberto had their child, shoot her in the head along with everyone at the party."

Gilberto leaned in the driver's side of the door and cut his eyes at me after speaking with the driver.

"Fuck with me! I'll kill you!"

I cried out and nodded my head. He handed the driver my phone and gave them instructions to text and call Aphrodite when we got outside her house. I thought he'd tossed my phone out with my purse in the parking lot but he must've removed it before. I was only hoping someone would track my location. When the car pulled out, I noticed I couldn't see out of the windows once the partition was let up. I tried opening the door and letting down the windows but to no avail. I was fucked and cursing myself so bad for being caught slipping.

"Are you okay?"

I forgot the little girl was in the back seat with me and had chopped it up in my mind that she was really a ghost. But she wasn't. Sitting with her little feet hanging from the seat and the purple and white dress on her tiny body was adorable. I blinked three times to make sure I wasn't going crazy. Reaching over, I lightly tugged at one of her ponytails, and when she smiled, showing that one dimple like Brock, I jumped to the door like she was the exorcist.

This man was fucking sick! How! Why! I didn't even know Brock when Athena was born! Why the fuck would he have them thinking their child was dead? This shit didn't make sense.

"You're bleeding."

Tears blinded my eyes and choked my voice as I began to hyperventilate. My head spun in agony to the point I needed fresh air to process this shit. This can't be!

"I'm...okay. What...What's your name?"

"You need a doctor."

Oh my God, she looked just like Aphrodite. This shit was so cruel! I'd been telling my man to seek help because he couldn't get over the fact that his daughter was no longer amongst the living, and the whole fucking time, she was! Oh my fucking God!

"I'm-I'm fine, baby. What's your name?"

"It's Ramira or A."

I shook my head. I didn't know how long we had before we got to Aphrodite's house, but I knew I was pressing for time.

I grabbed Athena's small hands and turned her to face me as the car moved through the streets of Jagoda Bay.

"That man is not your father!"

"I know. He's Tulsaire's father."

That shit had me sick to my stomach because it was true.

"Your name is not Ramira."

"Yes, it is, silly!" She gave off the cutest laugh.

"It isn't. It's Athena. You have a mommy, a beautiful mommy that looks just like you and-"

I was crying so hard my words were damn near inaudible.

"She loves you very much, Athena. You were taken from them, so they thought you were in heaven with God."

Athena leaned her head slightly.

"Like my cat Mr. Pea?"

I didn't know who her cat was, but I agreed.

"You also have a daddy. He's the best daddy in the whole wide world. You will know him when you see him because he has a dimple in his cheek just like you and he is wearing all white. He has a big ole head too."

Athena laughed.

"They will be crying and so confused, but please, don't be afraid of your parents. They are the best people in the world, and you will have the best life."

Athena looked so confused, and I hated to spring this on her, but that was the least I could do for Aphrodite and Brock.

"Will I see my brother again?"

Before I could answer her, the door was snatched open, and I was pushed out of the car. Hugging Athena tight, I rang the doorbell.

That had to go down as one of the worst days of my fucking life. I constantly replayed that back in my head, but the only thing that brought me a little bit of peace was knowing Athena was with her parents. Aphrodite and Brock deserved that. They would go to war behind Athena. I prayed Brock didn't let Baguette shine through and was combing the city instead of spending time with his baby girl. Knowing him, he was most definitely combing the city. His soul wouldn't rest until he found out where the fuck Gilberto was, but that was pointless. Gilberto would only be found when he wanted to. Just like he gave them their daughter when he was ready.

The sharp pains in my belly had me curling in the fetal position. The water cured my thirst, but I was starving. Balled up like an embryo, I prayed harder than I ever had. I prayed for my foolish decision to abandon my son and my mother. I prayed that Athena nor my son had been fondled or abused in the past years. I prayed Brock was at peace now that he had his daughter. I prayed Aphrodite was just as smitten with her daughter as I was in the few moments I'd been with her. I prayed that if God let me live through this situation that I had the tools to kill Gilberto. I was tired, and I felt light as a feather.

Before I could close my eyes, light shined through, and momentarily, I could see. I was in an unfinished basement, and there were no windows. I couldn't see anyone, but when I saw a bag of food be placed at the top of the stairs, I all but ran to get it.

I tripped up a few stairs, but when I made it to the greasy bag of McDonalds. I ripped it open and bit into the double cheeseburger. I was eating so fast I'd bit my fingers a few times. Thankfully, there were three burgers and two fries in the bag. I ate it all in the dark except one of the burgers, just in case it would be days before I ate again. Grabbing the burger. I carefully walked back down the stairs and hopped back onto the bed. This couldn't be life!

. . .

I was right to save that burger because forever passed by before the process was repeated. After a while, I was used to the cycle. I estimated about three days had passed before I received a meal, and it was always the same meal. Three double cheeseburger and two fries. I didn't even care if I was being poisoned. I was starving. The double cheeseburger I always saved was split in half to be eaten a day at a time, and the very next day, the process would repeat itself. If my calculations were right, three weeks had passed, and I was still naked, taking soap less showers, and anytime I had to shit, since there was no tissue, I had to rinse the boo boo out of the crack of my ass in the shower. I was so disgusted that I had to hold my vomit in because I needed all of my food to stay down. This shit was pure torture.

At the head of the three week mark, I'd collected enough bags to carry out my plan. I was going to scarf them all down and suffocate. I couldn't live like this. There was no life beyond this. My body was physically tired. This shit wasn't for the weak, and I was the weak. I just hoped and prayed whenever Gilberto and Baguette had their time, he spared my son. He didn't deserve to be killed behind his father's actions, but in the streets, there were no rules.

Stuffing the paper down my throat, my eyes watered as I began to choke. This pain was worse than Gilberto's beating, but I was welcoming it. I could see the light, but when I felt a hard hand slapping down on my back and a hand being jammed down my throat to pull out the paper, I began coughing and threw up all of my half a cheeseburger.

"Chile, what the hell are you down here doing!"

An elderly voice that I'd never heard before was standing over me as I continued to vomit all over the floor.

"I know it's bad, but it isn't that bad. The lord is keeping you here for a reason. Come on, let me help you to the shower, and then I can get this cleaned up and some food on your stomach."

I didn't have the energy to fight, and hearing her mention food had me letting her help me to the shower.

"Cut these darn lights on too."

She flicked a switch outside of the bathroom door, and when my eyes met with hers, a warm feeling came over me. I had to adjust to light since I'd been in the dark since forever. My eyes were super sensitive to light. I felt safe with her, but being that Gilberto had kidnapped me, anyone associated with him was an enemy.

She turned the water on and reached under the bathroom cabinet for soap and a rag. I could see the tissue and felt so foolish.

Once she cleaned my body like I was her child, instead of a grown ass woman that shared the same body parts as her, she went back under the cabinet and grabbed shampoo and conditioner. She hummed as she washed my hair, and it felt so good it brought me to tears.

"It's okay, darling. Come on. Let me braid you down."

She wrapped a towel around my body, brushed my hair and gave me two braids to the back. I sat on the toilet as she disappeared and came back with clothing. Once I was dressed, I finally turned to face her.

"Where am I?"

With a shake of her gray coils, she looked off into the distance.

"If I knew, I would tell you. I was put on a plane and brought here. With those dark windows, honey, I couldn't see nothing. What's your name, besides Tulsaire's mama?"

I snapped my head at her.

"You look just like him. I'd always wondered what his mommy looked like. I'm Haddie. I'm the kids' nanny, cook, and everything else."

"Why?"

That was the only word I could muster. Gilberto was a fucking nightmare, so anyone that worked for him was suspect as fuck. She looked like a sweet old woman and all, but again, she couldn't be trusted.

With a look of distress on her face, she peeked her head out of the door and then turned the water on of the sink and then the shower.

"Look, I've been working for this man for five years. I was a bit lonely with my grandson away in prison, and I wanted to make some coins. I'd been watching children my whole life, so with the help of my church, I created a profile, and a week later, I was interviewed. Mr. Gilberto explained he was a high-profile CEO, so secrecy was his number one priority. He was fidgeting too much if you asked me, but the moment I laid eyes on the most handsome little boy and newborn baby girl, I knew I was going to take the job.

The man was clearly unhinged, so I figured I'd work for him to keep my eyes on the chirren. I wanted to ask questions so many times, especially when we were always being whisked on planes and doctors came to the house to see about the kids rather than them going to a clinic."

The grease she slid down my scalp was soothing.

"Then he brought in home school teachers. One day baby girl had an allergic reaction, and I almost had a heart attack. I tried going to the emergency room, but he almost fired my ass. The doctor showed up when she was near death, and that's when we found out she had an allergy to almonds and peanut butter. That man clearly didn't have any relation to the child, but again, I kept my mouth shut. When she began to talk, and he didn't allow her to call him daddy, I knew shit was all wrong. I was so scared for the children, and their safety was my number one priority. I wanted to go to the police so many times, but I've seen Mr. Gilberto in action. Those chirren have seen him kill and harm more men than the devil himself."

My hands shot over my face as I smothered a sob.

"I have a grandson, but he'd just done time in jail. I wouldn't dare get him involved. I didn't know what else to do but to stay. I haven't seen baby girl in close to a month and only could hope that she is safe."

Haddie fanned her face and blinked back tears. Gilberto was so wrong for pulling this old lady in his bullshit. Her back was against the wall, and she truly didn't know what else to do besides protect the children.

"The kids haven't been abused or anything because he knows I don't play that. Only I spank my babies when they get out of line."

That got a little laugh out of me. We both settled into a silence, but my thoughts were as loud as the running water.

"I was a kid. Gilberto used to beat me 'til I was black in the face. I was suffering. I had plans to go to school and be something in life. I'd already raised my brothers; I couldn't raise a baby. So, I pushed him out and ran. Didn't even do skin to skin. I ran like a coward because I didn't want to be tied to Gilberto. I never once thought about what that would mean for my child. He's going to hate me-"

"Hey, hey. Don't do that! You were a baby yourself. You don't owe anybody a thing. You did what you felt was best. Tulsaire is not going to hate you. He loves you already. He's been counting down the days for

Gilberto to leave so that he could see about you. He's even been sneaking and having one of the guards go to McDonalds for you anytime his – Gilberto isn't paying attention. Despite what he's been through, he is a good kid. Plays too much Roblox and PlayStation, and he acts like he's allergic to deodorant, but he's a good kid. Good grades and well-behaved."

I was balling my eyes out at the guilt. Haddie pulled me into her bosom, and I cried like a newborn baby. She rubbed my back and let me get it all out.

"It's alright. When we get out of here, you just do right by him. Gilberto is gone, but he took him with him, so we can only plan for now. I'm not leaving my baby. All we can do is try to survive and stay alive, you hear?"

All I could do was nod and thank God. I didn't know what was next, but at least I had an ally.

CHAPTER 14

Kymani "Kilo" Lantis

The unplanned dinner I had with Goal and Baguette was three days ago, and there still was no word from my grannie. I was losing my fucking mind and trying to stay sane for my cousin all at the same time. Quasie hated a nigga's guts, especially behind how I'd been bossing up on her ass, but even she'd reached out from a blocked phone to see if I'd heard anything. I barely got any fucking sleep from combing these streets. When we weren't checking every inch of Jagoda Bay, we were at the round table plotting and trying to piece this shit together. One man had managed to ruin all three of our fucking lives and was still doing so. For what, though? Losing clientele wasn't a good enough reason. There was no way Gilberto was mad enough about losing a few dollars that he put me behind bars and took Baguette's daughter.

My phone rang as I made a block in a random ass upscale neighborhood. Seeing that it was Kaisha, I hit her ass with the ignore button and pressed on. When Ree called me immediately after, I sighed and answered. I know I hadn't been around my kids much in the last two weeks, but they spent spring break with me as well as I'd just deposited three thousand dollars in each of their accounts. I preferred not to give them any money, especially Kaisha, since I funded both of the roofs over their heads, put groceries in their fridge, and bought all of my kids' clothes and shoes along with haircuts and braids. When they both texted me about money, I didn't have it in me to argue. I Cash apped the money and kept it pushing. Now, here both these damn girls were doing what the fuck they'd been doing since day one. Working my fucking nerves.

"What!?"

"Unh Unh. I didn't call you to be on no bullshit, so you ain't got to holler at me."

Pinching the bridge of my nose, I stopped at a four way stop.

"Wassup, Ree? I ain't in the mood for all this. My son good?"

I missed my children like crazy. No matter how much of an inconvenience they'd been on my life and in my marriage, they were innocent in all of this and my heart. It was best for now that I didn't have them with me while I was trying to figure this shit out. Gilberto had snatched B's daughter and had them thinking she was dead, so there was no fucking telling what he would do to either of mine if given the chance. After sending the money, I explained to both baby mamas that I would be MIA, but if the kids needed anything, I would have Big Red drop it off. I guess Kaisha couldn't fucking comprehend because she'd been texting and calling me nonstop. I didn't answer because the fucking texts were about nonsense. Hell, she was the reason I knew Quasie was in New York. When she sent me a blurred screenshot of her walking in Central Park, I wanted to kill Quasie's ass. For one, that weak ass makeup didn't hide her hickies on the pic and the way her hips were spreading in that brown dress let me know my wife had been fucked. She said she hadn't, so my delusional ass was taking her word for it.

"He's good. I was just calling you because my sister told me her daughter is acting a fool. Says she was on her way to drop Kyma off to you. You know she will leave that girl on the porch. I wish her ass would just give me my little cousin-"

"Bye, Ree."

Making a u-turn and almost running into a Priest, I headed to my grannie's spot. I'd still been staying there because again, I was delusional thinking Quasie would let a nigga come home when she cooled off. With the way it was looking, I needed to carry my ass to my own place.

It took me less than seventeen minutes to get to Haddie's house.

Seeing Kaisha sit my fucking crying daughter on the porch and attempt to walk off had me seeing red. I hopped out the car before I could even put it in park good.

"Bitch, is you fucking nuts, hoe?"

Kaisha whipped her head around at me, slanging her long ass hair that I fucking paid for.

"Nigga, you got me fucked up! You think I'm 'bout to play babysitter while you and the bougie ass bitch live it up in New York? Hell the fuck no! You need to get Ha'! This yo' fucking baby!"

I had to wring my fucking hands together to keep from squeezing the fucking life out of Kaisha. She was too fucking fine to be so fucking ignorant.

"You got three seconds to get my daughter off that porch and take her ass home."

"We not going home!"

"Bitch, well take her to a fucking movies! Skating rink! Zoo! Take her any fucking where but here!"

"Nigga, you been gone five years, and now you still not trying to be in your kids' lives. That lil' petty ass money don't mean shit, Kilo! Quality time!"

While I knew exactly what I needed to do when it came to my kids, this was the wrong bitch to deliver the message. She had no fucking right to try to preach parenting shit to a nigga when she held the number one spot for the worst fucking mama on the planet.

"You down to one second-"

"You so fucking stupid! You that mad that you got a baby by me and my auntie that you really try to act like they don't exist. Well, we do! We here and will be forever! Get over it and handle yo' responsibilities."

Swiping my thumb across my nose, I nodded.

"My responsibilities include and is limited to Kyma and KJ. That's it! But yet and still, I take care of both you hoes! I put y'all up in quarter million dollar houses that ya' don't even keep clean. I feed you, I pay for your fucking pads and tampons, and that nappy ass weave in yo' head down to that crusty ass thong resting in yo' ass cheeks all come from me! I got two fucking kids, but because y'all can't hold yourselves down, let alone a fucking kid, I gained four fucking children. I'm so fucking sick of yo' project ass! You the worst fucking pick for my daughter! You think she not gone remember this shit when she older? Nah, you think you gone switch shit up and be mother of the year by then. But knowing you, you probably not! I despise you, hoe! Take my fucking daughter home! Got her out here crying and shit!"

I turned my back to go to my baby girl and felt a hard ass thud in the back of my head. My shit was bald, so I knew it was gone leave a knot.

Without blinking, I wrapped my arms around Kaisha's neck as she clawed at my arms. Seeing the life drain from her pretty little eyes had my dick getting hard. When her lips began turning blue, a shot went off in the air.

"I know she stupid, but I can't have you kill my family, Kilo."

I snapped my head at Ree, who had a gun to her side. My daughter was really fucking screaming now.

My son ran out of the car and wrapped his arms around my waist. He was the only thing that calmed me because I was ready to kill both these hoes.

"I'm good, son. Take your sister in the house and give her some juice."

I watched until my son ran to his sister, wiped her face and led her in the house.

"Kilo-"

Ree was consoling Kaisha while she flung around on the ground like a fish out of water.

"I hate you bitches. Both of y'all. Y'all have been hell in my fucking life since the day I stuck dick in y'all. You both disgust me. You ruined my fucking life. When I take care of this business, y'all better fucking run because I'm not gone stop 'til both y'all asses in the ground, and the very bitch y'all jealous of is going to be raising y'all kids."

"Hey, I don't fuck with you." Ree held her hands up.

"Bitch, you throw rocks and hide yo' hands. Every screenshot this incompetent ass hoe sends me comes from your account because your picture be at the bottom. You too pussy to be a thorn, so you send yo' lap dog out. Quasie not thinking about you bitches. She bossed the fuck up and can buy both you hoes lives with her own fucking money. My biggest fucking mistake in life was cheating on my wife and making babies with project pussy!"

"She... don't even like our kids. She will never raise them. I heard she got a new nigga," Ree's messy came out as she spat.

"Look at me. Both you hoes want to suck the cum out of my dick right now. You think I can't get another bitch if my wife wants to call it quits? I can buy six bitches if I wanted to. Now get the fuck off my grandma's grass and pray like hell ion cut the lights off at y'all cribs. You can use the light from yo' phones since y'all like to page watch so fucking much!"

Both Ree and Kaisha ran to their cars and peeled out of the drive-way. I was so fucking mad at myself for even letting my dick get me into this situation. Even back then, I was getting too much fucking money to be sticking my dick in bitches of their caliber. Here I was trying to piece this shit together, and now I was stuck with my fucking kids. Grannie was missing, and Kassie had work so there was my fucking help. I didn't want to go around my kids in a pissed-off mood, so I walked the block to calm down.

When I got back to my grannie's house, I took a nap with my babies. I hated their mothers with everything in me, but I was smitten with my two. I was going to get them cleaned up, take them to a movie and pray their grandmothers would hold them down for me while I got my shit squared out. I was going to offer them both a stack, so I'm sure they would fold for that. Fuck my life. The worst thing I could have ever done was give two scum ass bitches the chance to have one up on my fucking wife. I can't even blame Quasie for not wanting shit to do with a nigga. A nigga can't catch a fucking break.

CHAPTER 15

Goal Navarro

Anytime my thoughts were all over the place I was at my weakest. An unfocused nigga is a fucking dead nigga and can't shit a muthafucka do with a dead nigga but rejoice in the fact that he's gone. I didn't like when shit was off track, and these days, the only thing to stop me from killing every muthfucka with a breath was watching my baby sleep every night. I knew she needed time to process the fact that her daughter had popped up out of nowhere and that she wasn't ready to introduce us, but in the same breath, I couldn't be away from Pretty Pretty. Since the day I laid eyes on her fine brown ass, I knew she was mine. I didn't give a fuck about my situation or what her situation may have been. No disrespect to that nigga B, but I wouldn't give a fuck if she would've had a fucking baby by Barack Obama. I wanted her, so I got her. Goal Navarro gets what the fuck he wants. That's Law.

The rise and fall of her perky chest was like rain on a muggy day for me. I'd been sneaking in her home like a fucking touched ass nigga seeing her baby girl wrapped in her arms. There were fucking two of them. Aphrodite was undeniably the most beautiful woman on the fucking planet. No, she didn't have colored eyes, exotic features, a model-like physique, or no other shit that muthafuckas deemed you had to acquire in order to be beautiful. She was just unapologetically a black woman. A beautiful Ebony fucking stallion. And God saw fit that she had a fucking mini. Athena's little ass was just as striking as her mother and a baby girl any man would die behind. She had all of her mother's features, and it pained me that my baby had missed a small portion of her daughter's young life.

I still hadn't been formally introduced to Athena, but I'd been knocking her mama's box out the frame every fucking night and peeking my head in her room to make sure she was straight. She hadn't come from my nut sac, but you couldn't tell my ass that. I was ready to add her to all my accounts, give her her own black card so that she could buy all the ice cream and plastic nails she wanted and just all out spoil her unconditionally. She was an extension of the woman I loved like crazy, so it was only right I loved her. But, I had pressing matters to tend to, so that would come later. Aphrodite could take her time introducing me to her baby because the truth of the matter is, I'm not going no fucking where. Plus, that nigga B needed to bond with his own child before stepdaddy came in regulating shit.

"Aye, yo' greedy ass be taking the fuck over, Power! Let both the fucking legs go! You get the right, and Money gets the left! Y'all need to be more like Respect and chew on them fucking brains!"

Watching my other babies eat their dinner had tension slowly releasing from my body. Aphrodite released most of it around three this morning, but my Gators feasting on their fourth body of the week was getting me back to where I needed to be. Blood and guts had their waters red and pink. Due to all the souls that had been lost in the waters in the last couple of days had me remembering to call my nigga Wilde to have his people come and clean out their home. He was the nigga that I'd got them from, along with my sharks at the club and seaquarium at the restaurants, and he was trying to get my ass to purchase some more exotic wildlife. I was good on it though. Money, Power, and Respect were enough for a nigga. Plus, Pretty Pretty was constantly calling a nigga Aquaman.

"You and these fucking Crocs creep me the fuck out."

I cut my head at Big Red, who had just turned his money in for his bricks. The nigga was a vet in the streets, and even though I was skeptical of him taking over for Kilo when he got knocked, his light-skinned ass had been putting in work. It wasn't that I didn't trust Big Red because his name was stamped. It was just at the time so much shit was going on with Kilo being caught with the pistol that everyone was suspect. Knowing I should have been looking at my own fucking sperm donor that I didn't even fuck with.

"They ain't no fucking crocs nigga, they gators!"

Big Red scratched the side of his head where one of his wicks sat.

"Whatever the fuck they are, them bitches got more bodies than Lake Lanier. You gots to get them niggas some deer, wildebeest or some shit. All these fucking humans gone have them breaking out this weak ass homemade habitat and eating yo' ass alive."

Every nigga that came through the warehouse was intimidated by my babies. No matter how many niggas they gobbled, they would never turn on daddy. When the warehouse was empty, I let their ass walk around this bitch, and the most they did was follow me around and sleep at my feet. My brother was the only person that didn't fear them, and that was because he was just as fucked up as I was.

"Yeah, you don't even believe that shit. I can have Leo lower yo' ass in there, and they won't eat you 'til I say. My babies trained. Edthang' good, though?"

Although I was still out here looking for Gilberto's ole cat-licked hair ass, business still had to be tended to. The Navarro Cartel needed it's head, so no matter what, I had to be present for my business. Shit had been smooth. The niggas they'd been eating were old ass Columbians that we'd been snatching up. They used to work for Gilberto, and them niggas was tough because they wouldn't tell me shit. That or they truly didn't know where the fuck he was at.

"Edthang' copasetic. Streets good. You good, though?"

Am I good? Fuck no, I wasn't good. My baby was hurt and confused, and although she'd stepped into motherhood like she was made for it, I knew she wasn't really herself. Still, I wasn't about to vent to this nigga like a hoe. I didn't even vent to the woman that pushed me out.

"I'm good."

Big Red nodded skeptically and then focused his attention on the Gators that were now swimming laps around their waters. They did that after being too full. Shortly after, they would be napping.

"Aite, let me take my ass to the crib. Sora and the kids want to go eat and shit."

Big Red had a beautiful ass family. I'd always known what they looked like because in the beginning, I kept close watch on the nigga, but I saw a glimpse of them at the housewarming. That son of his was bad as a muthafucka, but other than that, he had a nice lil' setup.

"Stay dangerous, nigga."

We bumped elbows, and he was out. I appreciated the fact that he didn't bring up Aphrodite. I know he was married to her family and shit, but again, I wasn't talking about my bitch to no nigga. Ion give a fuck whose pussy he was sucking on. I headed upstairs and made sure everything was good before I left for the day. It was still too damn early for me to be popping up on Aphrodite, but I had a few more stops to make anyway.

Anytime I was taking care of business, I was in my dark grey Range. I own so many fucking cars; I bought two Rolls trucks on accident. To keep them separate, I had one white and one grey. The hoes go crazy when a nigga hops out with them eyes matching the car but fuck them bitches. It was AP 'til the world blow.

The Range was the closest to a basic car that I owned and helped me blend a bit. Truthfully, I didn't give a fuck about blending. I'd kill a muthafucka in a crowd full of civilians and pay every witness out there to turn a blind eye. Sometimes that shit was too damn tedious, so I wanted to keep shit calculated.

Parking the whip, I pulled my dress pants up my waist a bit since this heavy ass gun was tugging at them. When I was on my Cartel shit, a nigga was Rico Suave. My bitch loved it when I dressed the fuck up like Malcolm X and shit. I even had some Cartier frames resting on my face. The pussy was gone go dumb crazy tonight.

Walking in the middle of the perfectly manicured lawn, I tossed my hand up and waved at the neighbors. Tom, a young Caucasian white male that couldn't stand the sight of my ass, gave me a fake ass smile while continuing to roll around the grass with his two red headed stepchildren. No, really, those were his step kids, and he didn't even know the shit because I saw his wife sneaking a cracker in the back door once that shared the same redhead trait. Bitch was a stay-at-home mom while Tom busted his ass at his corporate job trying to get that corner office. He should have made that hoe go to work.

"Hadn't seen you around here much lately! I thought you two had maybe broken up."

Tom stood from the lawn and placed his hands at his waist while his breathing labored.

"Get those kids some Benadryl, Tom, and stop thinking so fucking much. They gone be itching like a bitch with crabs tonight."

By now, the children were standing next to him with their heads leaning and cheeks flushed red. Opening the screen door, I lifted my foot and kicked the front door off the fucking hinges.

"Oh God. Let's get in the house, children!"

I wasn't worried about Tom calling the cops because he knew not to get in my fucking business. He knew that shit wasn't safe. Walking into Daphne's hoe pad was not something I saw myself doing after I'd not only given her a champagne shower, but a golden one, yet, here the fuck I was. The bitch came to my baby's house, got her ass whooped, and although Pretty Pretty stomped her ass out, she still had her reservations about me fathering this damn girl's unborn.

I really didn't want to acknowledge the so-called pregnancy shit. Daphne knew damn well she wasn't pregnant by my ass. If she was, then she knew that fetus wouldn't ever see the light of day. Call me what the fuck you wanted, but I wouldn't dare let another bitch bring a child in this world knowing I had a woman. I didn't want them Kilo ass problems, not now or never.

After searching every inch of Daphne's two story three bedroom rental home, I concluded her ass wasn't there. The only reason I searched high and low was because her truck was parked in the garage. I wasted my fucking time coming up in this bitch. I didn't like wasted time just as much as I didn't like a bitch playing on my bitch top.

Pulling my phone out of my pocket, I sent a text and went to the fridge to get me a bottled water. Seeing that she had just went grocery shopping, I grabbed a strawberry yogurt, a bag of Lays and two fruit snacks out the pantry. When I heard my people pulling up, I made my way out the door, snacks in hand and hopped in my truck. When I reversed out of the driveway so that the tractor could move in, I saw

Tom's nosey ass peek from his window, so I rolled mine down and nodded at the cracka. He almost snatched the blind down from trying to close it.

"We clear for demolition, boss?"

Opening the chips, I placed the bag to my mouth and tossed my head back as the salty potatoes evaded my taste buds.

"Do ya' thang."

No sooner than the wrecking ball blasted through the left side of the house, tearing through that shit like it was made of cardboard, my phone rang.

"My house! What the fuck are you doing to my house, Goal?!" Daphne's screeching ass voice pierced my ears. Crunching on another chip, I let her scream and cry for another few minutes, unfazed, while watching all of her belongings be exposed to the neighborhood. I think I saw a Chanel turn into rubbish. Shit was a sight to see.

"What the fuck am I doing to your house? What...the...fuck...am... I... doing...to your...house?" I ate a chip in between words.

"I should be asking you what the fuck were you doing at my bitch house, but I know the answer to that already. Getting the life stomped out yo' muthafuckin' ass," I cracked.

The way Aphrodite was doing her dirty on the camera was commendable as fuck. I could get paid big bucks for that shit on social media.

"You're knocking down my house! That's my fucking home! What the fuck! Oh my God! I didn't even do shit to you!"

"Daphne, you know, the world know, and that nonexistent ass fetus know, I'm not the nigga to fuck with. Still, you fucked with me. Since you making like a fucking weasel and popping up at Pretty Pretty's shit, I figured you didn't have a home. So, demolished. If you think you gone pin a baby on me, demolished. If you show your face back up over there or play with my baby's address, demolished. If I find out you had some-thing to do with Athena-" I waited for her to answer.

"D...d...demolished!" She cried out.

Opening the fruit snacks, I checked the bag after scarfing them down. Them bitches were fye, I had to order some for the crib.

"I knew you had a little bit of common sense, sewage mouth."

All of a sudden, all that whooping and hollering she was doing came to a cease. Letting me know exactly what I knew from jump, Daphne was full of shit.

"Who the fuck is Athena?"

I'd seen on camera how Daphne looked as if she saw a ghost when she saw Athena's face. It took me to watch the shit a million times to see it, but last night, I caught it. Even if I hadn't, it let me know that Daphne knew something, even if she wasn't directly involved with the kidnapping. She was fucking my pops, and I wouldn't put it past his ass that he wasn't pillow talking. Knowing that nigga, he'd probably had Daphne around her, and if that were the case, she was definitely going to be gator food.

"That answer right there, is the reason I'ma Miley Cyrus your ass when I find you. I was gone kill you anyway for being such a hoe and making me really like yo' ass, but it wasn't high on the priority list."

"M...Miley Cyrus me?"

"Yup. Come through like this big ass Wrecking ball on yo' ass. Miley Cyrus. Bitch, listen to more than fucking City girls and Kitty Kat for once. Expand yo muthafuckin horizon. You'n know music?"

Daphne began sniffling, and I was sick of her ass and all that pointless ass crying. I'd rather watch her life crumble in silence.

"Get dangerous, Daphne, because you gone need the strength of a trillion bitches to shake me off yo' ass. See you soon."

Hanging the phone up, I scarfed down the yogurt and left the construction site just as the alarm was going off on her truck from the impact of the machinery tearing through the garage. These muthafuckas were playing with me. Even though I liked a good chase, my patience was running thin as fuck.

CHAPTER 16

Lydia "Litty" Greer

So much has been happening since Athena popped up. Even though everything was all out of whack, I'll take all of that to see my baby cousin's gorgeous little face. She was truly a Godsend, and seeing my cousin in mommy mode was priceless. Between school and helping Aphrodite with her boutique, I've been dog tired. Still, I tried to keep myself busy because when I was idle, my mind had time to wander. I'd reached the five month pregnancy mark, and I was holding on for dear life to not show at school. I hated to admit it, but I was afraid of what, not only my peers would say, but the teachers and counselors as well. I had weeks left until graduation, and prom was still up in the air on the location, but I knew my school would find a spot soon to have it.

Since my belly was growing by the day, there was no way I was going to be able to hide much longer. I'd even thought about skipping out on the senior activities that were approaching, but Aphrodite insisted that I should participate. She spent way too much on the dress due to my constant refitting's. Sad to say, I may need another fitting or a new gown altogether when it is over with. I hated to even bother her because she was bonding with her daughter, my sweet baby Athena.

The school bell rang, signifying dismissal, so I raced to my locker to place my book inside and retrieve my purse, leaving my cognac

MCM backpack. I had an hour to get across town to my doctor's appointment and prayed my Uber was nearby. Savannah was out of school today due to her harsh cramps, so I was on my own. I wouldn't dare ask my daddy to accompany me to my appointment because he was still getting used to the fact that his baby was having a baby. A baby. Luda Greer cried for hours, and it made me feel terrible. He asked me what was I thinking, but ultimately, he boosted his premium on the insurance, and I was grateful because that allowed me to go to a real OBGYN instead of the ones I'd been seeing at the state clinic. Black women, especially young Black women, had the highest mortality rate when it came to maternal deaths, so I wanted to at least be given the best chance by having great doctors. Thanks to my daddy, I was able to go to Sora's doctor, who was amazing. She was always booked and had a small and intimate practice, but one mention of my big cousin's name as a referral, and I was able to bypass her waiting list.

Once I had my purse in hand, I checked my notifications to see if any were from Gage aka Big Gator. It was still surreal that we were having a baby together. On one hand, I really did feel bad for altering his future. But, on the other hand, where I was still smitten with him, I was sort of happy to be bonded to him. I'm smart enough to know a baby didn't keep a man, and even though I was scared shitless, in a way I was looking forward to seeing what we'd created.

The thing is, Gator and I hadn't talked in weeks. We didn't even exchange numbers. At the bizarre ass housewarming, when I fainted, we talked about how I was feeling, but that was it. Last night, I finally got the courage to DM him my appointment information. When he opened it and read it but didn't reply, I cried myself to sleep. At that point, I realized I'd really messed up by not getting a Plan B. I had to come to the realization that it was a big possibility that my baby was more than likely going to be my sole responsibility, and even though that left a bad taste in my mouth, I had to accept it for what it was. It was time to plan accordingly. My future was in question, and although that was enough to bring me to tears, it was no sense in crying over spilled milk.

A part of me felt like Gage wanted nothing to do with this baby, and that scared me. I really didn't intend to trap him, but I was so conflicted.

I was terrified of being a mom, and every month, I told myself I was going to get rid of it until it was too late to do anything about it.

Making my way through the crowd, I tried to avoid the rowdiness of high schoolers that were ecstatic that the school year was nearing its end. I masked my pregnancy in oversized tops and hoodies, and so far, I'd been in the clear. I could still hide it under my cap and gown for graduation, but prom, it was a wrap. Shaking my head about thoughts of doom day, I ordered my Uber, and it was pulling up in three minutes. The moment I hopped in the back of the Nissan Sentra driven by a girl who seemed to be a little bit older than me, my phone rang with Bestie splattered on the screen.

"I got my cousin's car. I can come drop you off," Savannah yawned.

"No, I'm good, bestie. I'm in the Uber. You can get your rest."

"Okay, turn on your location and Facetime me when you get there so I can hear my god baby."

Savannah was so supportive in my pregnancy that I thanked God for her daily. She had her own life and her own problems, along with her staying booked doing lashes, but she made time to be my shoulder to lean on. I always thought her ass was going to have a baby first, but she was team fuck them kids. Outside of her stepdaughter and my little cousins, she didn't fool with the littles, period.

I pulled up at the doctor's office with about thirty minutes to spare, so I signed myself in and began completing the paperwork. When I made the appointment, it was advised that I got here early because there would be forms that I had to sign. Being that I was nineteen, I didn't need my father to sign off on anything since I was technically an adult.

After getting everything all signed, I shot Aphrodite a text checking on her and Athena. Aphrodite had been on ten since she fought the Daphne girl. I still couldn't believe crazy ass Savannah jumped her ass in. She was always looking to fight though, so it shouldn't come as much of a shocker for me.

The door to the office opened, and out of habit, I glanced up and looked back at my phone. Once my brain caught on to my eyes, I did a double take and had to hide the excitement of seeing Gage walk through the door. He was looking so good in shorts and a matching hoodie with Jordan 1s on his feet. His slightly bowed legs carried him from the front door to in front of me, and when he reached down and pulled me up for a hug, it caught me by surprise. I felt so good in his embrace, with his arms wrapped around my lower back. He smelled just as good as he looked, and by the time he was pulling away from me, I was tearing up.

"Wuz' good, beautiful?"

When Gage saw that I was crying, he lifted my chin with furrowed brows.

"I'm sorry, this pregnancy has me so sensitive. Gosh, me and pregnancy don't even sound right in the same sentence, but thank you for being here. It really means a lot."

It did. I was so happy to see him. That same euphoric feeling I got the night we shared at his brother's house had returned.

"Lydia Greer."

"That's me."

The nurse ushered us to the back and asked me to stand on the scale to check my weight. I groaned as I noticed I'd gained twelve pounds in two months.

"It's not too bad. You carrying that shit good." Gator licked his lips, causing me to blush.

"What dad said. Dad, you can step in room three. Mom is going to give me a urine sample, and she will be right in."

Gage nodded while taking my purse and jacket with him in the room. I was ecstatic to have him here, so much so that I almost pissed on the floor trying to get my leggings down.

Walking into the room, my body tingled, watching his tall ass read the poster signs up against the walls.

"Damn, the woman's body is amazing. Shit scary."

Observing Gage had me tingling down below. His cologne wasn't overbearing, but it did circle around the entire room. His toned, curved legs held his chiseled body in place while his large hand rubbed down his head as he skimmed the posters.

"Yeah, I've been doing my research, and I'm shocked there is so much that I didn't know about my own body."

Tik Tok has been my best friend. I've been watching videos about childbirth, cravings, side effects, and prevention methods. I will not be getting pregnant again. Ever. This baby has me sick as a dog. I can truly say this isn't for me.

"Good afternoon, I'm Dr. Kodas. You must be Lydia, and this is the father? Gage Navarro?"

Gage turned and raised a brow.

"I'm sorry, mom completed a paper that entailed your name. I'm not wrong, am I?"

"Nah. Wuz' good, Doc? You gone be delivering my baby?"

My baby. The sound of that had me swooning. It was sickening. I know.

"I surely am. Luckily, it won't be too much longer, being that mom is halfway there. I see here that you don't know the sex yet. We can do that today."

All I have been thinking about is the health of the baby and Gage accepting my child. The sex really hasn't been much of a thought, but since our family was outnumbered with all these damn girls, I would love to have a son.

"Yeah, we can do that, Doc. I saw somewhere we can get a 3D scan done. Is that something we can do here?"

I grew warm inside knowing that Gage had been doing his research when it came to my pregnancy.

"We can do a 3D, but not for another few months. I'd like for your baby to be fully developed so that we can get some clear and precise scans. I'll add you all on, maybe your thirty-fifth week."

I nodded and so did Gage. His cat eyes were so hypnotizing I had to tear my eyes away from him and focus on the screen.

"Okay, I'm going to lower the lights and have my tech come in to perform the ultrasound. Hop up here and lift your shirt for me."

Gage sprang into action, helping me on the table bed. The doctor smiled and stepped out of the room.

"You ready to see what we having?"

Giving Gage a small smile, I shrugged. I was too nervous from just being near him. The effect he had on me was crazy and childish, and I needed to shake it quick.

When the tech came in, I lifted my shirt. Gage stood on the side of me with his eyes fixated on my belly.

"I remember that shit was just flat. Now you got a real bump. Shit crazy."

The way Gage licked his lips had me stifling a moan, thinking about him licking and tugging on my lower set. I had to shake off the thoughts because that's what got us in this situation in the first damn place.

"And it's going to get even bigger. Mom, I'm going to pull your pants down a bit more and apply the gel. It's warm though, okay?" The tech interjected.

The tech lowered my leggings, placed a napkin-like sheet at the band, and folded it. Thankfully, I shaved last night because half my coochie was on display. Gage didn't mind though, judging by the way he rubbed his chin, never tearing his eyes away.

"Okay, mom and dad. Here is your baby. That's the leg. The head. The belly. You've got a thumb sucker too. Look."

Seeing my baby on screen sucking it's thumb was bittersweet. Gage pulled his phone out and began recording, and the moment the little heartbeat filled the room, the tears fell. I was really having a little baby.

"Alright. Looks like.... We have a-"

"Boy. I can see him stand at attention. That's crazy."

Gage rubbed his hand down his head and chuckled while still recording the screen.

"Yes, dad. You have a mini you coming. Prayerfully, he's just as good on the field as you are," Dr. Kodas spoke up with a wink.

It wasn't shocking that the doctor knew who Gage was. Everyone knew and loved him here in Jagoda Bay. Hell, everyone knew and loved him all over America, I'm sure. Which was wild, considering he was still in high school.

"Nah, Doc. He has to be better."

The tech printed out extra pictures and wiped down my belly. When she stepped out, along with the doctor, I sat processing the information while Gage typed away on his phone. A boy. I was having a son. That was crazy! The doctor came back in and talked to us a bit more. For the most part, she was answering Gage's questions, talking football, and he'd even called his mom so that she could ask the doctor questions about the baby and our due date.

"Oh, mom. I'm so sorry for letting sports take over the last leg of your appointment. My husband used to coach college basketball, and my son just ended his fifth season with the Memphis Grizzlies. We are a sports home. I understand you want to have a blood test done-"

"No, Doc, that won't be necessary. I know this is my baby." Gage cut his eyes at me, and that had my cheeks growing warm.

"Okay. If you change your mind-"

"We won't."

"Very well. Congratulations, son. You have a bright and beautiful young lady here, and she's going to be an amazing mother. This baby will only push you to be even greater than you two were destined to be."

I've come with Sora a time or two to her appointments during her pregnancy with Rhea, and apparently, Sora kept the doctor up to speed with me, letting her know I was salutatorian. I expected to feel shame being in her clinic so young and being seen for pregnancy, but not only did she make me feel comfortable, she made Gage as well.

"I appreciate that, Doc. Tell that nig- I mean, tell E-Nice I said what's good. I'll be at a few of his games this year for sure."

They talked a bit more before the doctor made her final exit. I was waiting on my prescription to be brought back in by the nurse that was going to help with my nausea, but due to the weight gain, the doctor wasn't really concerned.

Gage lifted my shirt back up and placed his hand on my belly. I closed my eyes for a moment to savor the feeling because it felt so good.

He got level to my belly and pressed his lips to my stomach.

"Son, you can't be with that thumb sucking shit. You too G'd up for that. Aite?" Gage kissed my belly and helped me up. At the same time, the nurse was handing me my prescription.

I made my next appointment, which Gage promised to be present for, and we were walking out the door.

"You took a Uber here?"

I tucked my hair behind my ear, "Yes."

"Don't do that shit no more. I'll take you to your appointments. Come on, you hungry?"

"I can eat."

Gaged gripped my hand and led me to a forest green Charger. It was so pretty, and the smell of black leather seats made my mouth water for some reason. I hoped I wasn't going to want to chew on no damn leather. I'd seen TikTok's about crazy pregnancy cravings.

"What you want?"

"Pasta."

I'd been craving pasta so much, that Olive Garden was in my future.

"Pasta it is."

Once I was secured in the car, Gage pulled through traffic and headed off to get us something to eat. We drove in silence, with him bobbing his head to Future. Things were supposed to be awkward because we practically didn't know each other, but they weren't. We glided through traffic as he rapped and drove fast as hell. When we pulled up at Maggiano's, I almost did a happy dance in my seat. I'd heard plenty of great reviews about the fine Italian restaurant and was eager to try it. I was hungry too, so I was definitely going to sample as much as I could today.

Gage helped me out of the car at the valet and pulled me to his side as we walked into the restaurant. We were seated immediately, and I was grateful for that.

Opening the menu, I wasted no time compiling my list in my head.

"Get whatever you want. You ate at school today?"

It was kind of odd that we were preparing for a baby but still in high school. At nineteen, I'm grown. I'm still a minor since I'm in school, but I felt like a little girl playing a grown woman game.

"Yes, I packed my lunch. Turkey sandwich, baby carrots with ranch, grapes, an apple, popcorn, a pickle, and a lemonade."

"Damn."

Embarrassment flushed my face. Saying it out loud did sound like a lot, although it really wasn't. Especially since I was still hungry after I ate. I'd even had a full breakfast, but I wouldn't tell him that. I threw it all up though, so it didn't stick.

"I can't wait to have this baby so I can go back to my normal appetite."

Tears lined my lids, and I didn't know why. I was already tired of wearing leggings and joggers. I missed my skirts, jeans, and shorts.

"Aye, what you 'bout to cry for? Ain't shit wrong with you eating. You eating for two. I didn't mean to offend you. I love the lil' weight on you. Shit sexy as fuck. My son got you thicker than a Snicker. I ain't lying."

Unrolling the utensils, I dabbed at my eyelids to catch the tears. I was so darn sensitive it was crazy.

"Gage, I know we haven't really had much time to talk because everything has been so crazy, but how do you really feel about all this?"

The waitress came and took our drink orders before his grey eyes were back on me.

"To be honest, this shit crazy. I was mad at first. I ain't gone lie. Not at you or no shit like that, but more so at myself. I didn't want a baby right now."

The pounding of my heart blasting through my chest was so loud it made my ears ring.

"But I take full responsibility. I didn't strap up. On the real, I hadn't fucked none in a minute before you, so strapping up or pulling out wasn't even an option. You too fucking pretty for a nigga to pull out, so after you have my junior. We gotta figure some shit out."

I couldn't hide the smile on my face if I wanted to.

"I'm not having any more until I at least get my degree. Then, I'll revisit the topic of children. This little boy snuck in on me."

"Yeah, we gone see."

Gage's warning-like response sent chills down my spine as the waitress brought our drinks. We then placed our orders, and he told me to get whatever, so I ordered an entree of chicken and shrimp carbonara, a salad, and stuffed mushrooms as an appetizer. Gage got the steak.

"We both have big plans, though. I don't want to stomp on your future. You have football and-"

"Litty."

Gage sat up in his seat before propping his elbows on the table.

"I would never let you do this shit alone. I know you haven't heard from a nigga, but I was processing shit. It was a lot going on that day, so I just had to take some time to take it all in. If we being real, I been consumed with some shit that had nothing to do with you or our son. I been... fucking with my brother on some other shit, aite? My future good; your future good. Ion want you to change shit or switch shit up on account of the baby. I'll do whatever you need me to do. I've already reached out to JBU. You know they want a nigga."

Hearing Gage talk about going to JBU was a shocker. Especially since I didn't recall him ever mentioning the school even though we'd only talked the night we met. I'd even seen him hint at other schools in his stories in social media but never JBU.

"How have you been? I know this shit fucked you up. You the most important person at the damn high school."

Playfully rolling my eyes, I bit into the stuffed mushrooms that had come on and was going to tackle the bread next.

"I am not, but I'm embarrassed. No one at school even knows I'm pregnant. I feel like I have so many people rooting for me, and I'm scared to let them down. Prom is nearing, and my cousin spent a pretty penny on my dress. I feel so bad because I don't want to go. I keep having to get the thing altered, so I don't even know if it will look right. Savannah is looking forward to going, but I really have no desire to. Everyone wants me to go for memories, but the mere thought gives me anxiety."

Taking a sip of my tea, I focused back on Mr. Handsome.

"I have dreams of pulling up to prom in a pig costume, and right after everyone points and laughs, I get eaten by a big ass gator. I have even had dreams of giving birth to a gator, and then it turns around and eats me."

Gage's eyes widened before he dropped his head and snickered.

"I promise I always have dreams about gators, and either I get eaten or the baby does. It's so weird."

"You don't have to worry about that shit. Ever. Aite? And as far as prom, I can go with you, and if you're up to it, we can go to mine too. I'll buy you a dress for mine. I wanted to go with Kitty Kat the rapper, but her nigga blocking, so why not bring my fine ass baby mama?"

The gesture was nice, and I was extremely flattered, but I asked him to let me think about it. I still had my reservations.

"We gone be aite, Litty. I got y'all."

I believed him too.

When we were done eating, Gator wanted to go to the mall, and when I asked to go to the maternity store, me needing new underwear turned into him buying me nine hundred dollars' worth of maternity clothes. I told him no since I was halfway through the pregnancy, but he insisted. I even let him pick out everything and was loving his taste. Everything looked so modern and cute. I couldn't wait to wear it all.

After shopping, we got dessert, and then he was dropping me off at home and helping me put my things away. I couldn't believe he was standing in my room. Gage "Big Gator" Navarro was in my room! And he said it was cute. I had to stop fan-girling over my own baby's father, but it was hard not to. Especially when I'd been crushing on him so long.

"Gage, thank you for all this. I really appreciate it. We can get the blood test. I don't want you to think I'm that girl."

I'd walked him to the door because I wasn't ready for my dad and him to face off again.

"It's nothing."

Gage leaned down and spoke directly in my ear. "I know yo' pops got a Ring camera right here, so I'ma whisper this shit."

His voice went a few octaves lower.

"The way I sucked and fucked on that pussy, I know that baby mine. Go back in the house before I do that shit again. I need all my strength for practice tomorrow, but you tempting a young nigga. Fuck them dreams. I'm the only gator that's gone be eating on you."

I cleared my throat and had to refrain from fanning myself. It's been five months, and I still think about that night that turned us into parents.

"Gage, if you go to the college you wanted to from jump, I'll go to prom with you."

Gage looked at me with a raised brow before kissing my forehead and palming my belly.

"Go lay down, beautiful. Son, I love you. See you soon, baby boy. Be good for yo' mama."

Tucking my hair behind my ear, I watched as Gage hopped in his Charger and sped off with the pipes alarming the entire neighborhood.

I locked the door, assembled the alarm and went to warm up my leftovers with the biggest smile on my face. My phone rang and I shook my head at my bestie.

"Oh, so you acting funny since you been with your baby daddy and shit?"

Rearing my head back, I removed the fork out of my mouth.

"How you-"

"Check ya' texts."

Placing the phone on speaker, I went to my text messages, and there was a screenshot from Gage's page.

His hand was on my belly, and with the background, I could tell it was from when we were at the doctor.

She was so fucking bad that I had to put an Angel in her ultrasound. We can't wait to meet you son-son. Daddy love you.

The post seemed to have been up an hour and had already gained two point three thousand likes and fifteen hundred comments. I refrained from going through the comments because I'm sure there were some angry birds saying some not so pleasant things that would only upset me. To keep from getting my feelings hurt, I wasn't even going to indulge.

"I saw y'all shopping in his story too. The nigga was zooming in on that booty while you looked through the racks. You shol' done got too thick! I'm so happy for you, friend! I keep telling yo' ass you God's favorite! And itssss a boyyyyyy!"

I read his caption at least four times before I snapped back to reality.

"Yeah, I guess I am, bestie."

CHAPTER 17

Aphrodite "Ditey" "Pretty Pretty" "AP" Greer

I don't know if it was Goal's dick, his tongue, or just me being sick of being in the house that motivated me to get dressed for the second time this week after I combed Athena's hair and let her help me choose her outfit for the day. My baby girl was obsessed with dresses, but I was shocked that she let me put her on this jumper set. I'd done a Zara order for her days ago and went crazy! I'd been waiting five years to ball out on my baby and did just that. The pastel-colored, striped jumper was what I called Genie fitting but gathered at the ankles. The pink ties at the shoulders matched the pink ribbons that were placed on each of her five ponytails that I'd pressed out and put ring curls in. I was skeptical about putting heat in my baby's hair, but I was eager to see how long it really was. Let's just say the shrinkage was real in us black girls because my baby was getting her Pocahontas on.

The day before yesterday, I finally gave in and took Athena to the pediatrician. I didn't have a birth certificate or social, so I was lost as hell. I texted her square-headed ass daddy, and even though he'd been MIA, he texted me back with not only the address of a pediatrician but a pediatric dentist as well. He'd also Cash apped me a thousand dollars and assured me that he'd already taken care of the under the table payments. I wanted to ask him when he would be coming to see his child, but I let it go.

I'd dodged my mama long enough because her ass popped up last week to be with her "granniebaby" so I let her accompany us to her appointments. Baguette had come through in the clutch with the appointments because I was able to get my baby examined and her teeth cleaned. We refrained from giving her the kindergarten shots she would need for the upcoming school year because we didn't know if she'd already been administered. Shit like that made me mad all over again. I didn't even know if my baby had already had shots. I wanted to ask her so bad, but I was scared to let her even have to think about her past. She'd adjusted really well and hadn't mentioned anyone from where she was. I wanted to keep her that way.

I'd just gotten seventeen boxes of new arrivals but was waiting on Litty to come over this weekend so that I could model them. My cousin was glowing, and even though I was still kind of pissed at her, I was happy that she was having a baby boy. RJ needed somebody to play with so his bad ass could quit hanging so much with Big Red. Sora was forever sending his ass out the door with his daddy.

Dressing in a romper similar to my baby girl's in style except mine was all yellow and so happened to be one of my new arrivals, I let my curly hair bush out, added gold accessories and slid my feet in a pair of Gold Louis Vuitton sandals. Times know they've changed, and quickly. Just a few weeks ago, I prided myself on constantly switching up my hair because I had to with my weekly new arrivals. I was forever in a new frontal or a new unit. Now, I was wearing my natural coils more than I ever had, and although Goal loved it, I was ready for some braids or something. I was thinking about getting the goddess braids back that I had on Goal's and I's first date but wasn't ready for someone to watch Athena for the eight hours it took.

Once my perfume was on my pressure points, I grabbed my matching bag and was out the door.

"I want a purse like yours, Aphrodite. You look so pretty like me."

Athena was now toggling between calling me Mommy and Aphrodite, and I was okay with it. She would make the full transition in her own time, so I wasn't rushing her. I was just happy to have her here with me.

After setting my alarm, my baby girl and I walked hand in hand to the garage, where I helped her into the booster seat I'd ordered the same day I ordered the clothes, and we were off for the day. My mom drove us around yesterday, so this was my first time driving my baby. I chose my AMG truck since my Benz coupe is what I was going to use when I wanted to let my hair down. This crazy ass man really had gotten me two cars. That was insane. Driving had me nervous, even with the detail trailing us, so at every red light, I was looking through the rearview mirror. She had her face in the iPad Goal had left for her a few nights ago and was oblivious to her mama's extraness.

At first, I was going to pull up at my auntie's house in the Bricks because my mama and Sora told me everyone had been not only worried but cursing me the hell out for shutting them out. Before I went around my family though, there was somewhere else I needed to be. I drove in silence to my destination, dodging every damn pothole and driving slow as fuck because I was carrying precious fucking cargo. It took us twenty minutes longer than required, but we'd made it in one piece. When I hopped out of the truck and removed my baby, I held her in my arms instead of letting her walk. I thought she would get tired of me carrying her, but she didn't complain. I would carry her forever if I could.

Our detail parked directly behind us, and I appreciated the extra layer of protection. Because detail or not, before I let my baby girl slip from my fingers again, I'd die. It was by the grace of God that I'd even survived in the first place.

"Mommy? Who's house is this?"

Ringing the doorbell, I adjusted my baby in my arms and gave her a quick peck. She had so much lip gloss on her lips, it transferred to mine. She'd completely ruined all my high end makeup but I didn't give a damn. Whatever she wanted, she got.

"You'll see, my pretty baby."

When the door opened, Athena focused her big, bright eyes in front of us. A face that I hadn't seen in a while stared back at us and her hands shot to her face. Baguette's twin rubbed her back as she blinked back tears.

"Oh my God! I didn't expect you two, but this is such a pleasant surprise! I have been crying for weeks, and I promised myself I wouldn't cry today. So, I'm not. But I'm so happy to see you. The both of you. Aphrodite. She looks just like her father."

Playfully rolling my eyes, I smiled. Kelly Dianne Cherman was dressed up as she always was while her husband was on the side of her in a jogging suit. Although Baguette and I remained friends even after our relationship ended, I didn't see his mom much because she was always traveling. We all dealt with the loss of Athena differently. The Cherman's coping mechanism was traveling. They both retired long before she was thought of and used the money their son laced their accounts with to travel the world. Tuscany didn't really care for Kelly. I tried to tell her Kelly was just bougie and stuck in her ways, but she was cool people, loving, and loyal. Although Baguette was the center of their lives, back then, she didn't indulge in his bullshit. She was forever siding with me and letting his ass know he was wrong.

"Come on, come on in. Can I hold you?"

Athena looked at me first, and when I gave her the nod of approval, she went into her grandma's arms.

I gave Baguette's father a quick hug after he complimented me, and they both were googly eyes over Athena. Closing the doors behind me, it was weird being in Tuscany and Baguette's house. I could smell her perfume, and that shit had me sick to my stomach. Goal told me that I still cried in my sleep, and although it was over Athena, I missed my best friend too. I'd been having dreams of Tuscany. Mostly our memories. I hoped and prayed my girl was okay, but I was tired of praying. I needed answers.

I'd reached out to her mama on Facebook and sent her a message. I was hoping she saw my message soon and replied. She had grown brothers, but I would rather reach out to her mom first. I just asked her to call me and left my number. Still, she hadn't opened the message yet.

"I'm your grandma, but you can call me GG. This is your grandpa. I just finished your room here. Would you like to see it?"

"Is this your house, GG?"

"No, grandpa and I have our own house. You'll have a room there too. This is your dad's house."

"Okay, I want to see my room, GG."

Baguette's dad had turned his head, so I knew he was crying, and I had to make my way to find Baguette because I didn't want to cry my makeup off. I'd been doing enough of that. I found Baguette in his man cave that was basically his basement that he had customized to his liking. I loved my home, but their home was just as beautiful. Baguette and Tuscany was always at my shit before I moved like they weren't over here living large. Bored asses. Fuck! I missed my girl.

Baguette's Za met me before he did. He had the entire room smoked out. Fanning my hand in front of my face, I knew I was going to have to wash my damn hair. Baguette's weed was always so damn stanky.

I walked right in front of his line of view, and his low red eyes gazed up at me. Seeing me, he ashed his blunt and ran his head down his waves.

"Where my daughter?"

Shaking my head, I plopped down on the side of Baguette. With the exception of the Lakers highlights from the previous season on the tv, Baguette's thoughts were the loudest thing in the room.

"Up there with your parents. I'ma have to fight your mama over my baby, ain't I?"

Baguette smirked and licked his lips, "Ion know how the fuck you ain't know. My baby gone get sick of all y'all asses, your mama included."

We both laughed. He wasn't lying. Athena was going to be stretched thin as hell, fooling with us. She just didn't know, but she had a whole slew of people ready to love on her.

"You been straight, Baguette? I know I told you I was sick of your ass always smothering me, but damn, I miss my bestie."

Baguette looked over at me for a moment and then focused his attention back to the flat screen in front of us.

"You done replaced my ass with Goal. You ain't fucking with me no mo', Ditey."

I bumped my shoulder with his.

"That's my...lil junt. You my bestie. Damn, so you cut me off soon as I get a lil' friend? Where the outfits and shit at now? Niggas ain't shit."

We both shared a laugh again.

"Mane, only yo' ass can come around have my ass laughing. I miss yo' ass too. Shit just..."

"Crazy?"

"Very."

Although Baguette was dressed up in his normal street clothes, he was void of his signature chains, and he needed a damn haircut. I don't know when the last time I saw Baguette without a haircut.

"How the businesses been running?"

I knew Tuscany mostly handled everything with *The Bottom* Sports Bar and Lounge, and since she was MIA, I hoped everything was still going smooth.

"Shit straight. I went by all the spots yesterday. How the doctors and shit go?"

"Good. We didn't do shots because I don't know if she already had them but she doesn't have any cavities, and she had me ordering a Frozen electric toothbrush from Amazon."

My baby being five means she has to go to kindergarten come the fall. There was so much shit I needed to get in order, including having her removed from being deceased with the state. I don't even know how to do that and am only hoping Baguette or Goal had some insight. There was so much to fucking do, but I was pushing it all aside and focusing on one thing at a time.

"I'ma have to order her one for my crib." Baguette shook his head, and I knew it was because he was still trying to process that she was still here. I hadn't seen Baguette since the housewarming, but being in his presence, the resemblance that our daughter shared to him was uncanny. She'd gotten a tad bit darker due to her swimming in the backyard, and they both now shared skin the same hue as a worn penny, and that dimple embedded in their right cheek was identical. My baby chewed her food like her daddy, slept like her daddy and was clingy as hell to me, just like her damn daddy.

"Baguette. Brock. She's here. She's real. She's not going anywhere. You're going to be an amazing dad. Everything is going to work out as it should in due time, but stop being so hard on yourself."

I knew Baguette better than he knew himself, and it was vice versa. Even though Athena needed her father just as much as she needed me, I was going against everyone's wishes and letting the man process this shit. Hell, I was still processing this shit, but my motherly instincts kicked in overdrive. I've had my baby to myself for weeks. Now it was time for her people to love on her just as I had. I couldn't live my life in fear, nor could I shelter her any more than she'd already been. Whoever she was with, I'm pretty sure most of her time was spent indoors. She did know how to swim. I was grateful for that, so that let me know she wasn't locked away in a damn dungeon. She needed to know she was loved, and hiding out with me was no way to live. I was content with being in the house all these years only because I felt guilty living life and being outside with my baby gone. Now that I had her, it was time to show her off. I prayed on it, and after Goal fucked the lights out of me and forced me to leave the house, I did that shit.

Baguette grabbed my hand and turned his head to face me.

"Aphrodite, I appreciate you. I know I took you through so much shit, so many emotions. Even after we broke up, with me constantly crying over our daughter, and now it seems like she's here. I'm not- just, thank you. You constantly ask a nigga to give you space, and then you go and do shit like this to draw me back in."

"Do shit like what, Baguette?"

He swiped his thumb across the back of my hand.

"Do shit like be you. I fuck with you, Aphrodite. Thank you for always understanding a nigga and being my person. Thank you for giving me a beautiful ass daughter. Thank you for holding my lil' baby down while I get a handle on shit. Thank you for being patient with a nigga. I'ma always give you the world, no matter what."

Leaning in, I wrapped one arm around Baguette's neck and kissed his jaw.

"I already got a lil' junt that gives me the world, so I'm good. Give that same world to Athena though. She getting kinda expensive," I joked.

Baguette chuckled, and at the same time, I stood.

I walked up the stairs, and Baguette followed. I wanted to stick my head in Athena's new room, but I was having a hard enough time separating from her, so I just kept it mobbing toward the front door.

"Aye, where you going?"

Pulling my keys out of my cross bag, I faced Baguette and blew out a sigh.

"I received a package from Macy's. There was a note attached that said failed to pick up with the store's address. I'm going to go trace Tuscany steps, and BEFORE you talk shit, remember back to what I been telling you all these years?"

Baguette had a look on his face as if I'd just told him I was going to feed him a shit sandwich. I hated that they were just all in love, basically fucking on my couch a few months ago, and now he hated the girl and hadn't even gotten the facts. Was it weird that she brought Athena home? Fuck yes, it was, but it was time to move on from that shit and get some fucking answers.

"What you been telling me all these years, Aphrodite?"

"That if you left her, I was going to kill you," I let his ass know without a hint of sarcasm in my tone. Tuscany was missing. She would never in life drop my baby off and keep moving against her own free will.

"Something isn't right, Baguette, and I'm going to find out. No matter what, Tuscany would have never left me for dead if the shoe was on the other foot. It's been weeks, and I don't even know if my friend is dead or alive. She mentioned that Gilberto made her choose. I specifically remember her saying that. But, choose what? It's more to the story! Look, if anything, find her, Baguette. We owe her that. If she doesn't give us the answers we want to hear, I'll beat her ass, and we never have to speak again," I lied. I knew my friend. Baguette was acting hard, but he loved and missed Tuscany just as much as I did. You just don't turn that love off.

"Yo' heart so fucking big, Aphrodite. I hate that shit too. You tough as nails on the outside but soft as a fucking marshmallow for the people you love. Even when a muthafucka pulling the wool over yo' eyes, you still love on them. Tuscany ain't the bitch we thought she was, but gone go find her. You'll make my job easier because when I get to her ass.... They gone need a professional gum scraper to peel her from the bottom of my shoe."

I bit my tongue because the look on Baguette's face let me know he

was serious. I just hoped when I found my girl, she had a good ass explanation. The only thing making me feel like she's alive is the fact that the
same muthafuckas kept my daughter in one piece for five years. I prayed
they showed Tusc the same grace.

"You still ain't answer me. Where you going? And don't say no
fucking lil' junt or lil' friend for I tell that nigga you playing with his
title, Mrs. Navarro."

The mention of Goal always caused butterflies to swarm in my
damn belly. I still didn't know what to call him though, even though
he'd made it clear we were a couple. I'd been single so long. Plus, the
world boyfriend wasn't even fitting for Goal. He needed to be King or
some shit.

"I'm tracing my friend's steps. I'll be back to get Athena in a few
hours. I got to hurry up and leave before I change my damn mind. I'm
'bout to break out in hives just thinking about leaving her. Then, I'll
have to let my mama get her for a few hours tomorrow because if she
finds out your mama kept her before she did, she gone talk so bad about
all of us."

My mama was so protective of me and my baby with her jealous self.
She will drag Kelly over Athena.

"Well, I'ma head out too. I got some shit to handle."

I gave Baguette a look and shook my head.

"Aite, be safe, bestie!"

I tossed my hand up and began walking to my truck. I loved both
my vehicles so much. I felt like a real boss driving in it, and it was only
day one. Even after I was gifted with the house and cars, I was still
driving my old truck around because I was mostly running errands to
get settled in my home and prepare for the housewarming. I just let
them sit in the garage and look pretty. I was thinking about giving my
Lexus to Savannah since Litty wanted a damn Kia. Despite her being
pregnant, she still was salutatorian and deserved to be awarded.

"Aye, you need to get out the house more. Yo' ass sitting in there
getting thick as fuck."

I did the gesture as if I was sticking my hand down my throat as I
hopped in the driver's side.

"Don't be weird! Please don't turn into one of them baby daddies!"

Baguette smiled, showing off that perfect Athena dimple.

"Aye, you said he already give you the world? That's cool. There are at least seven other planets in our fucking solar system! I love you, kid!"

"I love you too, but I love Tuscany more!"

I stuck my tongue out at Baguette and pulled out of the driveway. Before I could hit a block, I saw him speeding past me. He would come around. I just prayed he wouldn't catch a charge behind my bestie.

* * *

Going to the Macy's was almost a dead end. The manager wouldn't let me see the cameras even though I offered to pay, and all he handed me was the name of a tow truck service when I mentioned Tuscany drove a pink Benz. The fat, middle-aged black manager was no damn help and had me walking out of the store pissed.

"Hey! Hey! Excuse me, ma'am!"

Slowing in my steps, I turned to face a young girl that looked to be around Litty's age. She didn't have on a name tag and was in leggings, Jordan's and an oversized screen tee, so I knew she didn't work in the store.

A scowl covered my face because I was already pissed and didn't want to be bothered. I came here for answers, and all I had was a fucking card to the tow yard. I was going to call and pay the fee for my girl's whip though, but still.

"Yeah?"

She held her hands up as if to say she came in peace.

"I heard you mention the pink Benz, and I remembered because I was here that day."

Drawing my head back, my nose involuntarily crinkled.

"What, you work here or sum?"

The girl rubbed the back of her neck, and I knew then her ass boosted for the store.

"Forget I asked. You saw my friend?"

"Yeah! Pretty chick in an off white jumpsuit? Look like money?

178

Kind of look like Yung Miami? I saw her. This foreign nigga had her hemmed up by the sheets sets and slapped her around a bit. She was begging him to let her go, and when she saw him, she looked like she saw a ghost. I planned on calling the police, so I followed them to get a tag number, but there were no tags. He tossed her purse out the car too. Here, follow me."

The girl looked behind her before sprinting to a beat up Kia and popping the trunk on it. All types of stolen goods were on display. The girl looked back at me with a shrug, and pushed everything out of the way until she found what she was looking for.

"Mrs. Navarro-"

Jett gently pulled at my elbow, stepping in to do his job.

She turned her head and looked him up and down with a smirk.

"I'm not going to hurt her, with yo' fine ass. I just have something for her."

I let Jett know it was okay, and he stood back a little but kept a watchful eye.

"Here."

She held up Tuscany's YSL purse, and for some reason, it brought tears to my eyes.

"I scooped everything back in it that had fallen out. I didn't steal shit or look at none of her info. Something just told me to hold on to it."

Holding Tuscany's purse in my hand had the tears falling. I had to find my damn friend.

"I'm sorry. I wish I could do more, but I was already hot and-"

"You did what you could. Thank you so much. What's your name?"

She held her hand out for me to shake, and although she was slim, her puffy jaws almost closed her eyes as she smiled.

"I'm Chia."

Returning her handshake, I introduced myself.

"Thank you, Chia. It's nice to meet you. How old are you?"

Chia looked off.

"Twenty three."

"Okay, you look younger. That's a good thing. Here. I want you to take my card. I own a boutique and would love if you modeled for me sometimes."

I fished for a card and placed it in her hand, along with a wad of money. Goal had been leaving so much money on the dresser, I lost count on how much he'd given me in total.

Gasping, Chia took the money and blinked back tears.

"Thank you so much. I'll be calling you, and I promise I won't steal from your boutique. I just have a baby and a sister that needs me-"

"No need to explain. In about eight weeks, call me, okay? I may need help packing orders, modeling clothes, taking pics-"

"Girl, whatever you need, I got you. Thank you. Thank you so much! I love you, and I don't even know you. You got a baby?"

I nodded, "Athena. She's five."

"Here!"

Chia turned back to her trunk and shuffled through her inventory. She grabbed a black garbage bag and began stuffing all types of cute clothing in the bag.

"She a 4/5 or a straight 5?"

"4/5."

I made money, and my Goal is paider than paid, but I loved me a good booster deal.

"That's all 4/5. All that shit is name brand. Ralph Lauren, NIKE, Juicy Couture, Adidas, and some Gap sets. That should hold her for the summer. I did an order for this hoe that canceled on me, so it's all yours. Thank you again!"

I grabbed the bag and thanked Chia. Athena put on clothes everyday so it was never too much.

"Thank you, Chia. You take care and stay out of these streets. That should hold you over until I'm ready for you."

Chia and I said our goodbyes, and I tossed my garbage bag full of goodies in the trunk before heading to the tow yard.

Just as I was pulling out, my phone alerted me of a text.

Baguette: *Good ass heart.*

I didn't reply back to him, but I did drive off with a smile on my face. He'd followed me, so that let me know he wasn't as Team Fuck Tuscany as he tried to pretend to be. When I located my friend, I was going to get back on my hunt to find my sister. I haven't forgotten, but shit just needed to cool down before I brought another person into our already complicated lives. For now, I did know one thing, however much my girl's tow was, I was going to get my shit back when I picked up my baby. Run me my coins back, nigga, since you tryna give a bitch planets and shit.

CHAPTER 18
Quasie Lantis

I was able to leave the office early today, and I was happy about it. My stomach's been cramping, letting me know my cycle was approaching. I hated that my body always cramps days in advance instead of just coming in like a normal ass woman. I had plans of showering, ordering Benihana on Uber Eats, and popping three Tylenol extra strength while letting the tv watch me. I had a few offers that needed submitting on tomorrow, and if the Tylenol did its job, I would get those in tonight.

Despite my business still being successful, we hadn't heard anything from Ms. Haddie nor have I reached out to Aphrodite. Tuscany was tied into this some kind of way from my understanding of the rundown of events from Kassie, and although I was scared for what this may mean for Kilo, I still missed my girls and had been praying for them every chance I got. I felt like such a bad ass friend for not shooting Aphrodite a text just to check in and give an explanation as to why I didn't make it to her housewarming. Hell, I wanted to congratulate her on her baby girl, which was still bizarre to me that she was even alive and in the flesh. Thinking about it all had my head hurting, so I shook it off and just prayed for the very best. I wanted nothing more than for everyone to be okay and for all of this to blow over.

Turning into my driveway, tension formed in my face as I watched

Kilo leaning against the door. That man just didn't get the hint and I was tired of arguing with him. Today, he wasn't getting anything out of me. I wasn't even about to fight with him. I simply wanted to rest and soak my body.

"Wassup, Quasie? You look nice."

I drew my head back at Kilo and walked into my house with him on my heels. I stopped dead in my tracks, seeing a bouquet of white roses sitting next to an Apple bag on my entry console table. First, Eleven came to me, but I quickly shook that thought out of my head since, outside of the occasional check-in, I haven't heard from him. Plus, he didn't know where I lived. That man was dead ass serious about me figuring my shit out. I guess it said a lot about me because I still hadn't made a move to get a divorce. A part of me was saying it was no point, and the other part of me was just dragging my feet. Kilo and I were done, that much I knew, but things were just... complicated.

"If you already broke in, why did you wait outside, Kymani?"

I kicked my heels off in the foyer and walked right past his gifts. I hadn't gotten a new laptop since the one his ass broke, so I was happy he'd replaced it, but I wouldn't have needed a replacement if his ass hadn't smashed my shit. Stupid ass.

"I didn't want you coming in here beating my ass, so I waited on the porch."

I dropped another one of my Hermes bags on the emerald ottoman and faced my husband. Kymani was looking good today. Instead of being dressed in his normal white t-shirt and joggers, he was in fitted navy jeans, a navy Burberry button down shirt and white Forces. The Burberry cologne seeping from his pores did him justice, and his bald ass head was shining hard as ever. His ass didn't look like he was in trouble with the cartel, so I was most definitely reaching out to my friend tomorrow. I was going to have to order her a month's supply of Giulia.

"What, Kymani? I don't want to argue today. I have a stomachache and I just want to bathe and go to bed."

"I came to take you out to dinner, and before you say no, hear me out."

I crossed my arms over my chest and tossed my bob out of my face, signifying for him to proceed.

"I just want to talk. I know I fucked up with you. I know I been handling you all wrong, Quasie. I just want to talk over dinner. Like two old friends. No arguments. No disrespect. Just dinner as friends. Nothing more."

"As tempting as that sounds, I'll pass. I'm not feeling good, Kymani."

"You always get like this when you about to come on. A hot bath, Tylenol, and a nap, and you'll be up and ready in about two hours. You know you can't sleep that long. It's only five thirty."

I hated how well he knew me. This was the same man that knew my body inside and out, so I didn't even have a comeback for him. He was right. I couldn't sleep the day away, no matter how hard I tried. My blackout curtains wouldn't even work.

"Okay. Come back in three hours. If I'm still sleep, don't wake me out. Just lock the door on your way out."

Without waiting for him to reply, I made my way to my room and ran my bathwater. After a nice hot bath, I snuggled in my robe and once I was in my bedroom, smiled at the mug on my nightstand. Picking it up, I took a sip of the Herbal tea and smiled. Kymani used to always make me this weed tea that knocked my cramps out instantly. I didn't smoke, but weed tea was my favorite, and I hadn't had it in six years.

After drinking in down, I snuggled under the covers and was out like a light.

* * *

"Anything else I can get you?"

I politely dismissed the waiter and took a sip of my water. Kymani was back at my house three hours later, and I was just adding the finishing touches to my look. I didn't want to dress too sexy so he wouldn't get the wrong idea. So I slid on a pair of jeans, a sage silk wrap blouse and matching strappy heels. The tea did wonders because after an hour and forty five minutes of sleep, I was up feeling like a brand new woman.

"You always knew how to put that shit on. Always dressed like you have somewhere to go. You look sexy as fuck, Quasie."

I bashfully blushed at the compliment. It felt good to be on good terms with Kymani. Every time I saw his face, I was reminded of his infidelity, but today, it didn't move me. I was tired of the back and forth and had to take the good with the bad. He'd done me wrong; we were done, and I had to let the hurt go.

"Quasie, I'm sorry for having them babies on you."

Clearing my throat, I took another sip of water.

"Excuse me?"

"I'm sorry. As a man, your man, your husband, I should have never stepped out on you. Even being that I did, I should have at least had the decency to strap my dick up. To be honest, I can't remember if I did or didn't with them. Then I came home, and you handed a nigga a bag when you didn't have to. I said you shitted on me when I got locked up, but you didn't. I was just jealous as fuck seeing you out here on yo' grown woman shit, living the life I always envisioned for you without me."

Suddenly, the large room felt as if it was closing in on me. I was beginning to feel uncomfortable listening to Kilo because, for so long, all we did was beef.

"The bitch I was with shitted on me. I shitted on you. I bought them hoes a house and didn't do shit for the woman who rocks my last name. A nigga was bitter. I can admit that shit now. I fucked up bad when I did you in, and I'll never forgive myself for the rest of my life."

I had to blink a few times to make sure I wasn't still gone off the weed tea. This couldn't be Kymani Lantis talking.

"I... I don't know what to say. You was just cursing my ass out. Kilo, what made you do a one eighty? Is it the stuff with Aphrodite-"

"What? Hell nawl. You still haven't talked to your friend? I told you I'm good on that tip. Just still looking for grams, but ion want to get into all that."

Kymani sat back in his seat, and although he was handsome as ever, he was physically stressed, and it showed all over his face. This man had abandonment issues like no other. That's why he was so mad at me for not riding his bid out with him and now with his grandma gone, it really wasn't good for his mental.

"I fucked up. I'm around here looking for my grandma. Looking for answers about all this shit, and I asked them to hold my kids down. I take... you know what, I'm good. These aren't yo' problems, baby. I just wanted to be in your presence tonight. I still get the best peace in your space, even when you telling a nigga how much you hate me."

Reaching my hand across the table, I placed it on top of Kilo's.

"You said we came out as friends, so speak your peace."

Kilo dragged his hand down his face.

"I take care of them. I know they come from nothing, and the only reason they kept them babies was for a meal ticket. All I asked is that they hold my seeds down while I handle my shit. You think I need to be having them with me while this shit going on? I had to go pay the grandmas to watch them. Ain't that some shit? Bitches don't even got a fucking job."

Kilo tossed back his drink and signaled for another.

"They always so fucking worried about you. Like, what the fuck? They fucked your husband and had a baby. Fuck they mad at you for? I fucked myself all the way up, but I'm proud as fuck of you. You have a successful ass business, and you look even better than five years ago, and that's saying a lot because even then, you was the baddest. Kid free, and living a- what's that word you used? Exhilarated. You living an exhila-rating ass life. On God. That's all I could hope and pray for for you. You doing yo' big one, and you did nothing wrong by kicking my ass to the curb. You know Grannie said I had a better chance of winning the lottery than I did for getting you back?"

Kilo chuckled.

"She said what now?" I tried to hold my laugh.

"Hell yeah, that lady said she pray you never take a nigga back. That's cold. But nah, she right. I got a daughter, and if she ran back to a nigga that did her how I did you, I'd kill his ass and curse her ass out."

"Whatever, Kilo. Let me ask you this though. Why'd you call me the baby of a side chick? What do you know that I don't?"

I didn't want to give him any advice toward his whores or gremlins so I got straight to what had been on my mental. My mama was secretive as hell about a lot of things and got upset most times when I asked her certain questions. So, if he knew anything, I wanted to know. Kilo kept his ears to the streets, so anything he was saying was facts.

. . .

"Look. I fuck with yo' mama. I was wrong for saying that shit. Anything pertaining to her, you got to ask her, baby, but back to us. I just can't let you go, Quasie."

Before I could reply with his off-guard ass statement, my eyes caught a body I'd become all too familiar with. When they got up from the table where the opposite sex was waiting, oh so radiantly, I stood and excused myself.

My feet felt like bricks as I trudged near the far end of the restaurant, and I could feel Kilo's eyes burning a hole in my backside. I was rude for getting up during our conversation, but my legs were already in motion before I could process what I was doing.

With all logic out of the window, I found myself walking into the men's bathroom, at the same time, an elderly Caucasian guy was peering upside my head. All my common sense must've been left at the table with Kilo because I was standing in the middle of the dimly lit men's restroom with my eyes staring darts at Eleven's backside.

"You want to come hold this big muthafucka too and shake it when I'm done pissing, Quay?"

His voice. His panty-dropping, leg-spreading, rugged voice had me melting right there in the middle of the tiled floor.

Once his stream of piss ended, he zipped his black jeans, kicked his leg out slightly to adjust his monster to lay right in his boxers and walked the short distance to the sink to wash his hands.

Our eyes met in the mirror, sending my heart plummeting. I was sure you could see faint beats through the thin silk fabric of my blouse.

"You look good."

Scoffing, I turned my nose up.

"I guess I know why you've been sending me those dry ass text messages. Becky with the good hair has been occupying your time."

I was outside of my fucking body. Quasie didn't do this. I'm the owner of a multimillion dollar producing firm and managed a team of top-earning agents. I didn't sweat niggas. I didn't do niggas period, especially ones of the likes of Eleven, yet here I was.

"Nah, you wrong, baby. I ain't with nobody. No bitches. I been big chillin'."

"So you telling me that I'm blind now? See, this is why I don't do street niggas! Y'all always out to make a woman look fucking dumb! What happened to all that, 'I'll be waiting for you and I know what I want' junk that you were talking in New York?"

This man not only catered to my mind, body, and soul that weekend, he licked, slurped and poked on every part of my body. Every inch of me has been in his mouth. Every inch. To see him at the table with another bitch infuriated me, and for him to be walking toward me with a grin had me wanting to wipe the smirk off his lips.

Each time he took a step toward me, I took one backwards until my back hit the door. I was trapped. Trapped into Eleven's hardened chest that was void of his jewelry today. Trapped in the Mandarin and Leather notes of his cologne that I loved so much. Just fucking trapped with nowhere to go, forcing me to peer into his naturally sleek eyes.

"I know what the fuck I said in New York. Do you know what the fuck you said? Because last I remember, you claimed you hated the very nigga you sitting across from tonight. You claimed you don't fuck with him at all. Unless I'm deaf?"

Eleven placed his arm above my head and leaned into my space. I could smell his breath, and the only thing I could smell on it was mint from the gum he spit out before entering the bathroom.

"Eleven, I said what I said. I don't do-"

"Street niggas. I heard that shit loud and clear. But, for you not to do street niggas, you sure in the fuck sitting across from him, making him think he got a chance with pussy that don't belong to either one of y'all to make decisions on."

"Who...who it belongs to then, Eleven? Enlighten me."

My breathing was staggered, so I had to force my words out.

Eleven brought his lips to mine and sucked on my bottom lip before pulling both in his mouth.

"That's a business acquaintance. If you looked hard enough, you would have saw that it's five of us at the table. Ask me about me. I'm the only muthafucka that can give you straight facts. Don't assume. Shit gone have you looking dumb and you too educated for that."

"Eleven-"

"Stop calling my fucking name. You know what that shit do to me. I'll forget yo' ass on restriction, pull them tight ass jeans down and make yo' ass cum eleven times before they can even bring the check to that nigga and send you home with my dick on your breath. Say I won't," he challenged. I was dripping so fucking hard that I was ready to take him up on his offer.

"You won't. Well...you can't. I'm about to come on my period."

Eleven smirked and let his eyes wander over my face and breasts before taking a step back.

"Period? No, you not... Take yo' ass back outside though, Quay."

I wasted no time opening the door to leave. I'd made a fool out of myself, and I for sure felt dumb as hell. I could no longer be in his presence. Not with the way he was looking. Instead of the normal street clothing, he was in a thin turtle neck sweater, black fitted pants and Chelsea boots. It was casual and not what I was used to with him, but Eleven was a big ass mystery to me. Still I didn't see myself flat out asking what it was he did, because, I already knew. If I didn't know anything else, I knew street niggas.

"Aye!"

I stopped in my tracks before I could let the door go.

"Looks like you lent that nigga a life jacket. But, if that nigga even sniffs my pussy, we gone have a problem. You still mine, and you got access to my fucking pockets and my mind but the dick on pause until I see some fucking paperwork. I can't keep fucking on a married woman." Eleven laughed as I pushed the door back and stomped back to the table with Kilo.

I thought Kilo was going to trip, but we finished the dinner off on a good note, even though my eyes kept wandering over to where Eleven was. He was at a table full of white and Italian people, and although he was the only black person, he kept their table laughing and engaged.

Kilo dropped me back off at home, and offered to stay and eat my kitty, but I declined and went home to call Eleven instead.

When he answered the phone and spit those five words out, I took my ass to bed, mad as ever.

Eleven's last words to me kept replaying in my head all damn night.

I'm not fucking you, Quay.
Ugggh! How'd this man pull a me on me?

* * *

Yesterday was crazy. After that unexpected ass dinner with Kilo's flip flopping ass, I came home and went to bed with an unattended wet ass and tossed and turned all night. When I finally was able to settle into sleep, I expected to wake up this morning either facing cramps again or covered in blood, but was glad I wasn't.

I decided to skip the office today, but I did go ahead and enter those offer letters for my clients on my new laptop Kilo's ass had purchased. My old laptop was a few years old, so I was happy to have the upgrade but still mad that he broke my shit. It was nice to sit down and have dinner with him without the name-calling. Shaking Kilo out of my thoughts, I made myself a healthy breakfast and dressed casually. I wanted to go sit down with my mother because Kilo's side chick jabs were still swarming in my head. I couldn't let the shit go.

My mom lived about twenty minutes away from my neighborhood *Shirah*, and even though I didn't call ahead, I knew she would be home. These days all she did was garden. She still worked from home, but she did that part time. I tried retiring her, but since she didn't have any grandchildren, she didn't want to get bored. Her words.

"Ma!"

I used my key to let myself in just in case she was gardening out back or working. Being that it was now May, the cool breezes were long gone, and summer was slowly appearing. I didn't want to sweat my makeup off in the backyard, so if she was out there, I was going to wait inside for her.

"Girl, stop yelling. What you doing here?"

My mother came out of the kitchen carrying a tray housing two mugs and a pitcher of tea.

"I came to see you, but looks like you already have plans."

My mom sat her tray down on the coffee table and placed her hand on her hips. She's a curvy woman but looked damn good for her age and had lost a lot of weight in the last few years by walking the neighborhood. She'd never been a slim woman, and it was one of the reasons why I was in the gym as much as possible. Chubby ran in our genes, and chile, I wanted to stay right and tight.

"Yes, but I have a few minutes to spare. What has Kymani done now?"

I don't know who we stressed out more, my mama or Kassie. They both had front row seats to all of our drama over the last few years.

"Ma, Kilo said something to me about being the baby of a side chick during a heated argument. What was he talking about?"

All my mama and daddy did was fight and fuck, fuck and fight. That was the main reason I was always at my grandma's house. They were so damn toxic before being toxic was a thing. That's why I had to free myself from Kilo because I'd be damned if I brought a baby into a world like that.

"Kilo needs to mind his damn business and worry about those two side chick kids he got," she spat, but then, her expression softened.

"We going to have to talk about this another day, baby. Just know it's a lot of things I didn't tell you about your daddy, and although his ass is dead and gone, he sure has been stirring shit from the grave lately."

I felt a gush of fluids from my vagina and knew that it was my period finally coming on. I excused myself and ran to the bathroom before I messed up my clothes. When I pulled my wide leg pants down and sat on the toilet, I was shocked to see that there was no blood, just some clear discharge. Putting it to my nose, I took a sniff to see if I could smell any blood, and when I didn't smell any, I wiped myself once more, washed my hands and pulled out my phone. Going right to the calendar, I began counting the days as I heard my mama go to her door.

Saliva thickened in my mouth before it dried altogether.

'You won't. Well...you can't. I'm about to come on my period."

"Period? No, you not..."

Deciding to deal with one disaster at a time, I cleared the tears from my eyes and washed my hands once more before walking down the hallway.

"Why are you here, Deborah Robin-"

"Don't be calling out my whole damn name like I don't know it. I'm here because my daughter has been asking questions about her sister. While I feel like she's not ready to meet in this moment, I want us to at least be cordial so that we can make that happen for our girls."

"I don't have a problem with that. It was you that kept her away-"

"Bitch, you didn't even let us come to the fucking funeral- You know what? Fuck it. Just let me know what it is that you want to do. I promised my grandbaby I would stop cursing so much."

"You have a grandchild?"

"I do. She's a pretty lil' sum' too. Here's her picture. She's spending the night with me, and I can't hardly wait."

"Wow. She looks just like her grandpa."

"And I hate it too."

I walked into the room and stopped dead in my tracks. Sweat trickled down my back as my stomach turned.

Both women's heads snapped up at me, and the one that wasn't my mother stood abruptly.

"Aphrodite is... my sister?"

What the fuck is going on here?

CHAPTER 19

Brock "Baguette" Cherman

S ome shit had to give. Those same nightmares that used to plague
me were no longer nightmares, but for some reason, I was still
disturbed. My soul was disturbed. I'd never felt like a fucking
failure than I did right now in this moment. I kept tracing my mind
back to that day. I'd even written down every name of every face I laid
eyes on from the time I woke up 'til the time I fell to sleep on April 16th.
For so many years, I blamed myself for causing Aphrodite to give birth
to a dead baby, and the entire time she was alive.

A muthafucka really had snaked me. Pulled the fucking wool over
my eyes. Snatched my fucking daughter right from under my nose
because he could. Because I no longer wanted to do business with him. I
would have rather him put a bullet in my head instead of taking my
fucking daughter and changing the lives of so many.

I pulled up to the same place I'd been frequenting for the last five
years, except this time, it was well after visitation hours. I popped the
trunk of my old school car and grabbed the shovel.

Being in a graveyard when it was night was frightening for some,
but for me, the opposite. Death was inevitable. But, for a nigga like me,
death was closer than most. I'd gotten out of the streets alive, but that
shit didn't mean shit. My life had been filled with cars, clothes,
diamonds, bitches, and riches, and although it was a good run, my

heart had been through some shit. I lost the love of my life, lost the center of my life, and when I thought I found love again, I lost that shit too.

Even though we were looking for Gilberto's bitch ass with a flashlight, it was time for me to get the tick out of my head. My baby needed me. I needed her. But in order to fully embrace God's mercy, I needed fucking answers.

Standing above what I thought was Athena's final resting place, I knocked the fresh flowers out of the view of her headstone. My parents were visiting family for birthday, so they had flowers delivered. We'd been getting a bit of rain, and they seemed to be doing the flowers justice. Speaking of rain, droplets fell from the midnight sky, but I was prepared. The Fendi raincoat that adorned my upper half kept me dry while I stuck the shovel in the dirt.

"I've been coming out here five fucking years. Talking to my fucking self and my daughter has been living, breathing and walking this earth."

Soggy dirt piled behind me. After a while, it turned to mud as I dug my way into the grave as rain lightly tapped my shoulders.

"I could barely fucking eat. I could barely fucking sleep. I lost my fucking mind times ten. My bitch thought I was going crazy! Making a nigga go to therapy and shit! While the whole fucking time! I was right!"

I was a few feet down now but still had a ways to go, so I kept digging.

"I prayed that my daughter came back into our lives, and the moment she does, I can barely fucking look at her! I failed my baby! How can I go around her knowing my weak ass lifestyle caused her to be snatched from the one person she needed more than anything in the world? Hunh? How the fuck can I love on her knowing I was the reason she was taken away?"

I tried to hold them back, but tears flooded my vision, but still, I kept digging.

"She must've been so fucking scared! Imagine being a newborn, and you can't smell the familiar scent of your mother, can't hear the deep sound of your father's voice! No telling what the fuck they did to my baby in five fucking years!"

Thunder shook the sky.

"I've been out here talking my ass off, and my baby was never here! So, I need to fucking know, who in the fucking ground?"

The shovel hit an object, causing a loud thud and when the muddy porcelain box showed, I wasted no time breaking the lock off the casket and opening it.

There laying in the casket was a fucking mermaid baby doll. Snatching it up, I couldn't believe my fucking eyes. Gilberto played. He played and woke up a fucking beast that I'd buried a long time ago. He'd took shit too far. Tossing the doll out on the grave, I dug my way out of the grave and fell to my knees. There in the pouring rain, I let it all out. I wasn't like the couple that usually visited when I did. I had a chance at life with my fucking daughter. My fucking baby. While death is inevitable, and I'm more than prepared for it, I would be leaving this earth before my child. She was going to be the one putting me in the fucking dirt. For that, I was grateful. Still, I yearned for redemption.

Pulling myself off the ground, I hopped in my whip and headed across town. The rain was coming down so bad that I needed to pull my ass over, but I couldn't. So much shit was running rampant in my mind that it was enough to drive a nigga into an aneurysm. As much as I didn't want her to, Tuscany plagued my thoughts too fucking often. I tried to think back to when we met and if she showed any signs of disloyalty. I couldn't. She came along with a pretty face, not so pretty past, great pussy, and empathy. Fucking empathy. She showed me empathy when Aphrodite was around this bitch pushing along with life. Strong as fuck like she hadn't buried our daughter years prior.

Tuscany let me cry on her fucking breasts and some days, cried with me. This bitch decorated my daughter's grave with me. She celebrated the short life of my baby with me. She fucking helped me become a better fucking man! Everything I did wrong with Aphrodite, I did that shit right with Tuscany! It's no way I let a snake ass bitch underneath my fucking roof and in my bed while she watched me mourn the loss of my only child, knowing damn well she knew my baby was living and breathing.

Mane! This shit hurt so fucking bad. If this is what fucking heart-break felt like, I understand why Aphrodite got rid of my ass. In the last five years, I'd cried more than I had my entire life! Muthafuckas thought I was crazy as fuck for mourning the loss of my fucking daughter for five continuous years, but it was because my soul knew some shit wasn't right. I was so consumed with guilt that it was hard for me to look my baby in the face.

Parking my car almost on the fucking lawn, I hopped out and made it to the front door just as lightning cracked the navy blue sky.

Ringing the doorbell once, I waited a few moments until Aphrodite was opening the door with her face in her laptop.

"Aye, fuck I tell you 'bout unlocking the door and shit? You didn't even ask who the fuck I was. No telling who was behind this door."

Aphrodite waved me off and scrolled on her laptop, still not looking up at me.

"Aphrodite."

She finally paid my ass some attention and balled her perfectly bare face up.

"What the fuck, Baguette? What you –"

I stepped into her home and ultimately, her personal space, causing her to take a step back.

I thought carefully about how to spit my words out, but it was so fucking hard.

"Aphrodite, I need you-"

"Nigga, you need what? What you NEED to do is go find yo' bitch and get the fuck away from mine!"

Goal's voice boomed in the entryway, and I was confused as hell. This nigga was nowhere, but somehow his ass was always every fucking where.

"Goal, stop playing and bring your ass in before this rain gets too bad. Don't be mad at me when I go to sleep."

Aphrodite yelled back. Then she faced me with red flushing over her pretty face.

"I'ma wake yo' ass up too. Act like you'n know."

"Bye, Goal. Stop always watching on that damn camera. How many of these do you even got in here? I bet you be watching my ass in the shower."

"And do."

"Bye, nasty."

Aphrodite shook her head and closed her laptop.

"I didn't look when I opened it because Jett and 'nem are out there. I thought maybe he was coming in to use the bathroom. Now, what were you saying? And why you so wet and muddy? You good, Baguette?"

"Before that lil' junt' of yours interrupted me, I was saying, I need you to let me spend the night with my daughter. I know I ain't been around much, and that's my fault. I just keep trying to process this shit. I'ma do better and be better. On God."

"Yeah, you better, 'cuz when step daddy come thru-"

"Nigga, shut yo' ass up!" I yelled at Goal's playful ass and slipped my boots off before taking off to find my daughter.

"Hold up, Baguette. You need to shower! You tracking all that-"

I kept walking until I couldn't hear Aphrodite anymore. Athena's room was cleaned and smelled of lavender. Judging by the fog on her bathroom mirror, I knew she'd taken a bath, but Athena was nowhere to be found.

Going back out of her room, I walked into the main area of the house where Aphrodite could be heard still talking to Goal in the entryway instead of calling his ass. My homie was in love, and I wasn't mad at it. Goal a solid ass nigga. Crazy as fuck, but solid.

"Daddy?"

My baby was at the top of the stairs, hair in a pink bonnet, looking just like her fucking mama. The pink onesie Barbie pajamas that she was wearing were adorable as fuck. I took the stairs two at a time and kneeled in front of her when I got to the top, resting my elbow on my knee.

"Yeah, baby, it's daddy."

Looking at her was so surreal. She resembled a collectible China doll that was meant to sit on a shelf. My baby is a muthafuckin' sight.

Taking my hood of my head, I pinched my tear ducts and then looked back up at my baby.

"I'm sorry for not being around, baby. Daddy just so happy you here that ion want to scare you. I might love on you too much, and you'll get tired of me or some'."

Athena smiled, revealing a missing tooth. I looked around for Aphrodite, but her ass was still caking on the camera speaker. *I missed her losing her first fucking tooth?* Fuck.

"I won't get tired of you, daddy. I miss Ms. Haddie and Tulsaire, but I still haven't gotten tired of mommy."

I hoped like hell we found Kilo's grandma. I wanted answers, but I could tell that nigga was really going through it without her.

"You been away from daddy for a long time, and that made me different. It made me sad. It made me mad. It made me angry, but I'm happy you're back. I love you, pretty baby. Can daddy have a hug?"

Athena stood back and crinkled her nose up. I noticed that she was holding a doll. Looking closely, it was the same fucking doll that was in her casket. *Talk about full fucking circle.*

"Eww, Brock, I can't hug you right now because you're dirty."

Aphrodite told me that she goes back and forward between calling her mommy and by her first name, so I guess I wasn't exempt from the shit neither.

With the same look on her face that her mom just gave me, I snatched her ass up and tickled her belly. Her laughs were so loud and contagious that it caused me to laugh.

"I love you, kid. It's me and you, aite?"

I placed Athena back on her feet, and the way she checked her pajamas for dirt was comical.

"Me, you and mommy?"

I looked down the stairs. Aphrodite had finally come from the entryway and had her feet tucked underneath her butt, watching tv.

"Mommy ain't cool like me, so we might have to ditch her some time. Plus, daddy got a restaurant with an ice cream machine in the back, and you can have all the ice cream you want."

Athena's eyes lit up, causing my heart to flutter.

"Sprinkles too?"

"Fasho!"

"Yayyyyyy!"

"Whatever he telling you, don't believe it, Athena!"

Aphrodite's salty ass yelled, but my baby was too busy celebrating that she didn't hear her.

"Now, when did you lose that tooth?"

Athena reached in the pocket of her pajama onesie and pulled out a short, skinny front tooth.

"Today! I'm saving it for the tooth fairy!"

"Yeap, and you gotta get in the bed so you can get paid. It's already one a.m."

I made a funny face at Aphrodite being a party pooper, and that had Athena tickled.

"How much do the tooth fairy send these days?"

"Like *fifty* hundred dollars or something! I'm going to have millions of dollars."

"You already got that, kid. But fifty hundred dollars coming right up."

After Aphrodite got Athena changed because my baby swore I'd gotten her dirty, I grabbed a bag out of my truck that stashed baller shorts and underclothes. I kept it in the trunk for the days I went to the hood to shoot hoops. I showered in one of the spare rooms and snuggled under my baby in her comfortable ass bed. We stayed up all night kicking shit, but when we finally talked ourselves to sleep, I got the best fucking sleep in my life. Better believe, my baby woke up to her *fifty* hundred dollars too. Oh yeah, it was fuck a bitch for life when it came to my fucking feelings too. All I needed in this world was me and my baby girl.

CHAPTER 20

Brock "Baguette" Cherman

These last few days with my daughter are what the fucking doctor ordered. I felt like a weight had been lifted from my fucking chest after ripping up that fucking grave. My daughter is alive, like my spirit had known the entire time, so she didn't need no fucking final resting place.

Athena and I have been stuck like glue, and being at the house with her and her jealous ass mama was the highlight of my fucking life. I loved them both with everything in me, and I meant what I said when I told that fucking therapist no one would ever come before my woe.

Being in my little snaggle tooth daughter's presence and witnessing her little personality showed me that not only was she perfect, but she was all Aphrodite and me. She had so many of our fucking mannerisms and even slept just like me. Genetics was wild. Prior to these last few weeks, she hadn't been around us at all and was still all us.

In the passing days, I'd had my fucking nails sloppily painted, played dress up, even though the dresses could only go on one of my arms and sang Let It Go to my cords couldn't take it no more. This child of mine was the funniest and full of plenty of energy. It wouldn't be me though, if I didn't ask her questions. I didn't necessarily bring up Gilberto's bitch ass, but I did ask her about her life. When she told me she used to hear the gun go boom, I clenched my fucking jaws. There was no telling what the fuck Gilberto had my child around, and for that, there was a special place in hell for his ass.

"Brock, I mean, daddy, you about to go?"

My baby was swaying in her pajamas with syrup on her face and fingers. She was a sticky mess, but still, I pulled out my phone and sent her picture to my parents and Ms. Deb. I'd sent them so many fucking pictures, I'm sure they was sick of my ass. I couldn't help it though.

Getting eye level to my baby, I smiled. Seeing Aphrodite's face in little person form was still not something I was used to, but I loved it.

"Yes, daddy got to get to work."

"At your restaurants?"

"Yeah, baby. At my restaurants."

"Can you bring crab legs back and sleep in my bed again?"

"I'm sure yo' mama sick of me crowding y'all space, so I'll tell you what. I'll bring you some crab legs by and watch a movie with you, but I'm going home tonight, Princess. But you can come spend the night this weekend, and I'll make sure your grandparents are there."

That got Athena to jumping because she loved her room at my house. Aphrodite was salty about that too.

"You leaving?"

Aphrodite walked in just as I scooped my phone in the pocket of my pants. Thankfully, Aphrodite had some of my shit in the garage, so I was able to have clothes every day. Because I wasn't leaving my daughter's side.

"Yeah, I got some shit to handle with yo husband. Is that okay with you, Mrs. Navarro?"

Aphrodite smirked and hid her grin behind her mug of espresso. That nigga had her wide the fuck open. It was a good look in her, though.

"Alright, be safe. Give yo' daddy a hug, Athena, so you can get dressed."

"Can daddy pick out my clothes?"

My heart swelled hearing my daughter's voice. A nigga ain't been around, and she was still a fucking daddy's girl.

"How 'bout this. I'll come by in the morning and pick your clothes out?"

Athena nodded, and I scooped her up in a hug and kissed all over her face. She loved that shit too.

"Aite, put my kid down. Bye, Brock."

Aphrodite had a little attitude with a nigga since I wasn't studying her damn friend. She could play Inspector Gadget all she wanted to and go find her ass, but I still had a bullet for the disloyal bitch.

A few minutes later, I was out the door. It took me about twenty five minutes to get to Goal's warehouse, and once I was parked, I hopped in the black truck that was waiting. Kilo's ass was already in, sitting on the back row.

"Took you long enough, nigga."

Goal's ass popped his fucking head in my daughter's room at 5 a.m. with his fucking gym clothes on, telling me that we had to ride the fuck out today. Ion know when the nigga slept because if he wasn't keeping Aphrodite out all night, the nigga was in the gym. He kept himself discreet from my child, and I appreciated that. It wasn't nothing against that nigga, but I needed to bond with my own kid first. Now that she was a certified daddy's girl, Aphrodite could do as she pleased. I knew my child was in good hands around his loose screws ass.

"I was with my daughter, nigga. I ain't but a minute late."

The car pulled out of the lot, and I was happy as fuck we wasn't seeing them damn gators today. Goal was batshit fucking crazy. Hell, they eyes told it all.

"Where we headed to any fucking way? The more time pass that ion got my grannie, the antsier I'm becoming," Kilo boomed.

"Nigga, you should have been that same kind of antsy when looking into who the fuck she was working for. But, if y'all must fucking know, we going way fucking back. The easiest way to connect the dots is to retrace the steps. Order of fucking operations. So, we gone start with the day AP gave birth. Tomorrow night, we gone do the same shit with the day you got locked up, Kilo."

I could dig it. I'd been thinking a whole lot about that day and even reached out to Gia's lil' fine Italian ass who was working the front desk that day, but she had a new fucking number.

It took us damn near a half hour until we were pulling up in front of a three story cream brick home. Judging by the Land Rover and the

Benz in the driveway of the newly built home, I knew who ever lived here had a little bit of paper.

"Aite, Leo had all the cameras cut off every house on the block. Let's go."

The driver opened the door for us but stood back as we approached the front door.

"Aye, one of y'all kick the door in. I fucked my shit up kicking Daphne's in a few days ago."

Looking at Goal, I didn't even want to know what the fuck the story was behind that, but I was sure it had something to do with that ass whooping Ditey gave her. Aphrodite told me her and D had gotten into a fight and that shit had me shaking my fucking head. That girl just couldn't let go.

Pulling my sweats up, I reared back and kicked the door three times until the door was busting open, slamming into the wall behind it.

When I walked into the home and saw the large portrait of the couple above the fireplace, I wanted to give this crazy ass nigga a hug, but I kept my fucking game face on.

Creeping into the master bedroom, we saw a white bitch sleeping with a baby on her chest. Knowing I would never get that chance with my daughter had me tight and caused my mind to fizzle. The shower was stopped, and a few minutes later, our culprit emerged.

He stopped dead in his tracks as his...eyes grew wide.

Goal pulled a gun from his waist and shot above the tufted head-board. The silencer on the gun produced only a zipping sound. When ole girl or the baby didn't startle from their slumber, this nigga put up prayer hands.

"If you don't want my next shot to send these two to the grave, shut the fuck up and bring yo' ass out the room!"

With his pajamas damp as hell from barely drying off, he ran in front of us, and we were hot on his tail. He didn't stop 'til he was in the kitchen, and I had to admit, his spot was dope as fuck.

"Look, I have not even looked Dasani's way! You can tell Don he doesn't have to send any more of his men. I have my own family to protect."

I cocked my head, and at the same time, Kilo scratched his.

With the hand his gun was in, Goal raised his wrist and covered his mouth with it.

"Oh shit! You in fucking trouble with the Rinaldi Mafia? Damn, nigga! No wonder you got a missing eye and shit."

Dr. Pretty Boy Phine had the fucking ladies lining down the block to be seen by him, including Aphrodite. I made sure I was present at every doctor's appointment and mugged that friendly ass nigga every time. He knew his shit though, and never was inappropriate with her, so I let it rock. The day Aphrodite gave birth, she was panicking because this nigga was out of town, and she wanted him to bring our daughter in this world. Ironically, he was on vacation.

"This ain't about no mafia shit. Five years ago, you saw my baby mama through her pregnancy. You assured us that she would be good when you went on vacation weeks before her due date. When she gave birth, the baby was stillborn, despite her being healthy the whole damn pregnancy."

I tucked my fist underneath my armpits as Dr. Phine's scary ass shook in his fucking pants.

"That shit ring a bell? Or do I need to show you how it feel to mourn a child?" Goal warned.

"That's not necessary. I remember! Aphrodite. Unique name. Beautiful woman-"

"Nigga, do I need to pluck yo' other eye, Jack Sparrow? Fuck you calling my bitch beautiful for? You the same nigga that done inspected her pussy! That shit a HIPAA Violation!"

Dr. Phine held his hands up and looked from me to Goal in confusion.

"It's complicated, now talk," I spat.

"Yes. I remembered getting the call on vacation, and I was devastated. While I know during child birth, things can happen, Aphrodite was healthy as a horse, and so was baby girl. When I found out she was delivering at Central, I was even more infuriated. That hospital should have been shut down a long time ago."

Dr. Phine rubbed his hand down his head of waves.

"I looked into it, and I have all the files at my office. I can get across town, get it for you and call you with what I find."

"Dr. One Eye, only because I'm in a good mood and had some good ass pussy last night, I'ma give you the benefit of the doubt. You got one hour. Pull up at Houston's on South. One fucking hour or you'll be putting them in the family Mausoleum that yo' parents had built."

Dr. Phine nodded, and we were gone just as fast as we came.

"You taking yo' ass home tonight, ain't it?"

Goal asked as he texted on his phone. Judging by the way his ass was grinning, I knew he was texting Aphrodite.

"Damn, nigga. I ain't welcome?" I snarled.

Goal pulled his head from his phone and matched my glare.

"You wore out yo' damn welcome. Take yo' ass to the crib. I like having loud, nasty ass sex, and although her room is soundproof, she be uncomfortable with her old nigga down the hall."

Kilo cracked from the backseat.

"Nigga, you bet not get my baby mama pregnant! Wrap yo' fucking dick up! Let her get adjusted to having Athena."

Goal gave off a sinister grin, "Too fucking late. Now, run yo' whole day back on the day of the hospital. Don't leave shit out. If you shoulder bumped the janitor, I wanna know that shit."

Thinking back to the worst day of my life, I ran the whole story down. I hated talking about this day and only hoped the doctor had some good news for us. We couldn't get to Gilberto just yet 'cuz he was hiding like the pussy he was, but we were touching every fucking body else that had a hand in that shit. That's on my daughter!

By the time I was done, we were pulling up to Houston's and being seated in the back. We opted out of a booth this time. I hated coming here now because it reminded me of Tuscany's fried shrimp loving ass, and she was a fucking opp in my eyes. I hated that I still even thought about her foul ass. I wanted to lay hands on her so fucking bad.

"Brock, hey, baby. How are you?"

I raised my head, and an involuntary sneer covered it. I didn't have a problem with Ms. Giselle, but she was cool with Tuscany, so it was fuck her too.

"Send us somebody else."

Both Kilo and Goal were confused, judging by their expressions, but I didn't go into details.

. . .

"I can do that. But first, can you answer a question truthfully for me."

Crossing my arms and slumping in my seat, I waited on the question I knew she was going to ask.

"Where is Tuscany and is she in trouble?"

I laughed my anger off and swiped my thumb across the tip of my nose.

"Ion know no Tuscany. You niggas know a Tuscany?"

"Nah, don't ring a bell."

"Only Tuscany I know is the pasta. Y'all got some of that on the menu?" Goal's dumb ass held the menu up.

Ms. Giselle looked around the table and the stress in her eyes couldn't be missed.

Placing her palms on the table, she leaned in and looked around before speaking.

"Does Gilberto have her?"

Before I could react, Goal had his gun underneath her chin, but she didn't tense up. Keeping her palms flat, her eyes stayed on me.

"I ain't scared to die. Your pistol don't scare me. Brock, if Gilberto has her, she's in trouble."

"Ion give a fuck about that bitch being in trouble. She snaked me! She betrayed me and ran off with that nigga! They plotted against me!"

Ms. Giselle narrowed her eyes and laughed.

"Tuscany and Gilberto? Nah, you got it all wrong."

"You too fucking calm for a bitch that's 'bout to be brainless. You still ain't told us how you know Gilberto."

"What he said," Kilo added.

"Look, I used to work for him over twelve years ago back in Memphis. I hate to tell you her business without her being present, but her life is on the line. I was Gilberto's housemaid and didn't know shit outside the man but his first name. I knew he was dangerous, but since he paid me under the table, and well, I stayed. Just when I couldn't take it no more, I was going to take my money and flee, but he brought home a girl. An underaged girl. That girl had unknowingly sold her fucking soul to the devil. That man used to rape and beat her black and blue.

Still, she put up with it because he took damn good care of her siblings. Brothers, to be exact."

Sucking my teeth, I clenched my jaw but continued to listen to Ms. Giselle.

"Her mom and I were finally able to get her away, and with the money we had all saved, she relocated right here to Jagoda Bay. Tuscany isn't an opp. She didn't plot against you. She's a fucking victim and has been living her life right. She loves you! If she's missing, and I know she is because I can't get ahold of her, you need to find her. Brock, whatever you're thinking, DEAD IT! She would never cross you. That girl has been on the run for years. She'd finally felt safe when she met you."

The information Ms. Giselle laid on me was enough to make me sick, but I held my composure. I realized I didn't know Tuscany like I thought I DID. I mean, I knew she had a rough upbringing and would go sometimes months without talking to her mom and visited maybe once a year, but I didn't pry. I was too consumed with Athena. To hear that my old plug had raped my bitch had me ready to fucking spray up this entire restaurant. How fucking small is this world? Still, there was some shit Ms. Giselle wasn't telling me. I'd been in the streets too long to not know when a muthafucka was holding out.

Goal lowered his gun, and Ms. Giselle turned to face Kilo.

"Kymani, where is Haddie?"

"Well, you just know every fucking body, Misses Bitch. Gooood damn. Seems like we should have been coming to you for answers."

Kilo frowned up and sat back in his seat.

"How you know my grannie?"

Standing straight up, Ms. Giselle gripped the back of her neck.

"That's my mama."

Kilo laughed. He laughed so fucking hard that it shook the table.

"Yeah, that's funny. Haddie's daughters are dead."

"No, they're not, son."

"Son?" Both Goal and I yelled.

"Look, my mama came in here a few weeks ago, and it was my first time seeing her in over thirty years. She had two kids with her. I thought they were my great-grandchildren, but she told me no, that they belonged to her boss. Before I could get anything out of her, she shooed me off and gave me her number. I'd been calling her with no answer. Is she okay?"

Kilo looked as if he'd seen a ghost and rubbed his hand down his face.

"What is you saying though?"

"Haddie wasn't always good. Much like Tuscany, my sister and I were raped, and we produced a child from the same man. Haddie felt bad, so she kept the kids and pushed us out of her house. I'm your mama, and Kassie's mama, Gloria, lives in Cali. I'm sorry, son, but we can get into that later. Where is my mama?"

Kilo opened his mouth to respond, but we were rushed by the doctor. Sweat was pouring from his forehead, and his jacket was on inside out as he sat at the table, almost pushing Ms. Giselle out of the way. When he opened his bag, he grabbed a stack of papers.

"I hope I'm free to talk here."

"Nigga, spit it out before you walk out of this bitch like Stevie Wonder."

"Okay, okay. As I was saying, the case was odd. I looked into everything and even had her urine sampled. There were traces of Pliforathane in her system."

"Fuck is that?" I pondered.

"Pliforathane is a narcotic that was designed to be used as an alternative of the epidural, but it didn't pass the trial because while it washed away pain temporarily, it speeds up labor and makes the fetus extremely sedated."

Dr. Phine snapped his head at Ms. Giselle.

"Yes, she knows her stuff. That's correct." He slid the papers across the table.

Ms. Giselle shrugged, "My sister is a nurse, and I used to help her with her papers sometimes."

"Not only that, the baby's blood samples also showed traces of not only Pliforathane that passed through the mother, but Nicrosion."

"Now, I don't know about that."

"Nicrosion is a drug we use to make a patient extremely calm. It slows the breathing and heartbeat for procedures that we don't deem necessary to go completely under. With both these drugs in your baby's system, chances of survival are slim." Dr. Phine gave a look of sympathy.

"You not hearing me. Some shit not right, Aphrodite. You know my intuition is what kept a nigga out the way for so long. Ion know why this bitch done started speaking out almost five years later, but some shit not adding up. I think I seen-"

Just as I was about to tell Aphrodite that I think I seen somebody sticking our daughter with a needle when she pushed her out, her phone rang, and it was Goal telling her he was outside for their date.

"Fuuuuuuuuck! Fuck! Fuck! Fuck!"

"Nigga, you got all this info, why the fuck you don't tell them this shit back then?"

That's exactly what the fuck I wanted to know. Because I was 'bout ready to kill Dr. Phine.

"As I stated, the hospital is very...crooked. The more I dug into the files, I must've raised suspicions. I was paid a visit. I had my ass kicked by some Colombians, and they snatched up all my proof, telling me that if I spoke up to anyone, I would lose my life. They didn't know I had copies, though. I'm sorry, I really couldn't risk my life."

I was pissed, but the doctor was green. Any weak ass green nigga would have turned a blind eye too.

"Anything else, Doc? 'Cuz you done pissed me the fuck off. The more I stare at that one fucking eye, the more I want to pluck that bitch from your skull. You's a stupid, scary muthafucka." If this shit were a laughing matter, I would have been doubled the fuck over dealing with Goal's ignorant ass. But wasn't shit funny.

"The baby survived. Someone drugged them both and faked the baby's death. That's what we are trying to get to the bottom of." Kilo was trying hard to suppress his emotions, but I could tell Ms. Giselle had put a stain on his brain.

"What? My fucking God."

Dr. Phine removed the glasses from his face.

"The baby survived this?"

"Ain't that what the fuck he said, Cuh? Now, anything else?"

Pinching the bridge of my nose, I just remembered one part of my day that I overlooked.

"Can you see who signed off on these drugs?"

Dr. Phine added his glasses back to his face and shuffled through the papers.

"Uhhhh...yes, here. Looks like Registered Nurse Daphne Peters?"

"Hold up, yo' old hoe Daphne?"

Ms. Giselle asked, and now I was wonder what all had Tuscany told this lady.

"Shit, our old Daphne. We all done fucked. Including the doctor."

When the Doctor didn't deny it, I shook my fucking head.

"Pliforathane. If you're looking for answers try maybe finding out how it was that Aphrodite got the drug in her system. Someone gave them to her. That's what put her in active labor. She was drugged way before she got to the hospital. Even Daphne couldn't get her hand on that." The doctor sympathized.

"Aite, you can raise on up outta here. We keeping these papers too. Leave that Louis bag too."

Dr. Phine stood fast as hell, leaving everything and almost knocking the chair on the floor.

"Aye, get a fucking blood test. I saw some red hair on that baby, and I know a cracker that likes creepin' with married bitches. Better go ask Tom." Dr. Phine nodded and scurried out of the restaurant.

Goal sat back in his seat with his eyes on the papers. This shit was too fucking much. I knew Daphne was a hoe, and she was jealous of Aphrodite, but the bitch played a hand in kidnapping my fucking daughter. This whole fucking time, the hoe had even been to my fucking new crib since she was dating Goal. This bitch was working with Gilberto and feeding him all the fucking details of our lives. Knowing damn fucking well, she knew my daughter was alive. I was livid! Red was the only color I saw, and for that, she had to fucking die.

"You ready to take our order now, ma'am? Oh, and Kilo, my bad for pistol playing calling your mama Misses Bitch. I ain't know, my guy."

This shit was too fucking much.

CHAPTER 21

Aphrodite "Ditey" "Pretty Pretty" "AP" Greer

The passing days have been dragging on, and I was happy that today was a new damn day. Baguette had been here every night snuggled under my baby, and while I was happy he was getting his time in, I grew tired of biting socks to hold my screams. Baguette and I were long past anything outside of friendship, but it was weird as fuck getting my back blown out while my baby daddy was down the hall. Baguette had gotten a call after he and Athena ate pancakes and went flying out the door, promising that he would come back to bring her crab legs and that he would get her this weekend so that she could spend the night. Athena had spent the night at my mama's house. Well, if you called that spending the night, because I had Goal drive me to her house around three and picked my baby up. My mama didn't even fuss. She just let Goal scoop her out the bed, and we drove her home. She still hadn't formally met him because she was sleep the whole car ride, but now that she'd spent some time with her daddy, I was ready to make the introductions.

I was still skeptical because I didn't want to confuse my baby, but Goal had done so much for us that I didn't want him to feel like he was just a damn booty call. The nigga came through when Athena was sleep and left before she was awake. I tried every night to make his ass tap out, but he doesn't go to sleep. Ion see how he still got time to run a fucking

Cartel when he be up early in the home gym and then back out the door after drilling me to a cross every night.

Jett brought my baby some lunch, which was shrimp scampi from Red Lobster, and I felt sorry for whenever his ass had kids. He did an excellent job at keeping us protected, but his ass was just as bad as us when it came to bending to Athena's will.

"Eat up, baby. I know you tired of meeting people, but I got one more person to introduce to you."

Athena nodded as she bit down on a shrimp and watched Trolls on her iPad. Kissing the top of her hair, I walked out of the kitchen. I still couldn't believe she had a tooth missing. Her daddy, Jett, and Goal had all put money under her pillow and I wrote her a cute letter from the tooth fairy. I didn't even bother to count the money because I know it was way too much. My baby was too excited the next day and of course, I cried.

Goal was walking in the front door, and all of a sudden, my palms moistened. He was looking so fucking good in a grey tee that didn't say much but looked expensive and matching his bold eyes. Today, he didn't have a chain on, but he was rocking his Richard Millie, a pair of shorts that showed the tattoos on his legs and grey and tan Chanel sneakers. Goal is the type of fine that you never got tired of gazing at. The nigga was so good looking that I couldn't even be mad at Litty for popping it on his brother and producing a baby. They looked damn near identical. I was almost mad at her because her nigga looked too close to mine, and mine was one of a kind.

"Wassup, lil junt?"

Playfully pushing Goal in the chest, he grabbed me by my waist and led me to the back room.

"You not gone let that go, are you?"

For the last few nights, he's been joking about me calling him lil junt, and I couldn't wait to curse Baguette's ass out for talking too fucking much.

Once Goal had the door locked, he pushed me down on the bed, causing my short silk robe to fly up, exposing my shaved pussy.

"Hold up, Goal. I got to tell you... shiiiit!!"

Goal sucked my lower set of lips in his mouth while ramming two fingers inside my awaiting hole. His kisses on my pussy were slow and dragging. The strong hardness of his lips sent new spirals of ecstasy through me. I loved when Goal put his mouth on me. It was something about his oral that had me feeling so invigorating... exhilarating. That was the word. All things Goal made me feel Exhilarated, and as he brought me to a climax with his mouth, I bucked all in his face.

"I love munching on that pretty pussy."

Climbing on top of me while I was struggling to catch my breath, Goal buried his face in the crook of my neck and smuggled a kiss there while ramming his dick in me. He never eased in. His big dick ass always just forced his way through. I still wasn't used to it, but I could handle it better now. Pushing my legs behind my head, he smother my lips with his demanding master as he drilled me into the fucking mattress. The dick was so fucking good that he'd brought a bitch to tears.

My hands explored the hard lines of his muscular back as he rocked in and out of me and moaned in my mouth.

"Fuuuuuck! I love you so much, nigga! Daaaamn!" I cried out as I came a second time.

Sex wasn't supposed to be this good. This nigga had a spell on his shit, I was for certain. He was so fucking skilled. So fucking cocky, and although we'd been sexing every fucking night, I couldn't see myself getting tired no time soon.

"You ... the ...fucking prize, PP. Remember that shit. You the fucking prize. Fuuuuck! I'm 'bout to nut in my pussy!"

We both came together and when the high ass bed broke underneath us, we both laughed.

"Come yo' silly ass on. We got to shower real quick so I could get dressed. That's all that damn Red Lobster you been eating. Broke the fucking bed."

Goal helped me up.

"Fuck you. I barely eat," I laughed.

We finally made it to the shower, where I had to fight him off me. He was trying to go another round, but we really didn't have time for that.

I dressed simply in a grey backless maxi, trying to match my baby because she was rocking a grey and yellow Nike skirt set that I'd gotten from Chia and white Forces. I hoped she was staying out of trouble and would stay that way until she called me so that I could give her a job.

I did a light beat while Goal kicked back on the bed, watching the tv. Some shit he rarely did. He was just always in business mode or fucking mode. I was starting to wonder if my man was even real.

"Sexy ass, come put that pussy on my face real quick-"

"No, Goal Navarro."

"Fuck, you stingy as hell. You know I'm addicted to you. Come give me a kiss then before Athena come knocking on the door, cock blocking."

I laughed out loud but went over to give my man a kiss. I could taste my pussy on his breath and was going to make him brush his damn teeth when we were done.

"Oh, I almost forgot."

I reached into my nightstand and pulled out a bag that I'd been meaning to give him since his birthday, April 16th.

"There was so much going on on your birthday that I forgot to give you this."

I reached in the bag and pulled out the two navy boxes.

Goal whistled, "Okay, you went to my nigga Wafi. Big money."

"Shut up."

Placing the two boxes on his stomach since he was laying back, I watched as he opened each one. The smile on my face indicated how much I loved giving gifts.

"Oh shit."

Goal sat up with bulging eyes as he held the boxes to his face. Sending me into a fit of laughter.

"You showed the fuck out, Pretty Pretty. Fuck, this shit icy!"

"I'm sorry your birthday didn't go as planned, but I had you covered. Better late than never, but if you look at the receipt, you'll see I purchased it on April fourth. I had to pay a fat ass rush fee to have it done in a week too."

Goal hadn't taken his eyes off the ring and watch. I'd gotten him an Audemars Piguet bust down and iced the fuck out a matching pinky ring. On the face of the pinky ring, Navarro was bedazzled in diamonds. Thankfully, Wafi knew his ring size with one mention of his name, so the ring slid on perfectly. My man wore rings most times, and that shit was sexy as fuck. I used to think men wearing diamond rings was pimp-ish, but not Goal Navarro.

"Bring yo ass here. How much this shit run you?"

Goal pulled the receipt out. When he tried to read it, I snatched it and balled it up. Hooking his arm around my neck, he brought my face to his lips.

"How you gone cop me a ring before mine for you finished getting made?"

My heart skipped hearing him say he was having a ring commis-sioned. I wanted to say he was lying, but Goal Navarro wouldn't tell me a lie.

"I love you, Aphrodite. I love you more than I love my fucking self. Ion know how this shit happened so fast, but you stuck with yo' nigga."

Pecking his lips again, I smiled.

"I love you too, Papi. Now, come on. I want to go to the mall, but before that, I want you to meet Athena."

"You sure?"

"Positive. Just don't spoil my baby too much, baby."

Goal replied with a smile while clamping his new watch around his wrist in the place of where the Richard Millie was. His smile meant he wasn't hearing shit I'd said.

Goal and Athena hit it off good. He'd had her doubling over in laughter, and she even dragged him to her gold toy chest and played with the dolls. Goal Navarro's gangsta ass playing with dolls was too damn funny, but my baby was enjoying him.

My Papi just couldn't let it go that I'd dropped stacks on his belated birthday gifts so he dragged us to the mall and balled the hell out. After dragging me to a jewelry store and picking out the biggest diamond they had, which was unreal, our second stop was Gucci to get Athena a purse to match mine, and she was too happy about it. He actually got her five little mini handbags and crossovers, but I loved it because they were so girly. We had an hour before the ring sizing was going to be ready, so we had time to burn. This man said this was my temp ring 'til the real one was finished. He was in his feelings that I'd gotten him a ring before he got me one. I'd only gotten his ass a pinky ring to wear for leisure, and he was acting like I'd purchased him a wedding band. Goal is a mess.

When we got to the toy store, and Athena pulled out a black card to swipe, I whipped my head over at his ass, and he shrugged. He'd already handed my baby his fucking black card. Fuck was she going to buy? Unlimited toys and crabs?

"Ohh, I like Disney! Can we go to Disney World for my birthday?" Athena asked as the Disney store approached. Jett had already made three trips to the car to place our bags, and that was just from the first floor. We were now on the second level with one more to go.

"Your birthday has already passed," I sassed.

Goal swooped Athena in his arms with his semi-bowlegged ass.

"We got the same birthday, and even though it's passed, fuck yea, we can go to Disney World. It's our birthday every day, Lil Pretty! Ain't that right?"

"Yayyyyyy!" Athena screamed and hooked her arms around Goal's neck.

"Can we go to the aquarium too?"

"Yeah, but I got lots of lil fishes. I have the best aquariums. I got some gators too. They babies. You can feed 'em."

I cut my eyes at his ass because wasn't shit little about his fishes. The gator shit was new to me, but my baby was straight on all that.

When he let her down, she came back to my side and held my hand.

"Mommy, can we go in the Disneyland store?"

There was a line outside the store and it was visible you could see how crowded it was. My feet were hurting, but I couldn't tell my baby no.

"Yeah, me and Jett gone chill out here. I got eyes on y'all, though."

I kissed Goal on the lips and walked hand in hand with Althena. I wasn't standing in that long ass line, so we slipped past everyone and walked right in. The line was due to the black Ariel being in the store, and even though she wasn't Halle Bailey, she was cute. I made sure my baby got her picture, and we scrolled the sections, picking up everything she didn't have.

The store was shoulder to shoulder, but I kept my baby close. When

216

I stopped to look at a life size Elsa, Athena ran off, causing me to drop our handbasket and sending my heart into a frenzy.

"Athena! Athenaaaa!"

I was shoving people out of my damn way and trembling because there was no sight of her.

"Ma'am, I think she's at the back of the store-"

An employee informed me, and I ran full speed in my dress to get to my baby.

She was facing a wall and looking up at the tv. The Little Mermaid was playing on the screen.

"Athena! You can't run off, baby! You scared me to death."

I grabbed her up in my arms. The moment I let her walk, she runs off and almost gives me a heart attack.

"Mommy?" She whispered in my ear.

"Yeah, baby?"

I was still hugging her and thanking God she was okay. She was only gone a few seconds, and it felt like five years all over again.

"*Tenemos claro el avistamiento de Gol Navarro. Haz el tiro. disparar a matar.*"

Pulling my face from the crook of her neck, I stared at her.

"You're Bilingual? What does that mean?"

Athena's eyes watered, and panic set in. She hadn't shed a tear since I'd had her back.

"We have a clear sighting of Goal Navarro. Make the shot. Shoot to kill. That's what the man that went out the back door just said inside of his earpiece. Mommy, I don't want Goal to die. He's my friend! We have the same birthday!"

All the color drained from my face as I looked out of the glass window at Goal. He was laughing with Jett, and when he noticed me looking, he blew a kiss.

"Goal!!"

Bullets rang out, and even though Jett was sharp with his gun, he was hit just before Goal's body was riddled with bullets. Athena's screams filled my ears as his body not only bucked but went over the glass railing. The last thing I saw was his smirk and those grey demon eyes filled with sorrow.

Five years...Five years.

Half a decade.

One Thousand eight hundred twenty-five days.

Forty-three thousand eight hundred hours.

Two million six hundred twenty-eight thousand minutes.

Measuring the time, a lot can happen in five years.

It took me five years to not only find true love but to get my baby girl back. So much had changed in five years, and although I'd experienced the worst of times, I'd finally begun to see the best of times. Never would I have imagined that in five seconds, my whole world that I'd waited to have for five years, was turned upside fucking down.

To be Continued...

Lisa Austin Books

Yayo: The Beginning
   Yayo: Riot's Revenge
   Riot 3 (Yayo)
   Death if a Nawf Memphis Trap King
   Boostin' around the Christmas Tree
   I choose you boo 1&2
   Annihilate your love
   You're My favorite Mistake 1&2
   Peek it's boo 1&2
   Bossed Up
   Bayb
   If Cupid was a Thug
   Giving it a try with a street Guy: The Valentines
   Forever Good in his Hood
   Bound to a Bandit
   Dreaming of Spring
   Big Boss
   Humbled by a Real n*gga 1-3
   Humbled on Christmas Day- lani & Rut
   Just like I taught you
   Honey, I f*cked the Plug 1-3

Daddy's Lil Baby
Pregnant by a Muthaf*kin Don 1&2
A Winter Crest Christmas: Pure & Luxe
A Winter Crest Valentine's: Snowy & Sphere
Exhilarated
Wealth over Riches and Bad B*tches
Summer Vibes in Paradise bay: Coastal & Bliss

Please join my group for a chance to win prices, get sneak peeks, and read FREE exclusive books!
www.Bit.ly/LisaAustinGroup

www.ingramcontent.com/pod-product-compliance
Lightning Source LLC
Chambersburg PA
CBHW030320020726
47493CB00004B/1097